Witch Is How The Biscuits Disappeared

Published by Implode Publishing Ltd
© Implode Publishing Ltd 2019

Chapter 1

"You can't leave him there like that, Jill." Jack grabbed my arm.

"Like what?"

"You know what. You have to turn him back into a man."

"He shouldn't have nicked my parking spot."

"We managed to get another one."

"That's not the point. It's the principle that counts. Only a rat would have done something like that."

"So you thought you'd turn him into one?"

"It seemed only fair. Come on or we'll miss the start of the movie."

"I'm not going anywhere until you've turned him back into a man. I'm surprised you'd do something like this. It's the kind of thing I'd expect your grandmother to do."

"That's a bit below the belt."

"It's true, though. We're supposed to have a no-magic pact."

"Okay, okay. Where is he?"

"Just there, under his car."

I glanced around to make sure there was no one else around, and then reversed the spell. Then I quickly cast the 'forget' spell.

The man scrambled out from under his car, a little dusty, but otherwise none the worse for his ordeal. He did, though, look very confused.

Until this year, the best Washbridge could do for cinema lovers (yes, Mr Ivers, I *am* looking at you) was the dilapidated Washbridge Astoria. That fleapit had started to crumble when I was a kid, and it had only got worse since then. The nearest modern cinema had been in West Chipping.

But no longer.

Two weeks ago, Washbridge Screens, a ten-screen multiplex cinema, had opened in the city centre. Ever since then, Jack had been bugging me that we should pay it a visit. And so it was that we were queuing for tickets to see Red Storm.

"I told you we should have booked the tickets online." I sighed.

"We've got plenty of time before it starts. And besides, you said you wanted popcorn, didn't you?"

"What if the movie is sold out before we get served?"

"That's hardly likely. It's showing in three different screens. What size popcorn do you want?"

"The giant one will suffice."

"This is a lot better than the Astoria." Jack led the way down a long corridor. On either side, were doors to the screens, numbered one to ten.

"Which screen are we in?"

"Nine."

Once we got inside, I could barely see what I was doing because the lights were already down, and the trailers were showing.

"Jack, where are you?"

"Shush!" someone hissed.

"Sorry."

"Here." Jack took my hand and led the way up the stairs to row 'E'. "We're in the end seats."

Five minutes later, the main feature began. I'd been

looking forward to this particular movie for months. An action thriller with a kickass hero, it was never going to pick up an Oscar, but it was massively entertaining.

Fifty minutes in, and I was beginning to regret having popped into the coffee shop on our way to the cinema.

"I need the loo," I whispered.

"I told you not to get that large coffee."

"I'll only be a minute."

When I came out of the cloakroom, I looked up and down the corridor. Which screen were we in? Jack had the tickets, so I couldn't check those. It was—err—number five. No, it was six. Definitely screen six.

I crept back in, and much to my relief it was showing Red Storm. I'd been a little worried I might have misremembered the number. Now all I had to do was feel my way up the stairs to row E.

A, B, C, D, E.

I took my seat, and whispered, "Have I missed anything, Jack?"

"Who's Jack?" It was a woman's voice. "Why are you sitting there? My husband has just gone to buy ice cream."

"Oh? Sorry." I jumped out of the seat, hurried back down the stairs, and out into the corridor.

Which screen had we been in? Think, Jill! Nine! It was definitely screen nine.

Fingers crossed.

I made my way into screen nine, and up the stairs to row E.

"Jack?" I whispered.

"I thought you'd got lost."

"There was a queue."

***

On the way back home, Jack drove.

"You were right about the movie," he said. "It was great. It's just a pity you missed the best fight scene while you were at the loo."

"I think I preferred the Astoria."

"You said it was a fleapit."

"Yes, but it had character. These new multiplexes all look the same. They have no—err—"

"Fleas?"

"I was going to say soul."

Our next-door neighbours, Tony and Clare, were standing on our driveway; they'd obviously just been to our door.

"I wonder what they want," Jack said.

"I don't think they've spotted us yet. Drive around the block until they've gone."

"I'm not doing that. It could be important. It might be about TenPinCon."

"Aren't those two things mutually exclusive?"

"Hey, Jack," Tony was practically bubbling over with excitement. "Did you see the local evening news?"

"No, we've been to the cinema."

"They ran an article on TenPinCon. How did you manage to swing that?"

"Yeah, Jack," I said. "How did you manage that?"

"It was nothing. I have a few connections."

"I can't believe there's only a week to go." Clare was every bit as excited as her husband.

Tragic really.

"We have a surprise for you two," Tony announced.

I didn't like the sound of that. Not one tiny bit.

"Yes," Clare said. "It's a thank you for all the work you've put into the marketing campaign. Go and get them, Tony."

Them? The alarm bells started to ring.

Tony disappeared into their house and re-emerged moments later, carrying — err — I wasn't sure what.

"Look!" He held up whatever it/they were.

Jack looked every bit as puzzled as I was. "Err, thanks. They're — err — "

Clare jumped in. "Tenpin costumes for you and Jill to wear on the big day."

"Wow! Thanks guys." Jack's face lit up. "You shouldn't have." He'd got that much right. "Aren't they fantastic, Jill?"

"*Fantastic.*"

"Do you want to try them on now?" Tony said.

Before Jack could say something I'd regret, I grabbed his arm. "We'd love to, but we both have an early start in the morning, don't we, Jack?"

"I — err — "

"Not to worry." Tony handed them to Jack. "Try them on tomorrow and let us know what you think."

"Will do." I started for the door. "Goodnight, you two."

"That was kind of them, wasn't it?" Jack said, once we were in the house.

"I'm not parading around Washbridge Arena wearing that thing."

"It'll be fun."

"Not. Happening." I started upstairs. "I'm going to get a

shower, and then I'm off to bed. I'm bushed."

I was still annoyed at myself for missing the best action sequence in the movie. I'd just have to watch the part I'd missed when the movie became available for streaming later in the year.

Wrapped in a towel, I stepped into the bedroom, only to be confronted by a giant tenpin with legs and arms.

"You just couldn't resist it, could you?"

"It fits great." Jack's muffled voice came from inside the costume.

"You look really sexy."

"Yeah?"

"No, of course not. You look ridiculous."

"You should put yours on. We could mess around for a while before we turn in for the night."

"If you think I'm getting kinky with a giant rubber skittle, you've got another think coming."

***

When I woke the next morning, the bedroom was freezing.

I went in search of Jack, who I found in the kitchen, wearing his coat.

"Why is it so cold in here?" I shivered.

"The boiler has packed up."

"Can't you mend it?"

"I've tried switching it off and on again, but that didn't do anything."

"Some handyman you are. I'm frozen."

"You could always put your tenpin costume on. They're

really warm."

"Not a chance. We'd better call the boiler man."

"I've already done it. He's coming between ten and eleven this morning. Can you stay in for him? I can't do it because I have a meeting I can't get out of."

"It doesn't sound like I have much choice. How much is this going to cost us?"

"Nothing. We have a maintenance contract, remember?"

"Oh yeah. I knew that contract was a good idea."

"You said it was a complete waste of money."

Not long after Jack had left for work, Daze phoned.

"Hey, Jill. Could I pop over to see you?"

"Sure, but you'll need to come to the house. I have to stay in because I'm waiting for the boiler man."

"No problem. Is it okay if I bring the surveillance imps over with me?"

"I guess so."

"We'll be with you in a few minutes."

Daze had asked the surveillance imps to keep an eye on the three CASS school governors. Hopefully, they would have something to report.

My phone rang again, and I assumed Daze had forgotten to tell me something, but it was Kathy.

"Morning, Sis!" She sounded obscenely pleased with life. "How are you?"

"Cold. The boiler gave up overnight."

"Bummer. What are you going to do about it?"

"Fortunately, I had the foresight to take out a maintenance contract. The guy is coming later this morning."

"I just wanted to let you know that Pete has set on that friend of yours."

"Reggie?"

"Yeah. Pete reckons he's a giant of a guy. He didn't have any references, but Pete said if you vouched for him, that was good enough."

"I'm sure he'll do a great job."

"Aren't you going to ask me how the new shop's doing?"

"I don't need to. I can tell from your voice."

"We had a blockbuster weekend."

"I'm really pleased for you. How is Pippa doing?"

"She's absolutely brilliant. Where did you find her?"

"Just a friend of a friend."

"She's doing so well that I don't feel the need to call in there today. I'm happy to let her run the show."

"That's great. How's Lizzie, by the way?"

"So much brighter since she started dreaming again. The only problem now is that she insists on telling me all about her dreams every morning."

"Jack does the same, and they're always so boring — usually bowling related."

"Anyway, how was your weekend?"

"Quiet. We went to the new multiplex last night."

"What did you go to see?"

"Red Storm."

"Really? Pete and I went to see that last week. That fight sequence in the middle was amazing wasn't it?"

"Amazing." Or so I heard, anyway.

"I'd better get going. I just wanted to tell you about Reggie. I hope you get your boiler sorted out."

"Thanks."

Ten minutes later, Daze appeared, accompanied by the three surveillance imps. Although Daze had vouched for her companions, I still had my doubts about them. They had untrustworthy faces.

Daze made the introductions. "Jill, this is Ray, this is May, and this is Jay."

"I'm very pleased to meet you all. Shall we go through to the kitchen? It's a little warmer in there because I have the small fan heater on."

"Why don't you just use magic to heat the place?" Ray asked.

"I try not to use magic in the human world unless it's absolutely necessary. Would you all like a drink? Tea? Coffee? Juice?"

"I'd love a cup of tea," Daze said.

The three imps said they'd have the same.

As I was feeling generous, and because I still had a cupboard full of custard creams due to the shopping app mishap, I put a few onto a plate for my guests.

"What are those?" May pointed to the biscuits.

"Custard creams."

"I've never seen those before," Jay said. "Are they nice?"

"*Nice*? They're much more than nice. They're the king of biscuits."

I thought the custard creams might be a little on the large side for the imps, but I needn't have worried.

"Hmm! These are delicious." Ray munched.

May clearly agreed with him because she was already on her second.

Five minutes later, the plate was empty, and yet Daze

and I had only managed to eat one each. Jay glanced at the empty plate, and then at me, but I ignored him. If he thought he was getting any more, he was sadly mistaken.

"Okay, you three," Daze said. "Why don't you tell Jill what you've seen so far?"

"I've been following Randolph Straightstaff," May said.

Ray confirmed he'd been assigned to Francesca Greylock.

"And I've been watching Adrian Bowler," Jay said. "It was the same story for all of us—there's been very little to report. Until yesterday, that is."

"What happened yesterday?"

"All three of them went to the same public house."

"In Candlefield?"

"Yes. It's called the Whisperer's Horse."

"I can't say I've ever heard of it."

"Do you know Bryan's Irons?" Jay asked.

"No, I don't think so."

"What about Bart's Tarts?" May said.

"No."

"You must know June's Spoons," Ray said.

"I'm sorry, but I don't."

"The Whisperer's Horse is between Bryan's Irons and Bart's Tarts, and across the road from June's Spoons."

"One of you should sketch a map to show Jill where it is." Daze suggested.

"Good idea." May took out a small notebook. "I'll do it."

"What happened in the pub?" I was doing my best not to let my impatience show.

"That's just it." Jay shrugged. "We don't know. All three of them arrived at the same time and went through to a private room at the back. There were a couple of huge werewolves on the door. They wouldn't let us in, so we staked out the two exits and waited for them to come out."

"And? What happened?"

"Nothing. We waited there for hours but there was no sign of them. None of them left the building. By midnight, we knew something was wrong, so May volunteered to go back to Randolph Straightstaff's house."

"He was there," May said. "Back in his own bed. So I checked on the other two. They were back home too."

"You must have missed them coming out of the pub."

"We couldn't have. We never took our eyes off the exits all the time we were there."

"So how did they get out? And what were they doing in there in the first place?"

"Your guess is as good as ours," Ray said.

"Can you continue to keep tabs on them? If they return to the Whisperer's Horse, let me know straight away. I want to see what goes on inside that private room."

"Will do."

Just then, there was a knock at the door. I checked the window to find the boiler man's van parked on the road outside.

"Sorry guys, the man is here to fix the boiler. You'll have to make yourselves scarce."

"Hi, lady. I'm here about the boiler." He flashed his ID. "The name's Doyle."

"Come in." I took him upstairs to the cupboard where the boiler was located.

Five minutes later, he came back downstairs. "It's going

to be a costly job, I'm afraid."

"That's okay. We've got a maintenance contract."

"Oh?" He tapped away on his laptop. "It doesn't appear so. You didn't renew it when it expired last month."

That's when I remembered seeing the renewal notice, and thinking that it was a total waste of money. And then, I remembered throwing it in the bin.

Oh bum! Jack was going to kill me.

Chapter 2

I was just about to get into the car when I spotted something on our front lawn: A small, smelly, unwanted gift from one of the neighbourhood felines. Could Lovely have done it? She surely wouldn't have repaid my recent act of kindness in that way. Not after I'd persuaded the Livelys to revert back to her favourite food.

And then I spotted him. Sitting in Jimmy and Kimmy's driveway was my nemesis, Bruiser, and he was grinning from ear to ear.

"If I get my hands on you, I'll—"

"Jill?" Kimmy appeared in her front doorway. "Why are you threatening my little fluffykins?"

Fluffykins? Who was she kidding? "I—err, no I wasn't shouting at your cat. It was the other one."

"Oh?" She looked up and down the street. "Which other one?"

"It was a horrible thing. A big tabby. I thought it was going to attack Bruiser, so I shooed it off."

Unseen by Kimmy, Bruiser was smirking at me—he was no doubt thoroughly enjoying my discomfort.

Kimmy took another look up and down the street. "Thank you, Jill. It looks like it's gone now."

"I hope so. I wouldn't want to see any harm come to your little fluffykins."

The vegetable du jour was a leek. It seemed that Mr Ivers had a never-ending supply of those stupid hand puppets. After the leek had collected my cash, the puppet master himself stuck his head above the counter.

"Morning, Jill."

"Morning. You must have nearly worked your way through all the vegetable hand puppets by now."

"Not even close. I've got at least another ten up my sleeve." He chuckled. "Or should I say, *on* my sleeve."

"Right, well I should get a move on. Time and tide, and all that."

"Have you been to the new multiplex yet, Jill?"

"Jack and I went there yesterday to see Red Storm."

"An excellent movie. And that fight sequence, I've never seen anything quite like it."

"It was really something, wasn't it?"

"The new cinema is so much more convenient for me. I used to have to travel to West Chipping. I've signed up for their All-Inclusive Pass. I can go as often as I like for one monthly fee."

"I imagine you'll get your money's worth out of that."

"You're not wrong. I'll be practically living there."

***

Mrs V was sniffing her wrists.

"Are you alright, Mrs V?"

"Morning, Jill." She held out her hands. "Which do you prefer?"

"Your hands both look the same to me."

"I meant the perfumes, silly. There was a closing down sale at Vera's Perfume Counter, so I grabbed half a dozen. The prices were so good, I couldn't resist. Armi prefers Love Halo, but I think Blue Indigo is nicer."

I sniffed her wrists. They both smelled exactly the same to me.

"I—err—I actually have a bit of a cold, so my sense of

smell isn't great right now."

"But which one do you like best?"

"Err, the left one, I think."

"Blue Indigo. Me too. Thanks, Jill. That's the one I'll wear on Saturday night."

"Do you and Armi have something special planned?"

"Just me, actually. It's my school reunion. It's the first one they've held for over ten years."

"Right. Where's it being held?"

I assumed it must be somewhere very small. Maybe a telephone kiosk? After all, how many of her classmates would still even be alive?

What? Sheesh, I was only joking.

"At our old school of course. It'll be lovely to see all the old faces."

There would be plenty of those. "Aren't partners invited?"

"Yes, but—err—Armi doesn't want to go. It isn't really his type of thing." Mrs V was possibly the world's worst liar, but before I could press her further, she changed the subject. "It's such a pity about Alistair. Both of him."

"It's probably for the best. I've always worked better alone."

"You're like the Lone Ranger."

"Precisely."

"I see you managed to get rid of that awful desk of his over the weekend."

"Err, yeah. Fifty quid."

"You did well to get anything for that monstrosity. Oh, and while I remember, you asked me to remind you about your dental appointment this afternoon."

Oh bum, I'd forgotten about that. "I don't think I'm

going to bother."

"But last week you said you'd felt a few twinges of toothache."

"It seems to have cleared up over the weekend."

"You should go and get it looked at or it may come back, and it could be worse next time."

"I suppose you're right."

Winky was sitting on my desk. As soon as I walked in the door, he held out a paw.

"What?" I pretended to have no idea what he wanted.

"You know what. It's time to pay your debts."

"Okay, okay." I took out my purse and handed him one-hundred and fifty pounds. "Satisfied?"

"You're short."

"That was the wager we agreed for the hula hoop challenge."

"True, but you're forgetting the fifty pounds for disposing of doliphant boy's desk."

"Won't you take pity on me? I've just had to fork out to get the boiler repaired."

"Not my problem. You should have taken out a maintenance contract."

"I'll be broke if I give you another fifty pounds. Just think of all the things I've done for you over the years."

"Hmm?" He thought for all of thirty seconds, and then said, "Nah, I can't think of anything. Hand over the cash."

"Here!" I threw my last five ten-pound notes at him. "I hope you can live with yourself."

"There's no need to get ratty with me, just because you're scared to go to the dentist."

"Don't be ridiculous. I'm not scared of the dentist. And

besides, it was only a slight twinge. There's probably nothing wrong."

"Hmm?"

"What does that mean?"

"One of those molars doesn't look too clever."

"What are you talking about?" I ran my finger over my teeth. "They're all in perfect condition."

"We'll see."

And now, to spend even more money that I didn't have.

"Mr Song?"

"Sid Song speaking."

"It's Jill Maxwell."

"Oh." I could almost hear his heart sinking. "What's wrong now?"

"I need another sign."

"Another one?" he warbled. "I thought you were only allowed to display the one."

"I am. I need a sign exactly the same as the last one you provided, but this one needs to be at least two centimetres narrower. It seems the last one was wider than is allowed under the terms of my lease."

"Wouldn't it have been a good idea for you to check that before you placed your order?"

"I realise that now. Can you make me another sign or not?"

"Of course. It will be the same price as the last one."

"But it's two centimetres smaller?"

"That won't affect the price, I'm afraid."

"Okay. Get on with it."

"I assume you'll need us to remove the old sign?"

"Actually, no. I've already taken care of that. How long

will the new sign take you?"

"I should be able to do it within two or three weeks."

"No quicker than that?"

"I'm afraid not. We're snowed under right now."

"Fine. Just do it as quickly as you can, please."

My ten o'clock appointment arrived bang on time.

"Do have a seat, Mr Claymore."

"Thank you, but I'd prefer to stand if it's all the same to you."

"Err, sure."

"It's just that I had a boil lanced on Friday, and it's still—"

"O—kay. So how can I help, exactly?"

"I own the large car lot on the road to Smallwash. You've probably seen it."

"Do you mean Bestest Motors?"

"That's the one. Maybe I've sold you a car?"

"No, I don't think so." I refused to do business with someone with such a weak grip on the English language.

What? Yes, I'm well aware that I have also been known to say 'bestest', but when I've used it, it's always been in an ironical way. Obviously.

"Someone has been stealing my cars."

"I see."

"And then bringing them back."

"Oh?"

"Sprayed green."

"Let me make sure I understand this correctly. Are you saying that cars are being stolen from your car lot, and then being returned after they've been sprayed green?"

"Yes, well it's a sort of greeny blue, actually. The wife

insists it's turquoise."

"Okay. I don't think the colour materially affects the main facts. Do you have CCTV installed?"

"No. I never got around to it."

"How long are the cars gone for typically?"

"Usually no more than three or four days."

"And only one at a time?"

"That's right."

"Does whoever is taking them favour any particular model of car?"

"No. They've taken all sorts. It's getting beyond a joke."

"That's all very strange. When you say the cars have been resprayed, what are we talking about exactly? Is it a professional job or just a quick once over with a spray can?"

"It's definitely a professional job. Really good quality, actually. It wouldn't be so bad if they'd chosen a more popular colour, but there's a limit to how many green cars I can shift."

"Do you have any disgruntled employees, or competitors who you think might do something like this?"

"Both, actually. There's Sandy Gascoigne. He used to be my top salesman, but he got too big for his boots. He was always trying to tell me how I should run my business, so I sacked him."

"How long ago was that?"

"About six months."

"Do you know what he's doing now?"

"No idea. Don't much care."

"And you mentioned a competitor?"

"Yes. Harry Wilde at Wilde Cars. He's always been jealous of the number of cars I shift."

"Do you think he's capable of something like this?"

"He's a pain in the backside, but I wouldn't have thought so. But who knows?"

"When did this business with the green cars start?"

"About a month ago."

"Anyone else you think I should take a look at?"

"Not that I can think of."

"Okay. I think I have everything I need for now."

"I hope you can get to the bottom of this soon. If you don't, I might have to rename the business Green Cars."

***

Winky had cleaned me out of cash, so until I could get to the ATM, I only had a little loose change—and I was starving. Where was I supposed to get something to eat and drink without any money?

"Morning, Mindy."

"Hi, Jill."

"Look, this is a bit embarrassing, but I've come out without my purse. Do you think you could let me have a coffee and a muffin, and put it on my tab, please?"

"I didn't know you had a tab."

"Oh yeah, the twins—"

"She doesn't have one." Amber appeared from the back room. "She's trying it on."

"Hi, Amber, I thought it was your day off today."

"It should be, but Belladonna rang in sick, so Pearl and I are taking it in turns to cover the creche. She's up there now."

"Where are Lil and Lily?"

"Mum's got them."

"About the whole *tab* thing. You realise that I was only joking, right?"

"Hmm."

"Look, I'll come clean. I don't have any cash until I can get to the ATM. The cat cleared me out this morning."

"Did you just say *your cat*?" Mindy obviously thought she'd misheard.

"Yes, it's a long, complicated story that involves hula hoops and an orange desk."

"Who would buy an orange desk?" Amber raised her eyebrows.

"Please, Amber. I'm starving. I promise I'll pay the next time I come in."

"Okay, but just this once. And only the one muffin."

"Thanks, you're a star. What's wrong with Belladonna?"

"Food poisoning, she said."

"While she's not here, there's something you should know about her."

"Don't start with that again, Jill. I don't understand why you have it in for that girl."

"Honestly, you need to hear this."

"No, we don't. We know all we need to know about her. She's brilliant at her job, and the kids and parents all love her. I don't want to hear another word about her."

"But, I—"

"Not another word."

There was no helping some people.

***

When I got back to the office, there was a chill in the air, and Winky was under the sofa. My mother's ghost had made herself comfortable at my desk.

"Morning, Mum."

"Morning. Don't you think it's time you spruced this place up a bit? Or moved to somewhere more modern?"

"I like it here, and I like it just the way it is."

"I can't imagine what your clients must think of it."

"Did you come over just to criticise my office or was there something else you wanted?"

"I'm here to invite you to the grand opening of Cakey C."

"You're still going with *that* name, then?"

"Why wouldn't we?"

"Well, let me see. Maybe because you blatantly ripped it off from Cuppy C."

"You fuss too much. So, will you come?"

"Do I have a choice?"

"No, not really. It's this Thursday, and every ghost who is anyone is going to be there. Harry and Larry are coming, and the colonel and Priscilla, of course."

"I trust there'll be plenty of free cake."

"Absolutely. We aim to make a big splash."

"Okay. Count me in."

"Someone else you know will be there too."

"Oh? Who's that?"

"She came to see me the other day, completely out of the blue. I wasn't sure if I should mention it or not."

"Who did?"

"Jack's mother."

"Yvonne? Are you sure it was her?"

"Of course I'm sure. She came to see me at the shop

while we were still doing it up."

"I didn't even realise she was in GT."

"I don't think she wanted you to know. Not until she was ready."

"What did she have to say?"

"She wanted my advice on the best way for her to make contact."

"With Jack?"

"Eventually, yeah."

"What did you tell her?"

"I said she should discuss it with you first. That you'd know if it was a good idea, and whether Jack could handle it."

"I'm not sure how he'll react. How did she seem?"

"Fine, but she was obviously nervous about contacting you or Jack. I think you should speak to Yvonne before you say anything to him. She'll be at the launch party on Thursday. You can always nip through to the back to have a quiet word with her."

"That would probably be best."

I was stunned. For some reason, it had simply never occurred to me that I'd ever see Yvonne again. I owed that woman my life; she'd sacrificed herself to save me. I wanted to call Jack and tell him, but I knew I had to wait until I'd had the chance to speak to Yvonne myself first. I wouldn't want to raise his hopes until I was sure this was really going to happen.

Chapter 3

No sooner had my mother disappeared than Winky started making a ridiculous grinding sound.

"Why are you making that stupid noise?"

"That's my impression of a dentist's drill."

Oh bum! Was it that time already?

Mrs V popped her head around the door. "You haven't forgotten your dental appointment, have you?"

"Of course I haven't!" I snapped.

"Sorry."

"No, it's me who should be sorry. I didn't mean to snap at you. The cat has been winding me up."

"*The cat?*"

"You know how he can be when he wants feeding. Could you put some food out for him, please? I'd better be making tracks."

"Alright, dear. Good luck."

Luck? What did she mean by that? Had she spotted a cavity too?

***

My regular dentist had retired a few months ago, and I hadn't yet been seen by his replacement, a Mr Payne.

"Good morning, madam." Needless to say, the young woman on reception had perfect teeth.

"Morning. I'm Jill Maxwell. I have a check-up at one o'clock."

She checked her computer. "I don't seem to have you listed for today."

"You probably still have me under my maiden name:

Jill Gooder. I don't think I got around to updating it."

"Oh yes, here you are. Take a seat, please."

While I waited to be called, I pondered an age-old question: Why was it that the only place you ever found light aircraft magazines was in a dentist's waiting room?

"Mrs Maxwell!" The dental nurse, who also had perfect teeth, showed me through to the surgery.

The dentist was young. Much too young if you asked me. He couldn't possibly have finished dental school.

"I'm Mr Payne, but please call me Max."

Max Payne? Seriously?

"I'm Jill."

The nurse manoeuvred me onto the reclining chair, and placed a pair of ill-fitting glasses over my eyes.

"Any problems, Jill?" Max said.

"None. Everything's absolutely fine."

"Excellent. Let's just have a quick look. Open wide." He poked around for a few seconds, and then said, "Hmm?"

What did that mean? Nothing good, I'd bet.

"You have a bit of a cavity in this one." He tapped one of my back teeth. "Nothing we can't sort out. Everything else seems fine. Okay, you can sit up now."

The nurse removed the glasses.

"Do I need a filling?"

"Yes. Just the one. If you make an appointment at reception on your way out, we'll soon have it sorted."

"Right, thanks."

I made the appointment for the following Monday. One small filling was nothing to worry about. I most likely wouldn't feel a thing.

After surviving that ordeal, I deserved coffee and a muffin.

But, hold on! Perhaps the muffins were the reason I had the cavity in the first place. I would definitely have to cut back on the sugary treats.

***

"Could I have a caramel latte and a blueberry muffin, please?"

What? Obviously, I meant that I was going to cut back from tomorrow. Sheesh, give a girl a break.

Instead of making my coffee, the young man behind the counter in Coffee Games began to make all kinds of weird gestures with his arms.

"Sorry?" I didn't have the first clue what he was trying to convey to me.

The woman behind me in the queue noticed my confusion, and said, "It's charades day."

"Oh? Right."

The man was holding up two fingers.

"Two words?"

He nodded, then held up one finger.

"First word?"

He nodded again, then held up two fingers.

Huh? "Second word?"

He shook his head.

"Oh, you mean the first word is *two*."

He nodded, and then put up two fingers again.

"Second word?"

He nodded, and then cupped his ear.

"Sounds like?"

He nodded, and then lifted his foot onto the counter.

"Foot? Sounds like foot?"

He shook his head, and pointed again.

"Sounds like toes?"

He touched his foot again, but this time held up one finger.

"Toe? Sounds like toe?"

He touched his nose with his index finger, and waited for me to work it out.

What sounded like toe? Bow, dough, foe —

"Go!"

He nodded.

First word is two. Second word is go? Hang on, I've got it.

"To go?"

He touched his nose with his index finger.

"No, thanks. I'm going to drink in."

I'd just taken my first bite of blueberry muffinness when —

"Jill? It is you, isn't it?"

"Norman?"

Norman, AKA Mastermind, was a long-time acquaintance of mine. He'd first entered my orbit when he'd been dating Betty Longbottom. It was Norman who had been responsible for introducing me to the wacky world of bottle top collectors. After he and Betty had split up, he'd opened his own shop, selling bottle tops. The last time I'd seen him, he'd been with Tonya, a fellow MENSA candidate, who had at one time worked at the local betting shop.

"Do you mind if I join you for a minute, Jill?"

"I—err—of course not."

"I was thinking of coming to see you, but when I looked for your offices, your sign had disappeared."

"That's kind of a long story. What did you want to see me about? Do you have bottle top issues?"

"No. It's got nothing to do with the business."

"What then?"

"It's Tonya."

"She's your girlfriend, right?"

"My wife."

"You're married? When did that happen?"

"We eloped."

"To Gretna Green?"

"To Wood Green, actually. Tonya got the booking mixed up."

"Right."

"She's changed, Jill."

"In what way?"

"We've always had common interests."

"Bottle tops, you mean?"

"Yes, and mailboxes."

"*Mailboxes?*"

"That's Tonya's thing, really, but I've always tried to be encouraging about them. Just like she does with my bottle tops."

"She collects mailboxes?"

"No." He laughed. "She likes to take photos of them. We've travelled all over the country doing it."

"You said she's changed? In what way?"

"It's hard to put my finger on it. She seems kind of distant. As though she isn't really with me even when she is."

"Relationships do change over time."

"I know. It's probably just my imagination, but I'm worried she might be cheating on me."

"I seriously doubt that."

"I'd still like you to find out for sure, just to put my mind at ease."

"Okay, but I'd have to charge for my time."

"Of course. That's not a problem. The bottle top business is going from strength to strength. I opened a website earlier this year, and that's now making more money than the shop. At this rate, I'll be able to retire by the time I'm forty."

I was clearly in the wrong line of business.

***

Back at the office, Armi was in conversation with Mrs V.

"Hi, Armi. Long time, no see."

"Hello, Jill."

"What are you up to these days?"

"I've mostly retired now, but I do like to keep my hand in with the cuckoos."

"I thought you and the Cuckoo Clock Appreciation Society had parted company?"

"I'm done with those officious idiots, but I still enjoy building the clocks. Would you and Jack like one for your house?"

"I—err—"

"Of course you would, wouldn't you, Jill?" Mrs V chimed in.

"Absolutely. That would be very nice." We had plenty of room in the spare bedroom now, so no one need ever see it. "It's a pity that you aren't able to go with Mrs V to the school—"

Mrs V cut straight across me. "You'd better be making tracks, my little gingerbread man." She took his arm and led him to the door. "Jill and I have a lot of work to get through."

"Okay, see you tonight." He gave her a peck on the cheek, and then took his leave.

"What's going on, Mrs V?" I pinned her with my gaze.

"I don't know what you mean."

"Yes, you do. You cut me off just as I was about to mention your school reunion."

"No, I didn't."

"Yes, you did. Armi doesn't know about it, does he?"

Even before she replied, I knew the answer; the guilt was written all over her face.

"No, but he wouldn't enjoy it anyway."

Now I was really intrigued. "Why don't you want him to know about it? There wouldn't be someone there that you don't want him to meet, would there?"

"Of course not."

"Mrs V?"

"Alright. If you must know, I'm expecting Roland Brass to be there."

"And who exactly is Roland Brass?"

"We dated at school. He was the captain of the football team and I was the—"

"The chief cheerleader?"

"Of course not. I was the captain of the knitting team."

"When was the last time you saw him?"

"At one of the early reunions, but that's over thirty years ago now."

"But you still have the hots for him?"

"Don't be ridiculous. I'm a happily married woman."

"So why don't you want Armi to meet him?"

"It's not that. I just don't think he'd enjoy himself."

"I hope you know what you're doing. I've seen this type of thing go wrong before."

I was thinking back to when Amber and Pearl had attended a school reunion in the hope of seeing their schoolgirl crush, Miles Best. That hadn't ended well.

Winky had company. And his visitor was someone I hadn't expected ever to see again. He and the professor were deep in conversation, studying plans of some kind.

"We won't be a minute," Winky said, without even looking up. "You can take a seat on the sofa."

"That's very kind of you."

I tried to overhear what they were discussing, but they were deliberately talking in hushed voices. After about five minutes, they shook paws, and the professor made his way out of the window.

"What was that all about?"

"Just a bit of business."

"With him? After what happened with the zip wire?"

"Cat Zip."

"Whatever. You were nearly killed."

"That wasn't the professor's fault. The wire was faulty."

"Don't tell me you're going to try the zip wire—err—Cat Zip again? It would be suicide."

"Relax. We've come up with a new project that promises to be even more profitable than Cat Zip could ever have been."

"Is it as dangerous?"

"No, it's perfectly safe."

"So? What is it?"

"I can't tell you."

"I don't mind signing an NDA."

"Sorry. It's top secret at the moment."

"Please yourself. It's not like I care anyway. I have more important things to concern myself with."

"Like the dentist's chair?" He did his impression of the dentist's drill again. "Didn't I tell you that you had a cavity? Those fillings can be really painful."

"Don't be daft. I won't feel a thing. And anyway, how do you know I have to go back for a filling?"

"Tommy the Tooth gave me the nod."

"Who?"

"Tommy the Tooth. He's lived at that dental practice for the last five years. There's nothing that guy doesn't know about teeth. Who do you think looks after mine?"

"You just make this stuff up as you go along."

***

The week had got off to a promising start. It was only Monday, and I'd already booked two new cases. Granted, one of those was for Mastermind Norman, but they all counted.

Luther would be proud of me. That reminded me, I needed to give him a call.

"Luther, it's Jill."

"Hi. Is everything okay?"

"Everything's just dandy, thanks. I thought I'd let you know that I gave some thought to what you said when you were here last."

"Oh?"

"About my new office manager. I ran the numbers and decided you were right. The business couldn't afford him, so I've let him go."

"So soon?"

"Yes, but it's okay because he had another job to go to. I've also decided to close the Coventry office."

"Is that a good idea? You seemed to get a lot of work over there."

"It's fine. Work is really picking up here in Washbridge. I've signed up two new cases just today."

"That's great. Thanks for keeping me posted, Jill."

"No problem."

Now all I had to do was to remember not to mark any of the cases with a 'C' from now on.

***

Britt was in her front garden, and on first glance, she appeared to be talking to their new tree.

"Come down. He's gone."

"Is everything okay, Britt?"

"Hi, Jill. It's Lovely."

"I agree. It's a very handsome tree."

"No, I mean *my* Lovely." She pointed to the top of the tree. "I think she's stuck."

Sure enough, Lovely was looking down at us from her precarious perch.

"She'll be okay," I reassured Britt. "They always find their way down eventually. They just like to scare us."

"It's all the fault of that horrible creature from across the road. Have you seen Jimmy and Kimmy's cat?"

"Bruiser?"

"He certainly is. A real horror."

"No, that's his name: Bruiser. They used to keep him at the office."

"I wish they'd left him there. He's been terrorising poor Lovely."

Just then, Lovely shot down from the tree, and rushed around the back of the house.

"See," I said. "I told you she'd be okay."

"Thanks, Jill. I really shouldn't get so worked up, but I can't help myself. You know what it's like with cats. You get so attached to them."

"Hmm."

"I'm glad I've seen you, anyway."

"If it's about Jack and the glockenspiel, I can explain."

"No, it isn't that. We really enjoyed the Normal's housewarming party, didn't you?"

"Err, yeah, it was great."

"Anyway, we got to thinking that we missed out by not having one."

"I wouldn't say that."

"But then we thought why not have one now? It's not like we've lived here very long."

"Isn't there some kind of time limit?"

"No, I'm sure there isn't. So, our big news is that we're going to have a housewarming party this Wednesday, and obviously, we'd love it if you and Jack could come."

I was just about to make our excuses when Jack's car pulled up on the driveway.

"Hi, you two!" He came over to join us.

"I was just telling Jill that we're going to have a belated housewarming party this Wednesday."

I jumped in. "And I was just about to tell Britt that we were already doing something—"

"We'd love to." He gushed. "We had a blast at the Normal's party, didn't we, Jill?"

"A blast. Yeah."

"I'm really excited about the party," Jack said when we were inside the house.

"Me too." Sigh.

"I see the heating is working. Thank goodness for that. Did the boiler man say what the problem was?"

"The paperwork is on the kitchen table." I started for the stairs. "I think I'll take a bath before dinner."

I was halfway up the stairs when he shouted, "Why isn't the *maintenance contract-no charge* box ticked?"

Chapter 4

The next morning, the traffic in Washbridge city centre was horrendous. It took me ten minutes longer than usual to reach the car park. As far as I could make out, the reason for the delay was a pothole that had opened up on the road outside my office.

Mrs V was looking particularly resplendent.

"What do you think, Jill?" She did a little twirl to show off the maroon dress.

"It's very nice."

"I bought it for the reunion on Saturday."

"The one you haven't told Armi about?"

"I told him last night."

"I'm pleased to hear it. Is he going with you?"

"No. He didn't seem very bothered."

"Hmm." Something told me Mrs V hadn't tried too hard to sell him on the idea. Still, at least she wasn't going behind his back now.

"I'd better go and change out of this. I just wanted you to see it."

"Remind me, do I have any appointments today?"

"Just the one. This afternoon at two o'clock with a Mrs Cheryl Warne. She called yesterday after you'd left."

"Okay."

The punch bag was back, and Winky was working up a sweat, knocking seven bells out of it.

"Why is that thing back in here?"

"I need to keep my paw in."

"Why? Bruiser has gone now."

"Of course he has. He knew what he was in for if he hung around here any longer."

"I'm not convinced that's why he left. I reckon it might have had more to do with the landlord."

"I can't believe you fell for that lame excuse of his. Anyway, that's all history now. I've got bigger fish to fry."

"What do you mean?"

"I'm in training for the Washbridge Feline Boxing Tournament."

"Please tell me you're joking."

"Why would I be joking? If I can scare off the likes of Bruiser without having to land a single punch, why should I be worried about anyone else?"

Oh bum! When I'd pretended to be Macabre, in order to persuade Jimmy and Kimmy to get rid of Bruiser, it had never occurred to me that it would encourage Winky to do something as crazy as this.

"But you'll be up against professional boxers."

"So? Bring them on. The bigger they are, the harder they'll fall." And with that, he went back to thumping the punch bag.

It was no good. I simply couldn't allow him to go through with this. He would end up getting badly hurt. There was only one thing to do. I'd have to come clean and tell him the truth.

"Winky, can you stop that just for a minute? There's something important I need to tell you."

"Can't it wait?" He landed another two punches.

"No. I need to tell you this now before you do something stupid."

"Okay." He stepped back from the punch bag. "But make it quick."

"When Bruiser was threatening to fight you, I was concerned for your safety."

"Because of Bruiser?" He laughed. "Do me a favour."

"I was so worried that I decided to use magic to make myself look like the landlord, Mr Macabre. I went to see the people over at Clown, and told them if they didn't remove the cat from the premises, their lease would be terminated. That's the real reason that Bruiser left. I'm really sorry, but I only did it to protect you."

He stared at me for a long minute without speaking. I was expecting him to berate me for what I'd done, but instead, he began to laugh. "That's very funny. You almost had me going there."

"I'm not joking."

"You'll have to come up with much better than that to fool Winky." He went back to thumping the punch bag.

***

The cases were beginning to pile up. From a financial standpoint, that was great news, but the logistics were a bit of a nightmare. Norman's case, in particular, was problematic. Suspected infidelity cases required around the clock surveillance, but that wasn't something I could do alongside my other workload.

I wasn't worried though because I'd had a brainwave.

What do you mean: Oh dear?

I'd arranged to meet Daze at Cuppy C. She was already at a table when I got there, so I went to the counter to order my coffee.

"Six-pounds-fifty, please," Amber said.

"*How* much?" I assumed she was having a laugh.

"That includes the coffee and muffin you didn't pay for yesterday. You hadn't forgotten, had you?"

"No, of course not. In fact, I was just about to remind you." Drat! Foiled again. "Is Belladonna still off ill?"

"No, she's upstairs in the creche. She seems to have got over the food poisoning, thank goodness. I'm not sure I could have faced another day in the creche. One child at a time is more than enough for me. I don't know how Belladonna manages it."

"Hmm." I had to bite my tongue because I knew the twins weren't interested in hearing anything bad about Belladonna.

"Thanks for coming, Daze. I hope I didn't drag you away from anything important."

"That's okay. Blaze and I are having a well-deserved rest in-between cases. How about you? Are you busy at the moment?"

"Very. In fact, that's the reason I gave you a call. I've just taken on a case that needs someone to carry out surveillance pretty much around the clock. There's no way I can do that and work on my other cases too."

"Couldn't you hire someone to help?"

"That's what I plan to do, but the thing is, I don't need someone on a permanent basis. Only when this type of case crops up. My father had the same problem when he was running the business, and on the few occasions he did bring someone in, it rarely worked out well."

"I'm not sure where I come in?"

"It was the surveillance imps that gave me the idea. I was wondering if you could recommend a sup who might be interested in the work."

"I see." She thought about it for a moment. "There is someone, but—no, I don't think it would work."

"Tell me, please."

"A few years back, when we had more work than we and the imps could handle, we sometimes brought in a fairy called Edna. She's retired now, so she probably wouldn't be interested."

"Could you at least ask her?"

"I can, but you need to know what you're letting yourself in for."

"What do you mean?"

"Edna can be—" She hesitated. "How shall I put this? A pain in the bum. She's a cantankerous old biddy."

"But is she any good at her job?"

"The best. She always got results."

"She sounds just what I need. Would you give her a call and see if she's interested?"

"Okay, but don't say I didn't warn you."

As Daze and I wound up our conversation, I spotted Belladonna coming downstairs and leaving the shop, presumably on her lunch break.

I followed her, and just as on the previous occasion, she stopped off at the market to purchase a bunch of purple and black flowers, and then made her way to the unmarked grave in the Shadows.

This time, though, I made no attempt to hide.

"Jill?" She almost dropped the flowers when I approached her. "What are you doing here?"

"I followed you."

"Why?"

"I know this is your mother's grave."

She placed the flowers in front of the headstone. "What of it?"

"I also know who she was, and what she did."

"Oh?"

"Is that all you have to say for yourself? *Oh*?"

"What else am I supposed to say? You've no doubt already made up your mind about me. Just like everyone else has done before."

"She stole the souls of hundreds of children, just so she could remain young."

"Do you think I don't already know that?"

"And yet, you put flowers on her grave."

"I'm sickened by what she did, but—" Her words faded away.

"But what?"

"But she was still my mother."

"And from what I've seen, you've inherited her power over children. No wonder you're able to control them so easily. When did you plan on stealing their souls? Or have you done that already?"

"Of course I haven't." She slumped onto her knees and began to sob uncontrollably. It was several minutes before she recovered her composure enough to speak. "I suppose you're going to tell the twins?"

"Of course I am. And the police too."

"It's the same every time." She got to her feet. "Sooner or later, someone realises who my mother was, and this happens. I'm tried and convicted without ever being given a chance to defend myself."

"It's indefensible."

"What my mother did was indefensible, I agree. But I've

done absolutely nothing wrong. Yes, I do have a certain way with children, but I've never abused that 'power' if that's what you insist on calling it."

"And you expect me to believe that, do you?"

"Of course I don't. No one ever does. But if you took the time to do the research, you'd find out that I'm telling the truth."

Much as I found her mother's actions abhorrent, I didn't believe that a child should be punished for the sins of their parent.

"Okay, I'm listening."

"What do you mean?" She wiped the tears from her eyes.

"Prove to me that the children have nothing to fear from you."

"How am I supposed to do that?"

"You can start by giving me details of the places you worked in the human world."

"I've never worked in the human world."

"But you told the twins that you had."

"I lied. I had to say that because I knew that if they contacted the places that I've worked here in Candlefield, they'd be told I was sacked, and that would have been it. Game over."

"So why would it be any different if I contacted them now?"

"It won't be unless you actually talk to the owners of those businesses. Ask them if there were ever any problems with any of the kids under my care. There weren't. Not once."

"Why were you sacked, then?"

"Because someone found out about my mother. Just like

you have. They were scared of what I *might* do. But I would never hurt a child. I couldn't."

"Okay, here's what's going to happen. First, you're going to give me details of every place you've worked with children here in Candlefield. Then, you're going to call Amber and tell her you're still having problems with your stomach. That you came back to work too early, and you need to take a few days off."

"But she'll sack me."

"No, she won't. Not if she thinks you're ill. The twins think you're the best thing since sliced bread."

"Do they really?" She smiled for the first time.

"Yes, but that won't save you if I find out there was even a hint of trouble at any of the places I contact."

"You won't. I promise."

***

Oh boy!

Mr Claymore hadn't been exaggerating about the green cars. Every third car on the lot was now green. All sizes, all models, there didn't seem to be any particular pattern.

"Hi, there." A young man approached me. He was wearing a sharp suit and pointy shoes. "Were you looking for something in particular?"

"Actually, I was hoping to find something green, but you don't seem to have any green cars."

"But, I—err—" He gave me a puzzled look, and probably wondered if I was colour-blind.

"It's okay. I'm just pulling your leg. I'm not looking to buy a car. Your boss, Mr Claymore, has asked me to investigate the green car thing."

"Right. Sorry. He told me he'd hired a private investigator, but I was expecting a — err — "

"A man?"

"I guess so. Sorry. I'm Ronnie, but everyone calls me Grease."

"Like the movie?"

"Sort of. I used to be a mechanic, and I was always covered in the stuff. That was before I moved into sales."

"How are sales, anyway?"

"Not great. 'Green' cars are the big thing at the moment, but not this kind of green car. My commission this month is going to be half what it normally is. I hope you can sort this out."

"Me too. Would you mind answering a few questions?"

"Fire away. It's not like we're overrun with customers."

"Do you know Sandy Gascoigne?"

"No. He left before I started here. In fact, it was his job that I took over. I believe he's working for Washbridge Prestige Motors now."

"What about Wilde Cars? Do you know much about them?"

"Not really. Only that they're the competition. Mr Claymore hates those guys. Do you reckon they're behind this?"

"It's too early to say. When was the last car taken away?"

"It was that one over there." He pointed to a Ford Fiesta. "They took it last Thursday, and when we got here yesterday morning, it was back. It used to be black. I can sell black Fiestas all day long, but no one will even look at it now."

"I assume the cars always disappear at night?"

"Usually, but not always. Do you see that Mondeo, three rows back?"

"Yeah."

"That one disappeared while I was on my lunch break."

"And no one saw anything?"

"Nothing. It makes no sense to me. I can't work out how they're doing it."

Me neither. "Is Mr Claymore in today?"

"No. Tuesday is his golfing day."

"Can you do me a favour, Ronnie — err — Grease?"

"Sure."

I handed him my card. "The next time a car disappears, call me, would you?"

"No problem." He glanced at my car, which was parked on the road, in front of the lot. "Are you sure I can't interest you in a new motor? It looks like you could do with one."

"There's nothing wrong with my car."

"You should leave it here. If you're lucky, it might get a free respray. It certainly needs one."

"Are you always this cheeky with customers?" I grinned.

"Only when I know there's no chance that they're going to buy anything."

Chapter 5

When I got back to the office, Mrs V was wearing a pained expression.

"What's wrong, Mrs V?"

"I'm listening to see if it happens again."

"If *what* happens again?"

"There's been a strange noise coming from down there." She pointed to the floor.

"What kind of noise?"

"A sort of rumbling sound."

I listened for a while, but I couldn't hear anything.

"Are you sure it wasn't your stomach?" I grinned.

"I know what I heard, Jill. I thought we were having an earthquake or something."

"Okay. Well, whatever it was it seems to have stopped now."

Sometimes, I worried about Mrs V.

I expected to find Winky working out on the punch bag, but there was no sign of him anywhere in the office. Perhaps he had another meeting with the professor to discuss their new top-secret project.

My two o'clock appointment would be here at any moment. Cheryl Warne had said she preferred not to tell Mrs V the nature of her business. I just hoped it didn't turn out to be another infidelity case.

Before she arrived, Daze called.

"Jill, I've just spoken to Edna, and she says she might be interested, but she'd like to meet you before she commits to anything."

"Fair enough, but I'm keen to get this sorted asap.

Where does she live?"

"Actually, she suggested she came over to your office."

"Better still. When?"

"She said she could come over later today if that works for you?"

"That's fine. I have a new client coming in any minute now. How about four o'clock?"

"I'll let Edna know. If you don't hear from me again, you can assume she'll be there at four."

"Okay, and thanks for doing this, Daze."

"No problem. Just remember what I said about Edna. She can be hard work, but she gets results."

"I'm sure we'll get on famously."

***

Cheryl Warne was a bag of nerves. If it hadn't been for the man standing by her side, who was supporting her by the arm, I doubt she would have made it through the door.

"Could I get a glass of water, please?" she said, through dry lips.

"Of course." I went through to the outer office. "Would you get Mrs Warne a glass of water, please, Mrs V?"

"Of course. Is she okay? She seemed to be hyper-what's-it-ing."

"I hope so."

"I'm sorry about this." Cheryl took a sip of water. "This business has got me rather rattled."

"That's okay. Take your time."

"I should introduce myself." The man looked like he'd

just finished working on a fashion shoot for an up-market men's magazine. His hair was immaculate, his skin blemish-free and his suit must have cost a king's ransom. "I'm Jonathan Langer."

"Pleased to meet you."

We shook hands, and I was surprised to see that his fingernails were bitten to the quick. They seemed strangely out of place on someone who clearly spent so much time and money on his appearance.

Cheryl took another sip of water. "It's my husband, Robert. He's been kidnapped."

"When did this happen?"

"Last Friday."

"Have you informed the police?"

"No. The note said if I contacted them that he'd be killed."

"I told Cheryl she should go to the police," Langer said.

"Are you a relative?"

"No, I'm Robert's business partner. I told Cheryl that you can't mess around in cases like this, and that she should contact the police immediately."

"I'm not going to the police!" She had found her voice. "They'll kill Robert."

"What do you think, Mrs Maxwell?" he said.

"It's Jill, and yes, I do think you should go to the police, but Robert is your husband, so it's your call."

"I'm not going to the police."

"Do you have the note with you?"

"No, I'm sorry. I didn't think to bring it. My head's been in such a spin."

"Not to worry. Maybe I could pop around to your house to pick it up?"

"Of course."

"What does the note say?"

"That I have two weeks to raise a million pounds. And that they'd be in touch again with further instructions."

"Does anyone know about this other than the two of you?"

"Just Simon Richards," Cheryl said.

"Who's he?"

"He's Robert's best friend. They've known each other since university. He was supposed to be playing tennis with Robert on Saturday. He came to the house to pick him up, and found me in pieces. I had no option but to show him the note. He was the one who said I should contact a private investigator. To be perfectly honest with you, I wasn't keen on the idea. I just wanted to pay the ransom."

"Can you raise that kind of money?"

"It won't be easy, but yes. Just about."

"Can you tell me exactly how your husband was taken?"

"It was while we were at the cinema. Do you know the new multiplex that opened recently?"

"Yes. In fact I was there with my husband on Sunday. We went to see Red Storm."

"That's what we were watching too. It's not really my cup of tea, but Robert was keen to see it."

"Are you saying that your husband was snatched while you were inside the cinema?"

"That's right."

"Surely there must have been witnesses?"

"Not as far as I'm aware."

"What happened exactly?"

"We had called at the pub for a quick drink on the way to the cinema. I had a soft drink because I was driving. About half an hour into the movie, I had to nip out to the bathroom."

"Right?"

"When I got back to my seat, Robert wasn't there. I thought at first that he must have gone to the loo as well, but after fifteen minutes, when he still wasn't back, I started to get worried."

"Are you sure you went back to the right screen?"

"I'm not stupid. Who would forget which screen they were in?"

Who indeed?

"Sorry, that was a silly question. What happened next?"

"I tried to phone him, but he didn't pick up. I didn't know what to do, so I went back to the car, and drove home."

"Did you expect to find him there?"

"I'm not sure what I expected, but by then, I wasn't exactly thinking straight. When I got back to the house, it was empty, but I did find the note on the floor in the hall."

"The ransom note?"

"That's right."

"What does your husband do for a living? Where does he work?"

"He's a property developer. All very small scale stuff."

"I see. And what about you? Do you work?"

"Yes. I'm the managing director of Joma Cosmetics. The business has been in my family for generations."

"I see. How long have you and Robert been married?"

"Just under five years." She wiped away a tear. "It's our wedding anniversary next month. Do you think you'll be able to help, Mrs Maxwell?"

"Call me Jill, please. I'm sure I will. I'll make a start straight away. Will you let me know if the kidnappers get in touch again?"

"Of course."

"And you'll need to tell me how I can get hold of Simon Richards."

"I'll jot his number down for you." She scribbled it on a scrap of paper.

"Thanks."

As I showed them out, Langer hesitated at the door.

"Do you box, Jill?" He gestured towards the punch bag.

"Err, yeah. I like to keep my hand in. I meet some nasty people in my line of work."

Cheryl Warne had only just left when Winky jumped in through the window. He was caked in dry mud.

"What on earth happened to you?"

"What do you mean?"

"You're filthy."

"It's just a bit of mud." He began to brush himself down.

"You're making a mess all over my nice clean floor."

"This floor hasn't been clean since the turn of the millennium."

"Cheek! How did you manage to get so dirty, anyway?"

"Never you mind. By the way, I need a small favour."

"What now?"

"It's nothing much. I just need you to run me over to the Feline Quarter next Wednesday night."

"Where's the Feline Quarter?"

"It's on the other side of Washbridge. Don't worry. I'll

give you directions."

"What's over there?"

"That's where the boxing tournament is being held."

"I really don't think your taking part in that tournament is a good idea. You could end up getting badly injured."

"Rubbish." He breezed over to the punch bag and gave it a thump. "You're looking at the next Washbridge feline boxing champion."

***

I thought I should drop in on Aunt Lucy, to see how she was coping with the growing mountain of artwork being produced by the prolific Barry.

As soon as I walked through the door, I could sense something was wrong.

"Aunt Lucy? Are you okay?"

"No, I'm not. That husband of mine is driving me insane."

"What's Lester done now?"

"It's that awful grim reaper business he works for."

"I thought you'd reconciled yourself to the work he does?"

"I had."

"What's changed?"

"His employers have introduced a new bonus scheme, so now Lester is working all hours to try to meet his target."

"A bonus scheme? How does that work for grim reapers?"

"How do you think? The more people that Lester can process, the higher his bonus will be. I find the whole thing very distasteful."

"Have you told him how you feel?"

"In no uncertain terms, but it hasn't made any difference. The only thing he can think about his how high he can get on the leader board."

"They keep a *leader board*?"

"Yes. I told you it was distasteful, didn't I?"

"He'll probably get fed up of it after a while."

"I do hope so." She sighed. "I'm sorry to burden you with my problems. Shall we have a cup of tea?"

"That would be nice."

By the time we had our drinks, Aunt Lucy had calmed down a little.

"How are Barry and Rhymes?"

"They're both fine."

"I'm surprised Barry hasn't come in to see me already."

"He's busy working on the plans for his exhibition."

"That's still going ahead, then?"

"As far as I know. I don't want to get involved, but if it means I can get rid of all these drawings, I'm all for it."

"And Rhymes?"

"He couldn't be happier. Ever since you brought those books over, he's had a steady stream of visitors wanting to get a copy of his book."

"That's good. Hopefully, none of them will give him any honest feedback."

"That's not very charitable, Jill."

"Come on. You've heard his poems. Don't pretend they aren't awful."

Just then, the baby intercom sprang into life.

"I think someone is calling me." Aunt Lucy got to her

feet. "Would you like to say hello to Lil?"

"Not today. I'd better get back to the office. I hope you and Lester sort things out."

But before I could magic myself back to Washbridge, Barry came charging down the stairs.

"Hello, boy. I didn't think you were going to come and see me today."

"Sorry, Jill. Dolly has asked me to get all my pictures together ready for the exhibition."

"Right." I hoped Dolly wasn't building up his hopes only to have them dashed. "How's that going?"

"The exhibition is next week. On Monday."

"Oh? I didn't realise anything had been finalised."

"Dolly has organised everything."

"That's good of her." Bless her. She had probably arranged for his pictures to be displayed in some small church hall in Candlefield. Still, just as long as it made him happy, I didn't care.

"That's what I wanted to talk to you about, Jill."

"Oh?"

"I won't be able to go to the exhibition."

"Why, because you're a dog?"

"Yeah. Dolly said that people wouldn't understand that a dog can be an artist."

"She may have a point."

"Will you and your Jack go?"

"My Jack?"

"Isn't that what your mate is called?"

"Err, yeah, but Jack can't come to Candlefield. He's a human."

"It isn't in Candlefield. It's being held here." He showed me a small business card.

"Washbridge Art Gallery? It's being held in Washbridge?"

"Yes. Will you go? Please! I want you to tell me what everyone thinks of my pictures."

"I—err—won't Dolly do that?"

"Yes, but she's biased. I know you'll be honest with me. Will you go, Jill? Please say yes."

"Okay, then."

***

Winky was half-asleep, sunning himself on the window sill when an elderly fairy suddenly appeared and pushed past him. "Get out of my way, cat!" Poor old Winky was so shocked, he toppled backwards onto the floor.

"Edna?"

"That's me, and you must be Jill. Daze said to be here by four o'clock, so here I am. Did you know that you had a mangy old fleabag of a cat on your window sill?"

"That's Winky. He lives here."

"Really? I've never liked cats myself. They're untrustworthy animals in my opinion."

By now, Winky had recovered from his fall, and was giving Edna his one-eyed death stare. Not that she noticed or cared.

"Thanks for coming to see me, Edna. Did Daze explain what I'm looking for?"

"She said you needed someone to carry out surveillance from time to time."

"That's right. She tells me you've done similar work for the rogue retrievers?"

"Amongst others, yes. Officially, I've retired, but sitting

at home can get boring, so I wouldn't be averse to taking on work occasionally. Provided the pay was right, of course."

"If you've worked for the rogue retrievers, I assume you've had experience of working in the human world?"

"Plenty. It's my second home." She glanced around the office. "Is this it, then? I was expecting something a little — err —"

"Bigger? More modern?"

"Cleaner. There's mud all over the floor."

"Oh that. It's not usually like that. The cat —"

"I might have known. Untrustworthy and dirty. I wouldn't give them houseroom."

"Right, so are you interested in the job?"

"I don't see why not. It's not like I have much else to do these days."

"Great. I'd better brief you, then."

Once I'd given her details of Norman's case, Edna took her leave, with a promise to keep me posted on her surveillance of Tonya.

"Where did you find that horror show?" Winky jumped onto my desk. "You manage to get rid of doliphant boy, and then you replace him with the fairy from hell."

"You're just saying that because she doesn't like cats. I'm sure Edna will be a great asset to this business."

"I thought fairies were supposed to be pretty? She's almost as ugly as your grandmother. Those two could play the ugly sisters in panto."

He wasn't wrong.

***

I'd promised Jack that I'd pick up a few bits and bobs from the shop on my way home. But why bother when I could simply place the order using the shopping app? There was no point in wasting energy unnecessarily.

What was wrong with the stupid thing?

Every time I clicked on the app icon, nothing happened. Great, that was just dandy!

When I arrived at the Corner Shop, I was a little surprised to find that the bike racks had disappeared from outside the door. Inside, the place was deserted except for Little Jack who was standing behind the counter—on his stilts.

"Hi, Jack. Did you know that your shopping app isn't working?"

"I've decided to do away with it."

"How come? It seemed to be very popular."

"Too popular. That was the problem. It was costing me a small fortune to pay for all the extra staff that I needed to make the deliveries."

"That's a shame. It was very convenient."

"I'm embarrassed by the whole episode. I'm afraid I may lose some customers because of this."

"I'm sure most people will understand. I'm a business woman too. I know how important it is to keep a tight grip on your costs."

"Thank you. That means a lot to me."

"I assume you had to let Peter Piper go?"

"I'm afraid so, but I did hear that he's managed to get another job at Peck's Peppers."

"That's good."

"I hope so, but I heard the owner likes a drink, and spends most of the time pickled."

"Oh dear. Poor Peter."

"What can I get for you today, Jill? More custard creams?"

"No. I've still got a cupboard full of them." I handed him my list.

"Why don't you help yourself to a drink while I get these for you?" He pointed to a small vending machine at the far side of the counter.

"Is that new?"

"It is. And all the drinks are free. I figured it was the least I could do to make amends for the shopping app fiasco."

The vending machine had an impressive selection of drinks. I opted for a raspberry tea.

"That's everything." Little Jack began to put my order through the till. "How's your drink?"

"I could have sworn I selected raspberry, but this tastes just like lemon. I must have pressed the wrong button."

"I should have mentioned that the buttons are mixed up. If you wanted raspberry, you should have pressed the ginger tea button."

Chapter 6

The next morning, Jack was still grumbling about the bill for the boiler repair. I couldn't really blame him—not renewing the maintenance contract hadn't been one of my better decisions.

I needed to take his mind off it by changing the subject.

"I don't think I mentioned, my mother popped in to see me on Monday. It's the launch party for their tea room this Thursday."

"Are they still planning to go with *that* name?"

"Cakey C? Yeah, it looks that way."

"It's a bit of a cheek, isn't it?"

"It is, but like my mum said, the two shops aren't even in the same world, so it probably doesn't matter."

"I assume you'll be going to the launch?"

"I don't have much choice. My life won't be worth living if I don't make an appearance."

"Poor you. Having to eat all those free cakes."

"It's a tough job, but someone has to do it."

"Are you still busy at work?"

"Yeah, the cases are coming in thick and fast at the moment. I'm not complaining, though. The extra cash will come in handy."

"You're right there. To pay for the boiler repair for example."

"Are you ever going to let me forget about that? I've apologised a dozen times."

"Sorry. I won't mention it again. I promise."

"Good. I do have one really weird case at the moment."

"Aren't all your cases a bit weird?"

"Quite a few of them, but this is exceptional even by my

standards. You know that car sales place, just outside Smallwash?"

"Best Cars?"

"It's actually Bestest Cars, but yes, that's the one. The owner came to see me because someone is stealing his cars, spraying them green, and then returning them."

"That makes no sense."

"Tell me about it."

"Why green?"

"That's not really the point, is it?"

"I suppose not. I just wondered why not red?"

"I don't know. When I find out who's been doing it, I'll ask them."

"Or blue."

"Sheesh, Jack. The colour doesn't matter."

"Sorry. Do you have any other interesting cases?"

"Yes, but not that I can discuss." There was no way I could tell Jack about the kidnapping because he would have insisted that I go to the police. "The only thing I can tell you is that it involves the multiplex cinema."

"Intriguing. Go on, you can tell me. I won't breathe a word to anyone."

"Sorry. No can do." Another change of subject was called for. "Oh, by the way, Little Jack has decided to scrap his shopping app."

"Why? Did you crash it by ordering too many custard creams?"

"Very funny. It proved to be so popular that it was costing him a small fortune to pay the additional delivery staff."

"That's a pity. It was very convenient."

"That's what comes of making business decisions

without thinking them through first."

"Hmm." He grinned.

"What are you grinning at?"

"Nothing."

"Come on, Jack. Spit it out."

"I was just thinking about your office manager. Or should I say *managers*."

"That was totally different. And anyway, I've now recruited someone to help me with surveillance. Only on an as-needed basis, though."

"Who's that?"

"Daze recommended her. She's a fairy called Edna."

"What's she like?"

"She reminds me a bit of Grandma."

"Oh dear."

"I'm sure it'll be fine. Oh, by the way, we've been invited to an art exhibition next Monday."

"That's a joke, I assume."

"Why would it be a joke?"

"You hate anything cultural."

"I do not. Where on earth did you get that idea?"

"I can't imagine. What is this exhibition?"

"It's by a new artist. Apparently, he's the dog's — "

"What's his name? Maybe I've heard of him."

"I forget. Are you up for it?"

"Definitely."

"Great."

"You haven't forgotten we're going to the Livelys' housewarming party tonight, have you?"

"Of course not." Despite my best efforts.

By the time I left the house, Jack had already gone to

work. I was just about to get in the car when someone called my name.

"Jill!" Lovely came running across the lawn. "Wait!"

This was getting beyond a joke. Before the Livelys had moved in, my homelife had been cat-free. But no longer it seemed.

"What is it? I'm already late for work."

"I need your help."

"If they've changed your food again, there's nothing much I can do about it."

"It isn't that. It's that monster across the road." She nodded towards Jimmy and Kimmy's house.

"Bruiser?"

"Yes, he's a bully. Every time I walk along the road, he chases me."

"Maybe he wants to be your friend?"

"He definitely doesn't. He says I should get off his territory."

"That doesn't make any sense. I thought he'd only have an issue with other males."

"He seems to hate all other cats. I've spoken to a few of them around the neighbourhood, and they've all said the same thing. He's even had a go at a couple of dogs."

"What a horrible piece of work he is."

"Can you do something about him, Jill?"

"Like what?"

"I don't know. Please, I'm desperate."

"Alright, I'll have a think about it, but I'm not making any promises."

"Thanks, Jill."

"Lovely's not bothering you, is she, Jill?" Britt shouted.

"Err, no." I gave the cat a stroke. "She's just after some

fuss."

"What time will you and Jack be coming over tonight?"

"What time do you want us?"

"Does eight o'clock work for you?"

"Yeah. Unless I have to work late, of course."

***

On my way into the office, I called at Cheryl Warne's house. I say *house* but it was more of a mansion. Located on the main Smallwash to Washbridge road, it stood in its own grounds, and even though I drove that route almost every day, I'd never noticed it before because it was hidden by a high wall.

"Come in, Jill." Cheryl looked much more composed than she'd been the previous day.

"You have a beautiful home."

"Thank you. It's a little big for the two of us. Can I get you anything to drink?"

"No, thanks. I just popped in to collect the ransom note."

"Of course. Come through to my study, would you?"

Her *study* turned out to be twice as large as my entire office.

"This is it." She handed me the sheet of A4 paper on which was printed:

One million pounds or you'll never see your husband alive again.

If you go to the police, he dies.

We'll be in touch.

"Do you have any CCTV cameras installed? I didn't notice any."

"No. Robert doesn't believe in CCTV. He says it encroaches on people's privacy."

"I take it the kidnappers haven't been in touch again?"

"No, I haven't heard from them."

"Do you have a photo of your husband that you could email me?"

"Not that I can email. I've never gone in for digital photography."

"Not even on your phone?"

"No, sorry. I'm a bit of a Luddite when it comes to technology. I do have some regular photographs, though. You're welcome to take one of those."

"That'll be fine. Maybe if you could let me have the most recent one you have of him."

"That would be the one I took when he won the bowling trophy."

"Your husband plays ten-pin bowling?"

"No. Crown green bowling. It was only a local competition, but Robert was so very proud when he won. Wait here, I'll go and get you the photograph."

While she was gone, I took in the view through the window, which looked out onto a beautifully landscaped garden. In the distance, a gardener was busy at work, tending to the flower beds. Why didn't I have a house like this? I should have married a rich man.

What? Of course I didn't mean it. I wouldn't swap Jack for a million pounds. A billion, though? That would be a different matter.

"Will this do?" Cheryl passed me a framed photograph of a man holding up a trophy. He was beaming from ear to ear.

"That'll be fine. I'll let you have it back."

We talked for a few more minutes, and then she showed me to the door. "Please bring Robert home unharmed."

"I promise I'll do everything in my power to do that."

***

This was getting beyond a joke. The traffic through the city centre was crawling at a snail's pace again. It was another pothole, but this time on the opposite side of the road. I was ten minutes late getting into the car park.

On my walk to the office building, I bumped into Jimmy and Kimmy.

"Did you get caught in the traffic jam too, Jill?" Jimmy said.

"Yes, that's the second time this week."

"Did you see the pothole?"

"I did. These roads are a disgrace."

"I'm glad we've seen you, Jill," Kimmy said. "I wanted to apologise for snapping at you the other day. I know you don't mean our little fluffykins any harm."

Hmm, I wasn't so sure about that.

"That's alright. How is he settling into the neighbourhood?"

"Okay, I think, but he's a nervous little thing. It will probably take him a while to get comfortable with his new surroundings and to make friends."

"Right." Delusional or what?

"Jill, would it be okay if we popped over to see you sometime today?"

"Sure. What about?"

"We'd like to talk about the stolen clown shoe incident."

"Okay, but it'll have to be this afternoon, though. I'm pretty much tied up all morning. Does two o'clock work for you?"

"That'll be fine. We'll come around then."

"It's been happening again," Mrs V said, as soon as I walked through the door.

"What has?"

"That rumbling sound."

"I can't hear anything."

"It stopped a couple of minutes ago. It was louder than ever this time. You don't think the boiler is going to explode, do you?"

"Of course not. Look, if I hear it, I'll go and investigate."

"I wouldn't like to get blown up."

"I'm sure we're safe. Oh, and before I forget, I've got the clowns from next door coming to see me at two o'clock."

"You're doing it again, Jill." She tutted her disapproval.

"Sorry. Jimmy and Kimmy are coming over. Is that better?"

"Much."

Once again, there was no sign of Winky. This was getting to be a habit. Where did he keep disappearing to? It probably had something to do with his new business venture with the professor—whatever that was.

***

When it was time for me to leave the office, Winky was still AWOL.

"Have you seen Winky this morning, Mrs V?"

"No, but then I try to avoid him as much as possible. Maybe the rumbling sound scared him away."

"I'm going to talk to someone about the Warne case. I should be back after lunch. If Winky comes back, give him some food, will you?"

"If I must."

Robert Warne's friend, Simon Richards, had agreed to see me at his office building. I'd taken the car, but after spending ten minutes stuck in city centre traffic, I was beginning to wish I'd magicked myself there.

He worked at Belvedere Software, which was located in the new high-tech business centre called Washbridge Innovation Park. Much as I loved my office, mainly because of the memories it held for me, I couldn't help but think it would be nice to work somewhere like this. I bet the occupants of these buildings didn't have to put up with rumblings in the basement, grumpy landlords, muddy floors, or clowns hanging out on the stairs and landing.

Richards was tall, slim and super geeky.

"I hope you didn't mind meeting me here." He led the way to a small meeting room. "I can never be sure what time I'll get away at night. Once I get coding, the hours just seem to whizz by. I quite often work through the night trying to debug a program."

"Sounds like fun."

"It is. This is my dream job."

Poor guy.

"Thanks for agreeing to talk to me, Simon."

"No problem. Anything that might help to get Robert back."

"I understand that you were the one who encouraged

Cheryl to contact me in the first place?"

"That's right. Not you specifically, but when she refused to go to the police, I suggested she should at least contact a private investigator."

"I understand that you've known Robert for some time?"

"Yes. Since university. His room was just down the corridor from mine. If it hadn't been for Robert, I would probably have spent the whole of my time at uni alone in my room. He's much more outgoing than I am." He laughed. "But that wouldn't be difficult. Robert tried to include me in his social circle whenever he could. We've remained friends ever since."

"Were you studying the same subject?"

"No, I took a degree in A.I., artificial intelligence. Robert was studying English Lit."

"What about Cheryl? How well do you know her?"

"She and Robert met after uni. She seems nice enough."

Talk about being damned by faint praise.

"And wealthy?"

"Very."

"Was that what attracted Robert to her?"

"Err, I—err—" My directness had obviously caught him off guard. Intentionally so.

"If I'm to have any chance of finding Robert, it's essential that you hold nothing back. What kind of relationship do they have?"

He hesitated, obviously unsure about how much he should tell me. "Cheryl was the one who made the running. She pursued him relentlessly."

"But he loves her, right?"

"Err, yeah. Of course."

"I get the feeling there's something you're not telling me, Simon."

"You have to promise you won't tell anyone you heard this from me."

"You have my word."

"A couple of years ago, Robert had a brief fling."

"An affair? Did Cheryl know about it?"

"Yes, it was one of her friends."

"What happened?"

"Robert ended it."

"Do you know where I can find this woman?"

"She moved to America two years ago. Shortly after Robert ended the relationship."

"Do you know why Robert chose Cheryl over the other woman. Was it for love? Or money?"

"I honestly couldn't say."

He didn't need to; it was written all over his face.

"If he was unhappy with the relationship, why didn't he just divorce her?"

Simon shrugged. "He can't afford to."

"But surely, he'd walk away with a healthy settlement, wouldn't he?"

"Probably not. Before he got married, Robert told me that he'd signed a prenup agreement. It was Cheryl's father's idea, apparently."

***

After more potholes and more delays, I eventually made it back to the office.

"Has Winky come back, Mrs V?"

"Yes, about half-an-hour ago. He's filthy."

"Have you fed him?"

"I have. He could do with a good bath. I thought cats were supposed to take pride in keeping themselves clean?"

"Thanks, Mrs V."

"That rumbling noise has been happening on and off all morning."

"Oh? It's weird how it only happens when I'm not here."

"Are you suggesting that I'm making it up?"

"No, of course not. It's just a coincidence that's all."

"It needs sorting out, Jill. How am I supposed to focus on my knitting?"

"As soon as I hear it, I'll investigate. I promise."

"Look at the state of you," I said to Winky. "Where on earth have you been?"

"It's only a bit of mud. I don't know what all the fuss is about. You're as bad as the old bag lady."

"What have you been doing?"

"If I told you that, I'd —"

"Be forced to kill me. Yeah, I get it. But this can't carry on. What will my clients think if they see this mess?"

"I could always give Billy the Broom a call if you like?"

"Who's he?"

"He runs a contract cleaning business. He could have this place looking shipshape in no time at all."

"And who's going to pay for that?"

"I would, obviously, but all my cash is tied up in my new business venture."

"Which is?"

He grinned. "Nice try."

Jimmy and Kimmy arrived at two o'clock, as arranged.

"Have you heard that awful noise, Jill?" Jimmy said.

"What noise?"

"From down in the basement. A kind of rumbling noise."

"What did I tell you?" Mrs V had popped into my office to bring our drinks. "I've been trying to tell Jill about the rumbling sound, but she thinks I imagined it."

"I never said that."

"You didn't need to. Just because I'm getting on doesn't mean I've lost my marbles."

"Mrs V is right," Kimmy said. "It's been happening on and off for the last few days."

"I reckon it must be the boiler." Mrs V put my cup of tea on the desk. "We could all be blown to smithereens."

"I'll check into it later today, and if it is the boiler, I'll give Macabre a call. He's always pleased to hear from me."

Satisfied, Mrs V went back through to the outer office.

"So, you two, you said you wanted to talk about the stolen clown shoes."

"Indeed." Jimmy took a sip of his tea. "When we discovered PomPom was behind the thefts, we were both in shock. Even after hearing the phoney maintenance man's confession, we still had our doubts. I'll be honest, I half-expected PomPom to deny it when I confronted him."

"Did he?"

"Quite the opposite. He openly admitted he was behind it."

Kimmy took Jimmy's hand. "Jimmy's quite upset about all of this, as you can see. We thought Raymond was a friend."

"He's quite unrepentant." Jimmy was angry now. "PomPom has made it quite clear that, far from welcoming the competition, he intends to do everything in his power to put us out of business."

"What do you think he has in mind?"

"We have no idea. We're a bit worried to be honest."

"He could be bluffing to try to scare you."

"Do you think so?"

"He'd be taking much more of a risk doing anything now that you're onto him."

"I guess so, but if he does, would you help us?"

"Help how? Wouldn't it be better simply to go to the police?"

"That could result in bad publicity, which is precisely what we're trying to avoid."

"Okay. If he tries it on again, give me a shout, and I'll see what I can do."

"Thanks, Jill. You're a star."

Chapter 7

I needed a *real* cup of coffee, not the slop Mrs V made. No offence intended, obviously.

As I was walking down the high street to Coffee Games, Julie came out of Ever. As usual, the head Everette looked like an oversize canary in her yellow uniform.

"Hi, Jill. If you're here to see your grandmother, she isn't in today. In fact, we haven't seen her all week." She grinned. "Not that I'm complaining."

"I'm actually on my way to Coffee Games. Are you on your lunch break?"

"No, it's my half-day. I'm just off to I-Sweat."

"How are the guys doing in their new place?"

"They seem to be going from strength to strength. It's always busy in there."

"Good for them. I kind of wish they were still next-door to me instead of the clowns who are there now."

"Who moved in when I-Sweat moved out?"

"Clowns."

"Yeah, but what kind of business is it?"

"That's what they do. It's a clown school called Clown."

"Oh? Right." She laughed. "I didn't realise such things existed. I should check it out. Clowns are such fun, aren't they?"

"If you like that kind of thing."

"I'm surprised you haven't mentioned our new uniforms." She did a little twirl. "I have to give credit to your grandmother, she's certainly been splashing the cash recently."

"And the uniform you're wearing now? What colour would you call that?"

"Purple of course."

"Right. I wasn't sure if it was more plum or lavender, but I guess purple covers it. How many different uniforms do you have now?"

"There's the horrible yellow one, of course. Then there's the original red. And now we have blue and purple."

"Fantastic. I'd better let you get going, then. Enjoy your workout."

It hadn't occurred to me until Julie mentioned it, but I hadn't seen or heard from Grandma for a few days.

Bliss!

When I walked into Coffee Games, I thought for a moment that a witch or wizard must have cast a mass 'freeze' spell because everyone was standing stock-still. I was still trying to figure out what to do when music came through the speakers, and everyone started moving around as normal.

Sarah was behind the counter.

"What was that all about?" I asked.

"It's musical statues. Didn't you play it when you were a kid?"

"I don't think so. How does it work?"

"While the music is playing, you move around as normal, but as soon as—" Just then, the music cut out, and everyone in the shop was frozen to the spot again. Eventually, the music started up again, and she continued with her explanation. "As soon as the music stops, everyone has to freeze."

"Isn't that a little awkward when you're trying to serve people?"

"Not really because the customers have to freeze too.

What can I get you, Jill?"

"Just a caramel latte, please."

"Aren't you having a—"

The music had stopped again.

The order process was made far more difficult than it should have been by the musical statues farce, but I eventually managed to get my coffee. I was just wondering where to sit when I spotted two familiar faces: Betty Longbottom and Deli were sitting at the same table, and were beckoning me to join them.

"Hello, you two."

"Have a—" Betty was cut off mid-sentence when the music stopped. Moments later, she tried again. "Have a seat, Jill."

"I didn't expect to find you two enjoying a coffee together."

"Betty and I are BFFs now," Deli put her arm around Betty. "Aren't we, girl?"

"We are, Deli."

"How did that happen?"

"It's a long story," Deli said.

The long story took even longer because she was interrupted every time the music stopped. The Cliff Notes version was that Betty's marine centre, The Sea's The Limit, had suffered a catastrophic loss of power. Although she'd had the foresight to install an emergency generator in case of such eventualities, that had failed too. For a while it had looked as though all the marine life would perish, which would have meant curtains for the business. But then, Nails of all people, had come to the rescue. When Deli had found Betty out on the street, in floods of tears, she had sprung into action. Deli had practically had to drag Nails out of bed where he'd been nursing a hangover. For all his faults, of which there were many, Nails was an experienced electrician. Wow, who would have guessed? He'd diagnosed the problem and made the repair in no time at all. As a result, Betty had decided not to sue Deli's salon for the mishap with the permanent marker. It seemed all was well that ended well.

Until the next time, that is.

I attracted a few dirty looks on my way out of Coffee Games because I refused to freeze when the music stopped. Life was too short for that sort of nonsense.

As I made my way back up the high street, I spotted Lester.

"Hi, Jill."

"I don't often see you around these parts."

"I'm covering a larger area than I usually do."

"Does that have anything to do with the new bonus scheme your employer has introduced?"

"It does, yes. I assume Lucy has been bending your ear about it."

"I got the impression she isn't a fan."

"I don't understand why she's got herself so worked up about it. The way she talks, you'd think we were going around killing people just to get our numbers up. That's just nonsense. All it does is make sure cases get cleared up more quickly, which is good for all concerned."

"How's it going?"

"Really well. I'm currently number six on the leader board. If I can make it to the top spot, I'll be in the big money."

"Right."

"Sorry, Jill." He checked what at first glance I thought was a watch, but which on closer examination I could see was some kind of monitor strapped to his wrist. "That's a code red. I have to scoot."

And with that, he hurried away.

I had no idea what a code red was, and I certainly had no desire to find out. I was with Aunt Lucy on this one; the idea of a leader board for the number of people *processed* was all rather distasteful.

One side of the street had been closed just outside my office building. The measure had been taken in order to allow workmen to repair the road, where yet another huge pothole had appeared.

I was halfway up the stairs when Edna landed on my shoulder.

"Edna? What are you doing here?"

"Reporting back. What do you think?"

"Someone might see you."

"Don't be ridiculous. You're the only one who can see me."

"But my cat could see you the last time you came to visit me."

"Okay. If you insist on being pedantic, I'm invisible to everyone except you and cats. And dogs. I believe gerbils can see me too, but I've never put that to the test."

"Fair enough. Let me get inside the office, and we'll talk."

"Who are you talking to, Jill?"

Oh bum! Kimmy was standing at the top of the stairs, giving me the strangest look.

"I—err—no one. I was just rehearsing my lines for the

play I'm in."

"Oh, how very exciting! What play is that?"

"Err — The Invisible Fairy."

"Get a move on!" Edna screamed in my ear. "I don't have all day."

"I don't think I've heard of that," Kimmy said. "Where's it being staged?"

"Just the local amdram."

"I must tell Jimmy. We might pop along and see you in it."

"It's only in the rehearsal stage at present. I've no idea when it will be on."

"Do keep us posted."

"I will."

"There's been more rumbling in the basement," Mrs V said.

"Not now, Mrs V. There's something urgent I need to attend to." I hurried through to my office where Edna jumped down onto the desk.

"What was all that rubbish about a play?" she said.

"It was the best I could come up with. Do you want to let me have your report?"

"I've been following that Tonya character, as requested."

"Right."

"That woman can certainly eat. Two Cornish pasties she put away. Two of them!"

"But what happened? Did she meet up with anyone?"

"No."

"So what exactly is it that you want to report?"

"Nothing really. Apart from the Cornish pasties of

course."

"You're reporting that you have nothing to report?"

"Correct. I like to check in every day with my clients, to keep them abreast of developments."

"Even when there aren't any?"

"Precisely. So, if there's nothing else, I'll get back to work."

"Okay."

Having made her report, she flew out of the window.

"I'm trying to think what she reminds me of," Winky said.

"Don't you mean *who* she reminds you of?"

"No, I definitely mean *what*. Ah, yes, I've got it now. The backend of a bus. She's a dead ringer."

"You're no oil painting yourself."

"Where did you find her?"

"She comes very highly recommended."

"By who? The same people who recommended the doliphant twins?"

"She was recommended by the rogue retrievers if you must know. Anyway, that's enough about Edna. Have you heard any strange noises?"

"What kind of noises?"

"Rumbling noises."

"Yes, I have."

"Oh? When?"

"Just now. It was my stomach. Time to break out the salmon, I think."

***

After a long and mostly fruitless day at work, I was

looking forward to getting home and having a quiet evening in front of the TV.

I thought I'd left the traffic delays behind me, but when I got over the toll bridge, there was a policeman in the middle of the road; he was diverting all cars down a side road.

When I got closer to him, I lowered the window. "I only live a couple of miles further on. Can I come through?"

"Sorry, madam. No one is allowed down this road. You'll have to follow the diversion."

"What's happened?"

"A tree has fallen onto the road."

"Oh dear. I hope no one was hurt."

"There's been at least one fatality I'm afraid: A car was crushed by a falling tree. The road is likely to remain closed until the morning."

It just goes to show how cruel fate can be. When your number is up, it's up. And what a horrible way to go.

The diversion took me all around the back lanes, and by the time I got home, Jack's car was already on the driveway. As soon as I stepped out of the car, someone screamed at me.

"Help!"

Lovely was perched high in the branches of the tree. Sitting at its base was none other than my dear friend, Bruiser.

"Hey, you. Leave her alone."

"Butt out. You've already caused me enough problems."

"You're nothing but a bully."

"Talk to the paw because this face isn't listening."

I'd had just about enough of this monster. I checked to

make sure there was no one around, and then I used magic to change myself into a lion. One roar was all it took. Bruiser screamed, and then bolted for the safety of his house. As soon as he'd gone, I reversed the spell, and encouraged Lovely to come down.

"That was brilliant, Jill. Thanks. I wish my two-leggeds were sups."

"I don't think you'll have any more trouble from that one."

"Hi, Jill." Britt came out of the house. "You seem to get on really well with Lovely. You obviously have a way with cats."

"Hmm."

"We're really looking forward to seeing you and Jack tonight."

Oh bum! I'd forgotten all about the housewarming party. "Right, yeah. I'm not sure if we're going to be able to —"

"I saw Jack earlier. He said you'd be over at eight."

"Did he? Great."

"Did you have to take the diversion too?" Jack was upstairs, looking through his vast collection of ties.

"Yeah. The policeman said it was likely to be there all night. Did you hear what had happened?"

"No."

"Apparently a tree fell onto the road. Someone was killed."

"That's awful."

"Talking of awful, you aren't seriously going to wear that tie, are you?"

"What's wrong with it?"

"It's purple."

"It's plum, actually, and I like it."

"Do you really want to go next door? We could have a sexy night in. Just the two of us."

"We promised Britt and Kit we'd go. We can't let them down."

"It'll be awful."

"Every time we go out socialising, you always think it's going to be terrible."

"And I'm usually right."

"That's not true. You enjoyed yourself at the Normals'."

"No, I didn't. It was terrible."

"Are you honestly going to stand there and tell me that you didn't enjoy the magnetic fishing tournament?"

"It was beyond bad."

"I thought it was fun." He grinned. "I won, if you remember."

"How could I forget?"

"How was your day?"

"So-so. I bumped into Deli and Betty. They seem to have buried the hatchet."

"In Nails' head?"

"Surprisingly, no. It seems that he was the hero of the hour."

"I find that hard to believe."

"Apparently, there was a power failure at The Sea's The Limit, and Nails sorted it out. Oh, and you'll never guess what else happened today. I'll give you a clue: Boilers."

"Don't tell me it's been on the blink again? It feels warm enough in here."

"Not ours. The one at work. According to Mrs V, and Jimmy and Kimmy, it's been making all kinds of weird noises. I haven't heard it myself, but it can't be good."

"At least you won't have to pay to get that one repaired."

"I hope not, but I wouldn't put anything past Macabre."

We were almost ready to leave the house when there was a knock at the door.

"You two scrub up nicely." It was Terry Salmon, the fish man.

"We're just on our way next door," Jack said. "It's their housewarming party."

"I like your tie. Plum, isn't it?"

Jack shot me that smug look of his. "Thank you, Terry. I didn't think you were due to call this week?"

"I'm not supposed to, but I have to attend a conference next week, so I thought I'd just check if there was anything you needed?"

"I think we're okay at the moment." Jack turned to me for confirmation.

"Don't ask me. I don't keep tabs on your cockles."

"Yeah, we'll be able to manage until you call again," Jack said. "What's the conference? Anything interesting?"

"Very interesting, actually. It's called Fish On The Doorstep, and the part social media has to play."

It sounded truly unmissable.

Chapter 8

You know how sometimes you have those horrible recurring nightmares? The ones where you wake up in a cold sweat, and when you drift off to sleep again, the nightmare picks up where it left off?

Welcome to my world.

After having endured the Normals' housewarming party, I rightly felt as though I'd done my penance. That I'd served my time. But no, the nightmare had returned in the shape of the Livelys' little shindig.

Despite my protests, Jack had insisted on buying them a card and present. I was convinced the only reason the Livelys had decided to throw the party was because they'd seen how many presents the Normals had received. We couldn't afford to go around splashing the cash on gifts for all and sundry. We had a boiler repair to pay for.

All the usual suspects were there: Norm and Naomi, Jimmy and Kimmy, Clare and Tony, Mr Hosey, and a cast of thousands.

"This is lovely, isn't it, Jill?" Kimmy had found me hiding in the kitchen.

"Yeah, lovely."

"I was just saying to Jimmy that we should have had a housewarming party." Oh no! Please no! "But it's probably too late now, and besides people will be getting fed up with them."

"You're probably right. You can have too much of a good thing."

"Where's Jack?"

"The last time I saw him, he was talking TenPinCon with Tony and Clare."

"It sounds like that's going to be really exciting. When is it?"

"A week on Saturday."

"I bet you can't wait."

"I'm counting the days."

She took a sip of wine. "You're a bit of a cat lady, aren't you, Jill?"

"Sorry?"

"I mean you know a lot about cats."

"Well, I wouldn't exactly —"

"I'd value your advice about our little fluffykins."

"Bruiser?"

"Yes. He came rushing into the house earlier today and hid underneath the bed."

"Maybe he'd been chased by a dog."

"I don't think so. He's not normally worried about dogs. In fact, he's usually the one who chases them off. He wouldn't even come out when I showed him a bowl of his favourite food. What do you think I should do? Do you think he might be poorly?"

"In my experience, cats and particularly male cats, are subject to mood swings. Take Winky for example, most of the time he's full of energy, but then occasionally, he retreats into himself for no apparent reason. He'll sometimes spend all day under the sofa, and nothing can entice him out."

"Really? That's good to know. So, you don't think I need to call the vet?"

"No. If you give it a few days, I'm sure he'll be fine."

"Thanks, Jill. I'm glad I've talked to you. I feel much

better now."

"No problem."

Snigger.

"I have bad news, Jill." Mr Hosey had appeared at my side, which in itself was bad news enough.

"What's wrong, Mr Hosey?"

"The doctor has said I won't be able to use the tree camouflage again."

"Oh dear. What about the bush?"

"I can't use that either."

"I'm sure Jack would be happy to stand in for you. He told me how much he enjoyed his stint as a tree."

"That's very kind, but I simply couldn't impose on him in that way. As chairman of the neighbourhood watch, it's my responsibility to provide surveillance for this community."

"That's very public spirited, but if you can't be a tree, I don't see how you'll be able to do that."

"Fear not, Jill. It will take more than one minor setback to derail Hosey. I have another plan up my sleeve."

"What's that?" But more to the point, why did I even care?

"I'd rather not say until everything has been finalised. What I can tell you is that if this works out as I hope, it will be even more effective than the tree or bush."

"That's certainly something to look forward to."

"Quite so."

"Why are you hiding in here?" Jack said.

"I'm not hiding. And besides, you knew where you'd find me."

"How did I?"

"Because I'm always in the kitchen at parties."

"You should mingle with our neighbours."

"I have been mingling. I've played the cat whisperer for Kimmy, and I told Mr Hosey that you couldn't wait to be a tree again."

"You didn't!"

"Relax. He doesn't need your services. He's going in an all new direction—camouflage wise."

"What's that?"

"He wouldn't say."

"I guess we'll find out soon enough."

"Not if it's as good as he reckons it is."

"True. Tony, Clare and I have been going over the last-minute plans for TenPinCon. It's hard to believe it's only a few days away. Do you think your grandmother will want a ticket? She did work on the marketing, after all."

"Somehow I doubt it."

"I think you should ask her. It's only fair."

"I will if I see her, but she seems to have disappeared."

"Why don't you come through to the living room with me?"

"I thought I might stay in here and do the washing up."

"Come on." He took my hand and led me into the lion's den.

"Jill, there you are!" Britt gushed. "We wondered where you'd gone."

Unless I was very much mistaken, that wasn't her first glass of wine of the evening.

"Here I am."

"We're really glad you two came tonight." She hiccupped.

"Yes," Kit said. "We wanted to let you see we're more than just keep-fit nuts."

"We never thought that." Jack was quick to reassure them.

I kept my counsel on the subject.

"We're both keen writers, aren't we, Britt?"

"Really?" Jack said. "What do you write?"

"Poetry." She beamed. "I'm not very good, though."

"Rubbish," Kit said. "She has a real talent for it. In fact, she's recently published some of her work, and the book was automatically entered into a competition, so fingers crossed."

"That's fantastic!" Jack gushed. "Isn't it, Jill?"

"Yeah. Fantastic." If Jack asked her to read us some of her poetry, I would be forced to kill him later.

Fortunately, he didn't. *Unfortunately*, he said something much worse.

"I've recently had a poetry book published for a friend. His book was entered into that competition too."

"Oh?" Britt was already halfway down the glass of wine. "What's his name? Maybe I know him?"

It was at this point that Jack realised what he'd done. "His name? It's—err—"

"It was Robert, wasn't it?" I prompted him.

"Oh yes. Silly me. I'd forget my head if it was loose." Jack laughed, nervously. "Robert Hymes."

"Hymes?" Britt was clearly racking her brain to bring him to mind.

"He's not local," I said. "It's unlikely you would have come across him. He's a very private person who tends to stay in his shell."

"What do you write, Kit?" Jack asked, clearly keen to

get off the subject of tortoise poets.

"I tried my hand at a novel, but it isn't very good, I'm afraid."

"He spent over a year writing it," Britt said. "I think it has real potential."

"But you're biased, darling." Kit gave her a peck on the cheek.

"I've told him he should publish it."

"Why don't you?" Jack said.

"Definitely not." Kit shook his head. "It was a silly idea for a book. No one would want to read it."

"Don't listen to him," Britt said. "It's about a woman who discovers she has magical powers. That she's a witch. No one else knows, not even her husband."

That sounded way too familiar for my liking. Thankfully, Kit, who was clearly embarrassed by the attention, changed the subject.

"No one wants to hear about my silly book. We should discuss our plans for the community band."

"That's a great idea," I agreed, much to the surprise of all concerned.

"Jack tells us that you were pulling our legs about his prowess on the glockenspiel."

"He's just too modest to admit it."

"Jill!" Jack shot me a look.

"Okay, sorry. It was just a joke. He actually plays the harp."

"We've booked the community hall for the inaugural meeting of the band," Kit said. "We can all decide what instrument we're going to play then. It's a week on Friday at seven o'clock. Everyone's going to be there."

"Great. I can't wait."

As you're no doubt already aware, small talk isn't exactly my strong suit. I didn't care where Tony and Clare were thinking of holidaying this year, and I certainly didn't give a monkey's that Jimmy and Kimmy planned on turning their back garden into a vegetable plot. And when the Normals brought out the photos of their grandchildren, that was my cue to run and hide. There was no point in going back into the kitchen because Jack would find me there. Instead, I crept upstairs to have a nosey around. If anyone saw me, I'd tell them I'd got lost looking for the bathroom.

I wasn't too surprised to find that the Liveleys had turned their spare bedroom into a mini gym. Just looking at all the equipment tired me out.

"Hi!" The voice almost made me jump out of my skin.

I spun around, but there was no one else in the room.

Or so I thought.

"Hello!" someone said.

Had I finally cracked up?

"I'm down here." Underneath the exercise bike was a tiny man wearing a green duffle coat.

"Hello. Who are you?"

"I'm Gerald. What's your name?"

"Jill. Do you mind if I ask — err — what are you? An elf? A sprite?"

"Certainly not. I'm a gremlin."

"Oh? I thought — err — "

"That gremlins were ugly creatures who cause carnage wherever they go?"

"Something like that."

"We get a bad press. We're really quite nice creatures

who take pride in our work."

"Right. And what exactly is it that gremlins do?"

"We don't all do the same work. Any more than all humans do."

"Sorry, that was very insensitive of me. I should have asked what *you* do."

"I'm a member of the tidy chapter of gremlins. We like to make sure everything is neat and tidy."

"A worthy vocation. And you live here, do you?"

"Yes, I was assigned to this house a few weeks ago, but I'm beginning to think this posting may have been a mistake. The humans who live here are obsessively tidy. There's very little for me to do."

"You may find there's more to do after tonight's party."

"I do hope so. I hate being bored."

"Jill?" Britt was standing in the doorway.

"Sorry, I was looking for the toilet and I stumbled in here by mistake."

"I thought I heard you talking to someone?"

"Err, no. I was just saying to myself how impressive this set-up is."

"You're welcome to pop around for a workout any time."

"Thanks. I'll bear that in mind."

As I followed her out of the door, I gave a little wave to my new gremlin friend.

By ten-thirty, I could stand no more, so I went in search of Jack who was talking to a man I didn't recognise.

"Jack." I nudged his arm.

"Jill, have you met Mr Nutt?"

"Please call me Don. Everyone does." The man had a

crooked smile and more than his fair share of teeth.

"Nice to meet you, Don. Would you mind if I borrowed my husband for a moment?"

"Of course not."

I dragged Jack to a quiet corner of the living room. "We have to go."

"Don's a really interesting guy. He collects phone books."

"Why?"

"He didn't actually say."

"Right. I can't stand any more of this. Let's get out of here."

"We have to say our goodbyes first."

"Can't we just sneak out?"

"That wouldn't be very polite."

"Okay then, but let's be quick."

Just then, Kit clinked a spoon against his glass to get everyone's attention. "Neighbours or should I say, friends. Thank you all for coming this evening. I hope you've had as much fun as Britt and I have. Before you go home, we have one last treat for you."

"Come on." I tugged at Jack's arm.

"Wait. We have to see what this is."

Kit continued. "We must give credit to our wonderful neighbours, Norm and Naomi for this idea. We enjoyed this so much at their housewarming that we persuaded them to let us borrow it."

Oh no! Please no! Tell me it wasn't so.

Jack's face lit up as Britt wheeled in the giant magnetic fishing game.

An hour later, we finally managed to escape.

"It's a stupid game," Jack said when we got back to the house.

"I thought you loved magnetic fishing?"

"It's a game of pure chance. There's no skill involved."

"Your change of heart wouldn't have anything to do with the fact that Don Nutt beat you, would it?"

"Of course not. The man's a complete bore anyway. I mean, who in their right mind collects phone books?"

"Speaking of books, where do you think Kit could have got the idea for that book of his?"

"It's just one of those strange coincidences."

"I guess so. I just hope he doesn't change his mind and get it published. Life is already difficult enough."

***

What a night! Thank goodness it was over. All I wanted to do was to climb into bed, and sleep for a week.

Before I even had the chance to clean my teeth, my phone rang. A phone call at this time of night was never good news.

"Aunt Lucy? What's wrong?"

"It's your grandmother."

"Grandma? What's happened?"

"It suddenly occurred to me that I hadn't seen her for a few days, so I popped over to check on her, and —" Her words trailed away.

"Aunt Lucy?"

"Sorry, Jill. I'm still a little shaken. I found her in bed."

"Is she okay?"

"No."

"She's not —?"

"No, she's breathing, but I can't wake her up."

"Have you called the doctor?"

"Yes, he's on his way over here now."

"I'm coming over."

"Okay. Thank you, Jill."

"I'm sure he cheated." Jack appeared in the bedroom doorway. "No way he caught all those fish fair and —"

"I have to go to Candlefield."

"Now?"

"Yes. Aunt Lucy just called. Grandma isn't well."

"What's wrong with her?"

"I don't know. Aunt Lucy says she's breathing, but she can't wake her up."

"Okay. I hope she's alright."

Me too. Despite everything I'd ever said about Grandma, I couldn't imagine life without her.

I magicked myself straight over to Grandma's house.

"The doctor has just arrived." Aunt Lucy was pacing the hallway. "He's upstairs with her now."

"I'll go up."

"No." She grabbed my arm. "He said we should wait down here."

Reluctantly, I did as she said. After what felt like hours, but was probably no more than a few minutes, the doctor came downstairs.

"How is she?" I got in first.

"All her vital signs are fine."

"So why won't she wake up?"

"I don't know."

"What do you mean, *you don't know*?" I snapped.

"Jill!" Aunt Lucy said.

"Sorry, I'm just worried. What happens now?"

"I'd like to take her into hospital, so we can run some tests, and keep a close eye on her. Would you have any objections?"

Once we'd given him our blessing, he made a call, and minutes later, the ambulance pulled up outside the house.

As they took Grandma away on the stretcher, Aunt Lucy became a little tearful.

"She's in the best hands," I reassured her.

"I know."

"Can we follow you to the hospital?" I asked the doctor.

"There's nothing you can do there. It would be better to wait until the morning before you visit. We'll be in touch if there's any change in the meantime."

Once the ambulance had left, Aunt Lucy broke down. "It's all my fault. I should have checked on her sooner."

"You weren't to know."

"I hadn't seen her in days, and all I could think about was how peaceful it was. If I'd been less selfish, I might have found her before things got so bad."

"That's enough of that. You have absolutely nothing to reproach yourself for. And you heard what the doctor said: All of her vital signs are fine. Grandma is as tough as they come. She'll be okay."

"I do hope so."

So did I. Despite what I'd said to Aunt Lucy, I was really worried. And like her, I blamed myself for not having checked on Grandma earlier.

I stayed with Aunt Lucy for the best part of an hour until Lester persuaded me that I should go home. He promised he'd let me know if and when they heard anything.

"How is she?" Jack said.
"Not great. They've taken her into hospital."
"Did they say what's wrong?"
"They don't know."
"What about you? Are you okay?"
"Not really. I could do with a hug."

Chapter 9

I didn't expect to get much sleep because I'd gone to bed thinking about Grandma. To my surprise, I actually slept like a log, and didn't wake until Jack gave me a nudge just after seven.

"I'm going to make coffee, Jill. Do you want one?"

"Yes, please. I'll give Aunt Lucy a call."

"Okay. I'll see you downstairs."

Aunt Lucy was obviously already up because she answered on the first ring.

"Have you heard anything from the hospital?" I asked.

"I rang them a few minutes ago. They said there'd been no change overnight."

"Do they still not know what's wrong with her?"

"It doesn't sound like it. They said we could visit after nine o'clock."

"Shall I come over to your house or meet you there?"

"The twins are coming too. We can meet you in reception if you like."

"Okay. What time?"

"About ten to nine?"

"I'll see you then."

"Any news?" Jack passed me the coffee.

"No. I don't understand why they can't figure out what's wrong with her."

"She'll be okay, Jill. Your grandmother is very tough."

"I thought so too until I saw her yesterday. She looked so fragile."

"Drink your coffee. Do you want breakfast? I could make you a fry-up."

"No, thanks. I couldn't face anything."

***

Aunt Lucy and the twins were already in reception when I arrived.

"I've told the receptionist we're here." Aunt Lucy gave me a hug. "She said the doctor wants to talk to us."

"Nothing's happened, has it?"

"No. She said there's no change."

"So why does the doctor want to talk to us?"

"I don't know."

We didn't have to wait long to find out because five minutes later, Doctor Plainspeke beckoned us into a small meeting room.

"What's going on?" I said.

"As I told your mother, we're rather baffled at the moment."

I didn't bother to correct him by explaining that Aunt Lucy wasn't my mother because I had more important things on my mind. "You must have some idea what's wrong with her."

"I'm afraid we don't, but the good news is all her vital signs are still looking okay. My gut feeling is that she's come into contact with something that has caused this."

"But what exactly is *this*?" My patience was wearing thin. "What's wrong with her? Is she in a coma?"

"It appears so. The best thing you can do is to try and find whatever caused this."

"How are we supposed to do that?"

"You could try searching her house. Maybe you'll find something there. If you do, then we'll know what we're up against."

"Can we at least see her?"

"Of course. I'll have one of the nurses show you to the ward."

It was the first time the twins had seen Grandma looking this way, and they were both visibly shaken.

"Is she going to be okay?" Amber wiped away a tear.

"Of course she is," Aunt Lucy said with as much conviction as she could muster.

"Wake up, please." Pearl took Grandma's bony hand in hers. "Don't leave us."

Grandma didn't stir.

After we'd been in the ward for twenty minutes, I suggested to Aunt Lucy that I should go to Grandma's house, to see if I could identify what might have caused this.

"I'll come with you."

"No, you stay here with the twins."

"Are you sure?"

"Yes. I'll be back as soon as I can."

Although I'd visited Grandma's house on a number of occasions, I'd never really taken a good look around. The woman was incredibly untidy. There was stuff everywhere, and I barely knew where to start. It didn't help that I had no idea what I was looking for. In the end, I opted to begin downstairs and work my way up.

It quickly became apparent that the problem wouldn't be finding something out of the ordinary; there was plenty of that. The challenge was sorting through the sheer volume of weird and wonderful concoctions scattered around the place; it was overwhelming. Fortunately, all the jars and bottles were labelled, many in Grandma's scrawl. Using a notepad and pen that I'd found on the small writing desk in her dining room, I began to make a note of everything I found.

Three hours later, I'd been through the whole house, and I'd ended up with a list that covered four sides of paper. Hopefully, the culprit would be somewhere amongst that lot.

"Any luck?" Aunt Lucy said, when I got back to the hospital.

"There are tons of bottles and jars in her house. I've made a list of everything I could find." I handed it to her. "Where are the twins?"

"They had to leave because Alan and William have to work. And to make matters worse, the woman who runs the creche is poorly, so that's left the twins in a bit of a pickle."

"What are they going to do about the little ones?"

"They're going to take them to Cuppy C. I said I'd let them know if there were any developments here." All the time Aunt Lucy had been talking to me, she'd been studying the list. "I don't recognise even half of these."

"Who might?"

"The best person to speak to would be Regina Darling. She's Candlefield's foremost authority on potions. If anyone will recognise these, she will."

"Where can I find her?"

"The last I heard, she was living in a witches' commune called Greenacre. It's to the west of Candlefield."

"I'll go and see her." I took back the list. "You'll let me know if there's any change?"

"Of course."

***

The Greenacre witches' commune turned out to be a small farm on the outskirts of Candlefield. The witches who lived there all wore the traditional witch's outfit. Traditional that is except for the colour. It was the first time I'd seen anyone sporting a green witch's outfit. Surprisingly, it seemed to work.

"Excuse me!" I called to a witch who was milking a cow.

"Hello, there."

"Do you have a minute?"

"Are you hoping to join the commune? I'm afraid there's quite a long waiting list."

"Actually, I'm looking for Regina Darling."

"I haven't seen her for a few days. You could check at the office." Unable to point because her hands were *udder*wise engaged, she nodded towards a small log cabin.

"Okay, thanks."

A witch was trying to shoo away a hen, which was sitting on her desk. "Go away, Gertie. You shouldn't be in here."

"Hi." I just managed to dodge the bird as it took flight. "I'm sorry to trouble you, but I'm looking for Regina Darling."

"Are you from the tax people? We submitted our return last week."

"No, it has nothing to do with your taxes, but I do need

to speak to her."

"I'm afraid that's impossible."

"I must insist. This is a matter of life or death."

"That's as maybe, but Regina isn't here."

"Where is she?"

"On a retreat."

"Where? How can I get in touch with her?"

"You can't. Regina goes on a retreat two or three times every year, and she never tells anyone where she's going."

"When will she be back?"

"Tomorrow morning."

"And you're sure no one knows where she is?"

"Positive. You're welcome to ask around, but everyone will tell you the same thing."

"If I leave you this list, will you ask her to take a look through it? I need to know if there's anything on there that might cause someone to go into a coma-like state. Do you have a pen?"

I jotted my name and number on the bottom of the list, and handed it to her.

"You're Jill Maxwell?"

"That's right, and my grandmother, Mirabel Millbright, is the one who is in the coma."

"I'm so very sorry to hear that. I'll give this to Regina as soon as she gets back, and I'll ask her to contact you."

"Thank you."

After I'd left the commune, I called Aunt Lucy to update her on the situation.

"Any change with Grandma?"

"No, she's just the same. The doctors say she's not in any danger while her vital signs continue to remain stable."

"You should go home and have a rest, Aunt Lucy."

"I'd rather stay here. The staff are all very kind. They've given me a reclining chair, so I should be able to catnap."

"Are you sure you don't want me to come over there?"

"There's no need. I'll let you know if there's any change."

***

Frustrating as it was, there was simply nothing more I could do for Grandma until I heard back from Regina Darling. To take my mind off it, the best thing I could do was to throw myself into my work. First, though, I had to get to the office. The traffic situation in the city centre, and specifically on the road outside my office building, was getting beyond a joke. It seemed that not a day went by that a new pothole didn't open up.

"Did you hear about that poor man, Jill?" Mrs V said when I eventually made it to the office.

"Which man?"

"The one who died in the freak accident? It just goes to show that when your number's up, there's nothing you can do about it."

"Do you mean the man who was crushed by a tree falling onto his car?"

"No, I hadn't heard about that. I'm talking about the man who fell down the open manhole on the high street."

"How come the manhole cover was missing?"

"No one seems to know. It just goes to show that you should treat every day as though it was your last."

Winky was hard at work on the punch bag.

"I take it you're still planning to go ahead with this crazy boxing tournament?"

"Of course I am. I've been trying to decide where to keep the trophy. What we need in here is a glass cabinet. We could put it over there, so that everyone can see it when they come into the office."

"That's a brilliant idea. Would you prefer metal or wood?"

"Wood, I think. Are you going to buy one?"

"No, I'm not going to buy one. Why would I fork out for a trophy cabinet that's going to remain empty?"

"You're tighter than a duck's —"

"That's enough of that! I'm not in the mood for your stupidity today. My grandmother is gravely ill."

"You can't stand the old witch."

"I've never said that."

"You're always moaning about her."

"Shut up, and go back to your boxing."

***

Robert Warne had supposedly been kidnapped while at the multiplex, so my next move was to pay the cinema a visit. The young man behind the counter was more interested in trying to sell me popcorn than in addressing my questions.

"I don't want any popcorn. I'd like to see the manager."

"It's half-price before six pm."

"I don't care if you're giving it away. I just want to speak to the manager."

Reluctantly, he gave up on his quest to meet his

popcorn sales quota, and made a phone call.

"Mr Rudd says he's busy. Can you come back tomorrow?"

"Never mind." I was getting nowhere fast, so it was time for a different approach.

I nipped into the nearest toilet, made myself invisible, and then went in search of the manager's office.

It took a while, but I eventually located it. After reversing the 'invisible' spell, I knocked on the door and went inside.

"Who are you?" The 'busy' manager had his feet on the desk and was reading a car magazine. "You can't come bursting in here like this."

"I just did."

"I'll call security." He reached for the phone, which thanks to a little magic, crumbled in his hand.

"What the—?" He stared in disbelief at the telephone dust on his desk.

"You're clearly stronger than you look."

"What do you want?"

"I'm investigating a kidnapping that may have taken place in your cinema."

"A *kidnapping*?" He scoffed. "Have you been drinking? Don't you think I'd know if there'd been a kidnapping on these premises?"

"Apparently not because there has, and you don't."

"Even if that was true, I don't see what you want me to do about it."

"I want to see your CCTV."

"That's not possible."

"Are you sure about that? How is it going to look if this man ends up dead because you refused to help?"

"I don't have to help you. You're not the police."

"Yes, I am. See?" I quickly cast a spell so that instead of seeing my library card, he saw a police ID.

"Why didn't you say so before?"

"I thought that would have been obvious."

"Sorry. We only have cameras on the outside of the building."

"None inside?"

"Sorry, no."

"Okay. You'd better let me see the footage you do have."

He led the way to a small office that contained all the usual CCTV monitoring equipment, which by now I was quite familiar with.

"Would you like me to get someone to help you?"

"That won't be necessary. I'll come and get you if I need anything."

I knew which performance Cheryl and her husband had attended, so I focussed my attention on the footage that covered the main doors, starting half an hour before the movie was due to start. Fifteen minutes in, I spotted Cheryl, walking arm in arm with a man wearing a large-brimmed hat.

According to Cheryl, her husband had disappeared about fifty minutes into the screening, so I fast forwarded the footage to that point. It was almost thirty minutes further in that I saw her leaving the cinema.

Robert Warne must have left the cinema somehow, but not necessarily via the main doors. It was quite possible that he'd been taken by force through one of the five fire exits. Fortunately, the CCTV covered all of them. I was hoping I might see someone leaving the building with something that could have contained the missing man—a laundry basket for example. But there was nothing like that; the only people I saw go in and out of those doors were employees on a cigarette break.

Before calling it a bust, I took another look at the footage from the main entrance, but there was still no sign of Robert Warne leaving the building. The timestamp now showed a quarter to midnight, and there had been no activity for the last fifteen minutes. I was just on the point of giving up when I saw a crowd of people going *into* the building. Over the next ten minutes, dozens more people arrived at the cinema. That's when I remembered seeing the ads for the new Marvel movie, which had been shown at five past midnight on that particular day—the day of its release. I'd said to Jack at the time that you'd have to be crazy to go to the movies at that time of night. Apparently, there were plenty of crazy people in Washbridge.

Those blockbusters lasted a minimum of two and a half hours, so I fast forwarded the footage until the timestamp showed two-thirty. Not long after, the crowds of superhero nerds began to pile out of the cinema. In amongst them was Robert Warne, still wearing the large-brimmed hat. As far as I could tell, he appeared to be alone, and he certainly didn't appear to be leaving under duress.

Chapter 10

"There, what did I tell you?" Mrs V said. "Now do you believe me?"

I had no choice but to believe her. I'd heard the rumbling sound as soon as I walked into the building.

"How long has it been going on this time?"

"Almost an hour now. Do you think we should evacuate the building?"

"I'll go down into the basement to see if I can find out what's causing it."

"Are you sure that's a good idea?"

"Not really, but I'll go anyway. If I'm not back in thirty minutes, call the emergency services."

"Be careful, Jill."

I'd never had occasion to go down into the basement before, and I wasn't particularly looking forward to it, but I had to find out what was causing that noise.

The door to the basement, which was underneath the main stairs, was locked. I could have called Macabre, but by the time he arrived, the rumbling sound would probably have stopped again. Instead, I used the 'power' spell to force the door, followed by the 'take it back' spell to repair the damage.

The wooden stairs creaked as I made my way down into the cavernous basement. If the number of cobwebs was anything to go by, it was a long time since anyone had been down there. Knowing Macabre, he wouldn't have spent a penny more than he had to on maintenance. The boiler probably hadn't been looked at since he bought the building.

Unbelievable! When I was halfway down the stairs, the rumbling noise stopped, and was replaced by an eerie silence. I considered turning back, but having come this far, I figured I should at least take a look around. A couple of the light bulbs had blown, so the huge room was still in semi-darkness. There was very little down there: a few boxes and some old furniture — that was about it. The boiler was in the centre of the room, and appeared to be purring along nicely.

What was I supposed to do now? Hang around in the basement in the hope that the rumbling sound would start up again? It could be hours, and I didn't have that kind of time to spare, so I headed back to the stairs. I was only halfway up when the rumbling noise began again. I spun around, fully expecting to see the boiler vibrating, but it was still purring along as quietly as before. That made no sense.

I hurried down the stairs and walked towards the boiler, but as I got closer, I realised that the sound was coming from behind it. Gingerly, and unsure what to expect, I slowly edged my way around the huge machine.

And then I saw it!

My initial thought was that we must have been invaded by aliens. There was some kind of weird machine face down in the ground; it was almost as if a tiny spaceship had crash landed. But that didn't make any sense; how could it have ended up in the basement? Unless, of course, it had landed centuries ago, long before the building existed. That must be it! The aliens must have been biding their time and were now about to rise and take over the earth.

Just then, a small hatch on top of the craft popped open.

I was about to come face to face with a creature from another world. What should I do? Would they be hostile or friendly?

"Winky?"

"What are you doing down here, Jill?" He clambered out of the—err—whatever it was.

"Never mind what *I'm* doing down here. Why are *you* down here, and what's that contraption?"

"Isn't it obvious?"

"I thought you were an alien from outer space."

"You need therapy. Urgently."

"What is that thing? And what exactly are you up to?"

"Do you remember the raison d'être behind Cat Zip?"

"I remember that it was supposed to make it safer for cats to cross the road. That didn't quite work out, though, did it?"

"Maybe not, but the problem still exists. And this—" He pointed to the strange machine. "This is the solution."

"I don't get it."

"It's not that difficult. If we can't go over the roads, then we have to go—?" He paused.

"Under them?"

"Bingo!"

"Hold on a minute. Is this some kind of digging machine?"

"The correct term is TBM or tunnel boring machine."

Suddenly everything started to slot into place.

"Are you telling me that you've been boring a hole underneath the road outside this building?"

"That was the plan, but there have been a few minor hiccups."

"These *hiccups*? They wouldn't by any chance have

resulted in subsidence in the road above? Potholes, that kind of thing?"

"I wouldn't like to comment on that."

"Do you even know how to operate that machine?"

"Well, I — err — "

"Yes or no?"

"The user manual is three-hundred pages long. It would have taken me months to read it all. I did consider hiring a trained operator, but it was too costly."

"I've heard enough. This can't go on. Move away from that contraption."

"Why? What are you going to do?"

"Just step back!"

As soon as he had, I cast the 'shatter' spell, causing the machine to disintegrate.

"What have you done?" He looked at what was left of his TBM.

"Made it safe."

"I'll never get my deposit back on that now."

"Tough luck."

"I've a good mind to report you."

"If anyone is going to do any reporting, it will be me. If you don't close this little operation down immediately, I'll let the authorities know the real reason for the subsidence outside."

"You're stifling innovation. That's what you're doing!"

"Think yourself lucky that I'm not stifling you!"

"Thank goodness you're okay, Jill." Mrs V was clearly relieved to see that I was still in one piece. "Did you find out what the noise is?"

"You were right. It was the boiler."

"I knew it. Shall I get on the phone to Mr Macabre, and tell him to get someone out here to see to it?"

"There's no need. It was just the high-pressure valve thingy. It was sticking. I've oiled it, and it appears to be working now. There won't be any more rumbling sounds."

"How on earth did you know how to do that?"

"I took a night class in mechanical engineering a few years ago. I always knew it would come in handy one day."

"Well, well. I have to say I'm mightily impressed."

Me too.

***

As the name suggested, Washbridge Prestige Motors specialised in top-end cars. The sort of car I could only dream of owning. On my way over there, I made myself a promise that I wouldn't waste time drooling over cars that I'd never be able to afford. I'd go straight into reception and ask for Sandy Gascoigne.

Oh, but look at that gorgeous Porsche. And that Lamborghini. Have you ever seen anything so fabulous?

"It's a beautiful car, isn't it?" The salesman must have picked up my scent as soon as I'd stepped onto the sales lot. "Have you owned a Lambo before?"

"Not recently."

"Once driven, never forgotten. What do you drive now?"

"I—err—" Fortunately, I'd had the foresight to park my car two streets away; he wouldn't have been impressed by it. "I'm between cars at the moment."

"Would you like to take a look inside? I can get the keys."

"Sure."

The guy, who had clearly sensed a bumper month-end bonus, scurried away and was back moments later.

"Jump in." He opened the driver's side door. "What do you think?" It was then that I spotted his name badge: Sandy Gascoigne.

"It's very nice, Sandy."

I wasn't lying. It was truly amazing, but that was hardly surprising given the price tag.

He climbed in beside me. "I'm sorry. I didn't catch your name?"

"Jill."

"Would you like to take her for a test drive, Jill?"

"Maybe later. I have an urgent appointment in a few minutes. I just thought I'd pop in and take a look around while I was passing."

"No problem." He took a business card out of his breast pocket. "Give me a call anytime, and I can set up a test drive for you."

"Thanks, Sandy. Have you worked here long?"

"Not too long. About five months."

"But you must have been in the business for some time? You have the air of someone who knows his way around car sales."

"You're right — I have. I used to work for an outfit called Bestest Cars, do you know them?"

"They're out Smallwash way, aren't they?"

"That's right. A guy called Burt Claymore owns the place."

"From what I remember, the cars they sell are a bit

different from the ones you sell here."

"True, but I enjoyed my time there."

"How come you left, then?"

"I was fired." He smiled. "I was trying to offer some constructive advice, but Burt took it the wrong way. He thought I was undermining him."

"That must have hurt? Getting the sack, I mean?"

"At the time, yeah. But to be honest, Burt did me a favour. I never would have landed this job if he hadn't given me the boot."

"Weren't your current employers put off by the fact that you'd been sacked?"

"No, I was lucky. They know Burt, and they know how he can be. They gave me a month's trial, and then offered me the job permanently."

"Good for you. Have you seen your old employer since you were sacked?"

"No. Never look back; that's my motto."

"I'd better be making tracks." I got out of the car.

"Call me about the test drive. Any time."

"I'll do that."

Gascoigne was a slick salesman, and I could see how he would do well in his chosen profession. My gut feeling was that he wasn't the one behind the mysterious green car situation because, even though he'd been sacked by Claymore, Gascoigne didn't appear to hold a grudge. Quite the contrary, his dismissal had worked out in his favour because it had resulted in him landing a much better job.

***

"A tunnelling machine?" Jack looked incredulous. "Please tell me that you're joking."

"I'm deadly serious. Winky decided that if he couldn't go over the road, he'd go under it. But not any longer. That TBM won't be digging any more holes."

"Still no more news on your grandmother, I take it?"

"No. According to Aunt Lucy, the hospital have confirmed her condition hasn't changed. Until I hear back from Regina Darling, the potion master, there isn't much more I can do."

"At least tonight's shindig at Cakey C should take your mind off things."

"I wish I could get out of it, but there's no way I can."

"You'll enjoy it when you get there. Just think of all those free cakes."

"That's the only thing that's keeping me going."

***

Wow! Just wow!

I thought ripping off the Cuppy C name was bad enough, but not satisfied with that, my parents had actually copied the style of the signage too. It was practically identical.

Word of the launch party had clearly got around because the shop was full to bursting. I spotted a few familiar faces amongst the crowd, including the colonel and Priscilla.

"Long time no see, you two. How are you both?"

"Couldn't be better, Jill." The colonel certainly looked well. "It's a great spread that your parents have put on tonight."

"I'll have to take your word for it. I haven't managed to fight my way through to the refreshments yet. How is Hauntings Unlimited doing?"

"Going from strength to strength, I'm pleased to say. And much of that is thanks to you. If you hadn't helped to sort out the issue with the spookberry licensing, I'm not sure we would have survived."

"That's great to hear."

"We're having such fun running it too, aren't we, Cilla?"

"Absolutely." She beamed. "Working together is the best thing we ever did. Have you and Jack ever considered doing it?"

"It would never work. He's too much of a control freak."

I eventually managed to find my way to the cakes, and boy what a selection; I was spoiled for choice. And they were every bit as yumcious as those at Cuppy C.

I hadn't expected Harry and Larry to be at the launch party because I wasn't sure how they'd feel about seeing their shop in someone else's hands. As it turned out, I needn't have worried because when I found them, they were laughing and joking with my parents.

"Jill!" Mum called. "I didn't think you were coming."

"I've been here a while."

"Come and join us. Isn't it a wonderful turnout?"

"Fantastic. What do you think of what they've done to the place?" I asked Harry and Larry.

"We love it," Harry said. "I'm sure it'll be a roaring success."

"And such a great name," Larry chipped in. "I don't

know how they thought of it."

"It is great, isn't it?" I turned to my mother. "How did you come up with it, Mum?"

She glared at me. "Oh, you know. Just a moment of inspiration."

"And the sign too." I was having fun now. "Such an unusual design."

"Could I have a quiet word in private, Jill." My mother took my arm and led me towards the back of the shop.

"I was only joking about the name and sign." I offered in self-defence.

"That's not what I wanted to speak to you about."

"Oh?"

"Yvonne's in the back room." She opened the door and ushered me inside. "I'll leave you two alone to talk."

What was I supposed to say to the woman who had sacrificed her own life to save mine? I was still contemplating that question when she came over and gave me a hug. We were both in tears for several minutes; it was Yvonne who eventually managed to speak first.

"How's Jack?"

"He's great. What about you?"

"I'm fine."

"I had no idea you were in GT."

"I thought I should find my feet before I made contact with anyone."

"I'm glad you have. What about Jack? Will you contact him too?"

"I don't know. I wasn't sure how he'd feel about it. I thought I should speak to you first."

"He'll be thrilled to bits."

"I'd like you to talk to him first, just to be sure. Do you

mind?"

"Of course not, but I already know what he'll say."

Chapter 11

I didn't want to tell Jack about his mother until we had the time to sit down and discuss it properly. The next morning, he was in a hurry to get to work, so I decided it would be best if I waited until the evening to have that discussion. Although I was sure he'd be pleased by the news, it was inevitably going to come as a big shock.

"I like that tie," I said.

"The answer is no."

"What are you talking about? I only said I liked your tie."

"Don't you think I know you by now? Most mornings, you don't even notice which tie I'm wearing."

"Rubbish."

"Okay, then. It's Friday today. Can you tell me which tie I wore on any other day so far this week?"

"I — err — the blue one."

"Which blue one?"

"The blue one that I like."

"Just as I suspected. You have no idea."

"It's only a teeny-weeny favour. I need to view the city centre CCTV. I thought you might put in a word for me."

"What did we agree about you asking me to use my position to help you?"

"That I wouldn't ask you to do it again."

"That's right."

"Is that a *maybe*?"

"No. It's an unequivocal no. N.O."

"I never did like that tie, anyway."

Jack had left for work, wearing that horrible tie of his,

and I was just about to leave when my phone rang.

"Is that Jill Maxwell?"

I didn't recognise the woman's voice.

"Speaking."

"This is Regina Darling."

"Thanks for calling. Have you had a chance to look through the list I left for you?"

"Yes, just now. It didn't take long because there's only one item on there that could cause the symptoms you described. That's the dark hazel. Do you know where your grandmother got hold of it?"

"I have no idea."

"It's extremely dangerous to sups and humans alike."

"She's been in a coma for a number of days. How much longer is it likely to last?"

"Indefinitely."

"What?"

"Left untreated, your grandmother could remain in that condition until the end of time. Neither alive nor dead."

"You said if left untreated. That suggests there may be a treatment."

"Just the one. The only way to reverse the effects of dark hazel is with the sap of the rainbow lily."

"And where would I find that? Is it available in the pharmacy?"

"I'm afraid not."

"Do you have any?"

"No. It's a very rare substance. The only place you'll find it is in Rainbow Valley, which is inhabited by the rainbow fairies."

"Where is that?"

"Do you know the Black Woods?"

"I do, yes."

"Rainbow Valley is north of there."

"You wouldn't happen to know who's in charge there, would you?"

"I believe it's Queen Munch, but I could be wrong."

"Okay. Thanks very much for all your help."

"No problem. I hope your grandmother gets better soon."

I magicked myself over to Aunt Lucy's house.

"I know what's wrong with Grandma." I explained what Regina Darling had told me about the dark hazel, and about the cure being available only in the Rainbow Valley. "What I don't understand is why Grandma would have the dark hazel in her house if it's so dangerous."

"You know what she's like. She thinks she's indestructible."

"At least there's something I can do now. I just wanted to update you before I go over to Rainbow Valley. Have you heard of the rainbow fairies?"

"I can't say I have, but then there are so many different kinds of fairy that it's hard to keep track. Do you want me to go with you?"

"No. You keep Grandma company. I'll be back as soon as I can."

***

From the Dark Woods, I headed north as instructed. Rainbow Valley turned out to be remarkably easy to locate, mainly because of the beautiful rainbow that appeared above it. It hadn't rained, so I was at something of a loss to understand why there was a rainbow, but it certainly made navigation easier.

As always when dealing with fairies, I thought it advisable to shrink myself to their size. At the head of the valley was a checkpoint with a rainbow coloured barrier and guardhouse.

"Can I help you?" A rather overweight fairy, dressed in a rainbow coloured uniform, came out of the guardhouse. She had a half-eaten slice of toast in her hand.

"I'd like to see Queen Munch, please."

"You're plain out of luck, then." She took a bite of the toast.

"It's a matter of the utmost importance."

"That's as maybe, but you can't see Queen Munch."

"Why not?"

"Because she's been dead for over two years."

"Oh? Sorry, I was misinformed. Who's in charge here now?"

"Queen Chomp. She's Queen Munch's eldest daughter."

"Can I see her, then, please?"

"Do you have an appointment?"

"No, but like I said, this is a matter of the utmost importance."

"Says you."

"Would you at least ask if she'll see me?"

The guard shoved the rest of the toast into her mouth. "What's your name?"

"Jill Maxwell."

"How do you spell that?"

"M-A-X—"

"No, I meant your first name. Is it with a G or a J?"

"It's a J."

"Wait there."

She went back into the guardhouse and made a phone call. Through the window, I could see her trying to juggle the phone while at the same time, popping more bread into a toaster. She spoke so loudly that I could pretty much hear every word she said.

"No, she doesn't have an appointment—A witch, I think. A very tiny one—Maxwell. Jill with a J—Okay, I'll hold on." There was then a pause for a couple of minutes. "Hello? Right, okay. Bye." Only when she'd buttered the toast, did she come back out to deliver the verdict. "The queen will see you."

"She will? Excellent."

The fairy guard pressed a rainbow coloured button to raise the barrier.

"Just follow the rainbow road; it leads directly to the rainbow palace."

"Thanks. Before I go, I have to ask, how come there's a rainbow in the sky? It hasn't rained recently."

"It's always there." She shrugged. "Why else do you think this is called Rainbow Valley?"

The rainbow road weaved through woods and fields before it eventually reached a small city. As I walked through the streets, towards the palace, I seemed to attract a lot of attention from the residents, who were all dressed in rainbow coloured clothes.

When I reached the huge rainbow coloured gates of the palace, they were closed. I was just wondering what to do next when they opened.

"You must be Jill Maxwell." The rotund fairy shook my

hand.

"Queen Chomp?"

"Goodness, no. I'm Felicity. One of the queen's fairies-in-waiting. Would you follow me, please?" She led the way up a rainbow coloured staircase to a huge hall. "The queen will be with you momentarily."

"Thanks."

I was busy admiring the rainbow coloured furniture when the roly-poly figure of Queen Chomp entered the room.

"This is an honour," she said, through a mouthful of donut. Cinnamon, if I wasn't mistaken. "I've read a lot about you, Jill Maxwell."

"Really?"

"Yes, indeed. The Rainbow Weekly has carried articles on your various exploits."

"I had no idea."

"What brings you to our valley today?"

"I'm here in search of the sap of the rainbow lily."

"Why do you need that?"

I told her about Grandma, the dark hazel, and that I'd been advised that the only cure was the sap of the rainbow lily. "Can you help?"

"I'd like to, but it isn't quite as simple as that."

"Do you have the rainbow lilies?"

"Yes, of course. Unfortunately, the Rainbow Kingdom Charter does not allow me to give away the rainbow lily sap."

"But surely, you're the queen?"

"True, but my powers are still restricted by the charter. There is a way, though."

"Tell me, please."

"Although we can't *give away* the sap, we can barter it for certain commodities that can't be found here in Rainbow Valley."

"What do you want? Tell me and I'll get it for you."

"Would you be able to get something from the human world?"

"Yes. Just name it."

"A Bakewell pudding."

"A pastry?"

"Not just any pastry. Only an authentic Bakewell pudding from the village of Bakewell will do. It's considered by the rainbow fairies to be the most revered of pastries."

"How many do you want?"

"Just one will suffice."

"And in exchange you'll let me have the rainbow lily sap?"

"Indeed."

This whole exercise was proving to be much more complicated than I'd first anticipated. Still, if it meant that Grandma would be cured, it would all be worthwhile.

Bakewell was a delightful market town in the Peak District. I'd never been there before, and under different circumstances, I would have loved to have explored it properly, but today my mission was to get hold of a Bakewell pudding as quickly as possible, and to take it back to Queen Chomp.

Several shops in the town claimed to sell the 'authentic' Bakewell pudding, so to be on the safe side, I bought one from each. Laden with these, I magicked myself back to the queen's palace in Rainbow Valley.

"That was quick." Queen Chomp was now eating a chocolate éclair. "Are those what I think they are?"

"Bakewell puddings, as requested."

"From Bakewell?"

"Of course."

"You only had to buy one."

"It's fine. It'll be well worth it if it means Grandma will be cured."

"May I see them?"

She took the boxes from me and peeked inside each one. "Excellent. You did very well."

"And the sap?"

"I had it prepared in readiness for your return." She picked up a rainbow coloured phone. "Felicity, bring it through, would you?"

Moments later, the fairy-in-waiting appeared, carrying a vial containing a rainbow coloured liquid, which she handed to me.

"Thank you. How much of this do I need to give my grandmother?"

"It's very potent," the queen said. "Just a couple of drops will do the trick."

"Will it take long to work?"

"It should take effect pretty much immediately."

***

When I got to the hospital, Aunt Lucy and the twins were seated beside Grandma's bed.

"Did you get it, Jill?" Amber said.

"I did." I held up the vial of rainbow coloured liquid.

"Are you sure this is going to work?" Pearl was staring

at the vial.

"According to Regina Darling, this is the only way to reverse the effects of dark hazel."

"I'll go and find the doctor." Aunt Lucy hurried away down the ward.

"I never thought I'd miss her criticising me." Amber looked down at her grandmother.

"She'll soon be back to her old self." I did my best to reassure the twins. "Regina Darling reckons the lily sap should work pretty much straight away."

Moments later, Aunt Lucy came charging up the ward, with the doctor a few paces behind her. I could tell from her expression that something was wrong.

"He says we can't give the rainbow lily sap to her." She sounded close to tears.

"You can't go around administering your own potions." The doctor glanced at the rainbow coloured liquid. "What is it, anyway?"

"It's the sap of the rainbow lily. It's the only thing that can reverse the effects of dark hazel."

"We can't be sure that's what caused her current condition."

"It's the only thing in her house that could have done it."

"How do you know that?"

"Because I spoke to Regina Darling who is Candlefield's leading authority on potions, poisons and the like."

"I still can't authorise this."

"So you intend to do what?" I snapped at him. "Sit around, hoping for a miracle?"

"I'm very sorry. I simply can't allow it."

I'd heard quite enough of his excuses, so I moved over

to the bed, and gently lifted Grandma's head.

"What do you think you're doing?" The doctor started towards me.

"It's her only hope." I opened her mouth, and tipped the vial, so that a little of the rainbow liquid dripped onto her tongue.

Five minutes later, and there had been no change in Grandma's condition.

"I thought it was supposed to work straight away?" Pearl said.

"That's what Regina Darling told me."

"Be patient," Aunt Lucy said. "I'm sure it will work."

But it didn't. One hour later, Grandma's condition hadn't changed; she was still in a deep coma. The doctor had left us to return to his duties.

"I don't understand." I was close to tears.

"You did your best." Aunt Lucy took my hand.

"But it didn't do any good."

"Sorry, but we really do have to go," Amber said. "Belladonna is still off work, and we don't know when she'll be back. Let us know if there's any change, Mum."

"Of course I will. You two go and take care of the little ones and the shop." After the twins had left, Aunt Lucy said. "You should go too, Jill."

"No, I want to stay."

"You have your own life to live. I'll let you know if there's any change."

"I should stay with you."

"There's no need. Please, Jill. I'll be fine here by myself."

"Okay, but you must promise to let me know if anything happens?"

"Of course."

Had Regina Darling made the wrong diagnosis? Had something other than dark hazel caused the coma? I couldn't remember the last time I'd felt so helpless. I'd been so sure that the rainbow lily sap would cure Grandma. What hope was there for her now?

Chapter 12

I'd been so busy that I'd almost forgotten about Belladonna until the twins had mentioned that she'd called in sick.

I owed it to all parties concerned to talk to her previous employers. If she was following in her despicable mother's footsteps, she needed to be stopped once and for all, and I was quite prepared to do whatever was required to do just that. On the other hand, if what she'd told me was true, and she really was innocent, she should be allowed to live her life without the fear of persecution.

Belladonna had given me a list of five places she'd worked in Candlefield: three nurseries and two creches. The first on my list was Candle Kids, a small nursery not too far from Aunt Lucy's house.

When I arrived at the colourful building, I spotted a notice in the window that said they had a few places for kids between the ages of one and four.

"Hi! I'm Layla, the manager." The young witch had a large rubber pen stuck behind her ear. "Can I help you?"

"I see you have a few free places at the moment?"

"That's right, but they're likely to go very quickly. They always do. Are you looking for somewhere for your little one?"

"I am."

"What's his or her name?"

"Name? Err—" My mind went completely blank. I really should have thought this through first. "Her name is—err—Pen."

"Pen?"

"Penny."

"And how old is Penny?"

"Err, two."

"The terrible twos, eh?"

"Yeah."

"I can get someone to give you a quick tour if you like?"

"That would be great, but I'm due at work in a few minutes. Maybe I could come back later for that?"

"Of course. We're open until seven."

"Great." And then, as if as an afterthought, I said, "A friend of mine sent her little one here. She was full of praise for the staff."

"That's always good to hear."

"In fact, she mentioned one person in particular. What was her name? It's on the tip of my tongue. Bella, no, Belladonna, that was it."

The woman's expression changed immediately. "Belladonna no longer works here."

"Oh? That's rather disappointing."

"I can assure you the current staff all have excellent qualifications."

"I'm sure they do. It's just that my friend mentioned that she'd never known anyone who had such a calming influence on children. She said she'd seen nothing quite like it."

"Belladonna was really good with the children, that's true."

"Can I ask you why she left?"

"I'm sorry, but I can't discuss that."

It was time for me to come clean. "I'm afraid that I've been less than honest with you. I don't have any children."

"I don't understand."

"Are you familiar with Cuppy C?"

"The tea room?"

"That's right. My cousins own it, and they've recently opened a creche above the shop. They've employed Belladonna to run it."

"Oh?"

"It's alright. She isn't working there at the moment. I persuaded her she should take sick leave."

"I'm not sure what you want from me?"

"I know all about Belladonna's mother."

"Such an evil woman." She shuddered. "I couldn't believe it when I found out."

"I can understand why you wouldn't want Belladonna working here, but can I ask, and please be honest, did you ever have any problems with her?"

"Well, no. Not as such."

"Are you sure? No complaints from any of the parents?"

"None, thank goodness. In fact, many of them were sorry to see her leave, but what could I do? If word had got out, it would have been the end for us."

"Right. Thank you for your honesty. I appreciate your time."

And it was exactly the same story at the other nurseries and creches. None of them had a bad word to say about Belladonna's work, but they'd all felt compelled to let her go once they learnt about her mother. More importantly, there hadn't been a single report of any child being harmed in any way while in Belladonna's care.

It seemed that what Belladonna had told me was true: She was being punished for the sins of her mother, which wasn't fair. But even if I didn't tell the twins what I knew, it was bound to come out sooner or later. If things were ever to change, a radically different approach would be needed, but that would require the agreement of both the twins and Belladonna.

"Any news on Grandma?" Pearl asked, as soon as I walked into Cuppy C.

"Not yet."

"Do you think she'll be okay, Jill?"

"Of course she will. You know how tough she is."

"It's just that I can't stop thinking about all the horrible things I've said about her." Pearl was clearly struggling to hold back the tears.

"Don't be silly. We've all done that, but none of us meant anything by it."

"Do you want a latte?"

"No, I can't stay. I was hoping to have a quick word with you and Amber, but I imagine she's at home, isn't she?"

"No, she's upstairs in the creche."

"Do you think you could get someone to cover the shop while I speak to you both?"

"I suppose so. Is it about Grandma?"

"No, actually, it's about Belladonna."

"Not again! Come on, Jill. You have to let it go."

"I can't. This is way too serious. I need to speak to you and Amber, and I need to do it right now."

Somewhat reluctantly, she agreed.

I wasn't looking forward to telling the twins what I knew, but it had to be done, and there was simply no way to predict what their reaction would be.

***

After I'd finished my meeting with the twins, I called Belladonna to make sure she was at home before going over to her house.

She must have been watching for me because she answered the door before I'd even had the chance to knock.

"Nice house," I commented as she led the way through to the kitchen/diner.

"Thanks. I share with two others."

"Are they in at the moment?"

"No, they're both out at work. Would you like a drink?"

"Tea would be nice."

When we had our drinks, I told her what her previous employers had had to say.

"I told you, didn't I?" She began to cry. "I would never hurt a child. Never."

"Everyone spoke very highly of you."

"Does that mean you won't tell the twins who my mother was?"

"I've already told them."

"What?" She screamed. "You promised you wouldn't do that."

"I never said that."

"That's it, then. I'm done for. I'll never be able to work with children again."

"Wait a minute. Hear me out. I had to tell the twins about your mother. I had no choice in the matter. But I also told them everything that your previous employers had to say about your work. Most importantly, I told them that no child had ever come to harm while in your care."

"How did they react?"

"Just as I expected them to. They said they couldn't take the risk that word of who your mother was might get out."

"See, what did I tell you? There's no hope."

"Hold on. I haven't finished yet. I think I may have come up with a plan that will allow you to continue to work at the creche."

"What's that?"

"It seems to me that you have two choices. You can leave Cuppy C and try to get a job elsewhere—"

"Where? I've run out of places."

"Even if you did find somewhere else, the same issue will inevitably raise its head again sooner or later."

"You said I had two options?"

"That's right, but the second one isn't going to be easy for you."

"I'm willing to consider anything."

"You have to leave Belladonna behind."

"I don't know what you mean."

"I can use magic to change your appearance permanently."

"I didn't realise there was a spell that could do that."

"There isn't, but I'm sure that by combining and reworking some of the existing spells, I could do it."

"So I'd be someone else?"

"Inside, you'd still be you, but to all outward appearances, yes you'd be a totally different person."

"That's a big step."

"Probably much bigger than you realise. For a start, you'd have to leave all your old friends behind."

"I don't have that many."

"That will make it a little easier, but there'll be lots of other adjustments too. For example, you'd have to find a new place to live. This is not going to be an easy option."

"If I did this, would I still be able to work in the creche in Cuppy C?"

"Yes, but Belladonna would have to resign first. The twins would then employ the 'new' you."

"And the twins have said they're okay with that?"

"Yes, but they're still a little nervous about it. So am I for that matter. If I've got this wrong, it will all come back on me. That's why I'll still be watching you like a hawk."

"I'm not worried about that. I have nothing to hide." She hesitated. "There is just one thing. What about visiting my mother's grave?"

"I thought you might mention that. That may prove to be the hardest part of your decision. If you do make this change, you'll no longer be able to go there. If you did, it wouldn't be long before someone put two and two together."

"I'd feel so guilty. Abandoning her like that."

"This may sound harsh, but there's no other way to put it. That woman brought this on herself. She chose to steal the souls of those poor children; no one made her do it. She's the one responsible for all the problems you've been forced to face in your life. In my view, you owe her nothing."

"Even so, I don't know if I can just abandon her like that."

"You'll need to give it a lot of thought." I stood up.

"Take the weekend to think it over, and then let me know what you decide."

"I will, and Jill—"

"Yes?"

"Thank you for at least giving me this chance. No one has ever done anything like this for me before."

***

The fact that time stood still for me while I was in Candlefield could be advantageous sometimes, but it could also work against me. Take today for example, I felt like I'd already done a full shift, what with the fruitless search for a cure for Grandma, and the work involved in checking on Belladonna.

And yet, when I magicked myself back to Washbridge, it was still early morning.

"Morning, Jill." Unlike me, Mrs V was clearly feeling bright and breezy.

"Morning."

"Are you okay?"

"I'm fine."

"Are you sure? Didn't you sleep? You look tired."

"I'm okay. Any messages?"

"Just the one from a Mr Tune. He wouldn't say what it was about, but he left a number for you to call him back on."

"Okay, thanks. Do you think you could make me a coffee, please? Better make it black and very strong."

Winky was hard at work on the punch bag.

"Don't you ever get fed up of hitting that thing?"

"I just pretend it's someone I don't like, and that motivates me."

"Anyone in particular?"

"It varies. Today, I'm pretending it's the person who cost me a small fortune by destroying my TBM." He turned the punch bag around, so I could see the photograph of me, which he'd pinned to it.

"That's not a very nice thing to do."

"Neither was destroying my tunnelling machine. I'll be paying for that for months."

"Just think yourself lucky that I haven't told the local authority who was responsible for all the subsidence."

"I'd love to hear that particular conversation." He put on a silly high-pitched voice. "Excuse me, is that the highways department? I'd like to report that my cat is responsible for the potholes that have recently appeared in the city centre. Yes, I did say my cat. How did he do it? He was driving a tunnelling machine." Winky dissolved into laughter.

"Was that supposed to be my voice? I don't sound anything like that."

"Yes, you do. I had you down to a tee. I could make a living as an impressionist."

"And you can take that photograph down."

"No chance." He gave it another thump.

Who was the mysterious Mr Tune, I wondered? A new client, hopefully.

"Is that Mr Tune?"

"Terry Tune speaking." I was speechless for a few seconds because the man had the same weird sing-song voice as a certain Sid Song. "Hello?"

"Sorry. This is Jill Maxwell. You called me earlier?"

"Oh yes, Mrs Maxwell, thanks for returning my call."

"How can I help?"

"Actually, I was calling with some rather sad news."

"Oh?"

"I believe that you're waiting for a sign from It's A Sign?"

"That's right. It's a replacement for one that they made recently. Do you work for Sid?"

"No. I'm very sorry to have to tell you this, but Sid died two days ago."

"What? I had no idea."

"He was killed in a freak accident. The sign on his own building fell on top of him. I'm told he wouldn't have known a thing about it."

"That's terrible."

"It is. I've known Sid for many years. Although he and I were competitors, we remained close friends. His widow, Cissie, contacted me to ask if I'd take on all the work he has on the books. I was of course only too pleased to oblige."

"I see."

"I'm currently working my way through the list; I'm giving everyone on there a call. I just wanted to check that you'd have no objection to my company, A Sign Of The Times, fulfilling the order, but also to warn you that there may be a slight delay."

"Right. Well, thank you for letting me know, and yes, I'd like you to continue with the sign."

"Thank you, Mrs Maxwell."

"Please give my condolences to Mrs Song."

"I will."

Poor old Sid.

Chapter 13

Shortly after lunch, Kathy popped into the office.

"Did you know your sign is missing, Jill?"

"Really? I had no idea."

"It's true. There's only the Clown sign out there."

"Gee, thanks for telling me, Sis. I wonder who could have stolen it."

"You're being sarcastic, aren't you?"

"What gave it away?"

"What happened to the sign?"

"The landlord made me take it down because it was too big. The replacement is on order."

"You haven't had a lot of luck with your signs, have you?"

"Not a lot."

"What's with the punch bag?"

"I — err, it helps me to work off the stress."

"Why do you have your photo pinned to it?"

"Err, that's just Mrs V's little joke. She's such a kidder. Did you come over for anything in particular?"

"I just wanted to have a quick word about Reggie."

"There's nothing wrong, is there?"

"No. Not really. Pete says he has a great work ethic. He's always punctual and he picks things up really quickly."

"Why do I feel like there's a *but* coming?"

"But —" She hesitated.

"But what? What has he done?"

"Nothing bad. It's more kind of weird."

"Are you actually going to tell me?"

"It's some of the stuff he talks about to Pete and the

other workers."

"Such as?"

"Someone asked him where he used to work, and he said at a school called Gas, I think."

"It's CASS."

"You've heard of it?"

Oh bum! "Err, no. Well, yes, but only because Reggie mentioned it to me."

"Do you know where it is?"

"I've no idea."

"Apparently, neither does Reggie. When one of the other guys asked him where the school was, he said he couldn't remember, which is obviously nonsense."

"Peter isn't thinking of sacking him, is he?"

"No. Like I said, he's a good worker. It's just that the other guys are starting to think he's a bit weird, that's all. You were the one who recommended him, so I thought maybe you'd know where this school is?"

"There isn't a school."

"Oh? But he said —"

"That's my fault. I told him to say that."

"I don't understand."

"Reggie has been in prison for the last few years."

"*Prison?*"

"He was totally innocent of all charges, I promise you."

"Don't you think you should have told Pete?"

"Yes, I should have, but that's all on me. It wasn't Reggie's idea to lie. He's an honest guy who I'd vouch for all day long."

"I wish you *had* said something."

"I'm sorry. I can have a word with Peter if you like?"

"That's okay. I'll tell him."

"Do you think he'll sack Reggie?"

"Come on, Jill. You know Pete better than that, which is precisely why I don't understand why you didn't just say something in the first place."

"I can only keep repeating that I'm sorry."

"Okay, let's forget about it. How did the housewarming party go?"

"It was every bit as awful as I expected. And then some."

"Did Jack enjoy it?"

"Up until the point where he lost at magnetic fishing."

"*Magnetic fishing?*"

"Don't ask. How are things with you?"

"Both shops are going great guns, and Pete is having to turn work away."

"And the kids?"

"They're driving me crazy."

"I don't believe that for a second."

"It's true. I swear they get more and more untidy every day. It's got to the point where I hate going into their bedrooms. I dread to think what it'll be like when they're teenagers."

After Kathy had left, Winky jumped onto my desk. "Do you know what you need?"

"I have the feeling you're about to tell me."

"A Rolodex."

"And why would I need that?"

"To keep a record of all the lies you tell." He laughed. "Prison? Seriously?"

"She bought it, didn't she?"

"Which just proves how gullible you two-leggeds are.

Do you think that sister of yours would like to buy a half-share in a gold mine?"

"How's that new girlfriend of yours doing? When do I get to meet her?"

"You don't. I've already told you, she prefers to maintain a low profile."

"I don't believe she even exists. Why don't you just admit that you aren't seeing anyone? It's nothing to be ashamed of."

"You can believe what you like. It's no skin off my nose."

"You could at least tell me her name."

"Okay. It's Myndya."

"Myndya?"

"Yeah. Mind ya own business."

***

Seeing as how my mean husband, who had a terrible taste in ties, wouldn't arrange for me to view the city centre CCTV footage, I would just have to sort it out myself. It was at times like this that I really appreciated my magical powers. In the old days, before I discovered I was a witch, it would have been practically impossible to gain access to the council's security offices, but now it was easy peasy. I used the 'invisible' spell to get into the small control centre, and then the 'sleep' spell to make the on-duty operator nod off for a while.

These days, fortunately, most of the city centre was covered by cameras. I started by identifying the one that was closest to the main entrance to the multiplex, and then brought up the footage for the exact time and date that I'd seen the man in the hat leaving the cinema. Initially, the street was pretty much deserted, but then a bunch of people appeared. This was obviously the same crowd who had been at the midnight showing of the Marvel movie.

The large-brimmed hat made it easy to pick out my target. He was clearly alone and in something of a hurry. As soon as he disappeared from view, I switched to the next camera. Provided he didn't take any of the side streets where there was less likely to be CCTV coverage, this would be a piece of cake.

And so it proved.

I followed his progress from one camera to the next until he reached the edge of the city centre, where he stopped outside a house, took a key from his pocket, and let himself in.

Bingo! I had him.

This was beginning to look less and less like a kidnapping to me. If what Simon Richards had told me was true, Robert Warne had clearly fallen out of love with his wife. That's if he'd ever been in love with her at all. It may well have been her money that had attracted him to her in the first place. If he did want out of the marriage, the prenup agreement could have meant he would walk away with only a fraction of Cheryl's wealth. What if that wasn't enough for him? What if he'd worked out another way to extract money from her?

By getting her to pay his ransom for example.

All this was, of course, pure speculation. The only way to find out for certain was to confront the man himself, which is why I was headed to the house I'd seen on the CCTV.

Rather than take my car, I decided the walk would do me good. I was halfway across town when Edna appeared on my shoulder.

"I wish you'd give me some warning when you're coming. You scared me to death."

"What would you like me to do? Blow a trumpet before I appear?"

"Never mind. What's happening with Tonya?"

"She had a wax. Would you like to know what kind?"

"Definitely not."

"She bought some sausages and a can of peas."

"This is all fascinating stuff, but did you see her do anything suspicious?"

"I was just getting around to that. She went to that coffee shop on the high street."

"Coffee Games?"

"That's the one."

"Did she meet someone there?"

"No, but she did put on a blindfold, and then she stuck a pin into a young man's bottom."

"Is that all?"

"What do you mean *is that all*? Isn't that enough?"

"It must have been *pin the tail on the donkey* day. Tonya must have stuck the pin in the man by mistake."

"Are you telling me that's some kind of game?"

"That's right."

"Humans? I'll never understand them. Do you want me to continue to follow her?"

"Yes, please."

"Very well." And with that, she disappeared.

I was beginning to have my doubts about Edna.

I retraced Robert Warne's footsteps until I reached the house where I'd seen him let himself inside. I'd only seen the row of houses in black and white on CCTV, so the pastel coloured walls and doors came as something of a surprise. I rang the doorbell of number ten, and when there was no answer, I hammered on the door. There was still no response and no sign of movement inside. That didn't necessarily mean the house was empty because if Robert Warne had faked his own kidnapping, he would no doubt be cautious about opening the door.

To get to the rear of the property, I had to walk to the end of the row of houses, and then duck down the narrow alleyway that ran behind them. I knocked on the back door, but again with no response. On a whim, I took a look through the back window.

Lying on the tiled kitchen floor was a man's body.

Moments later, with the aid of the 'power' spell, I'd gained access to the property. The man lying on the floor was obviously dead, and the blood on his head and on the floor-tiles was clearly fresh. Was whoever did it still in the house? I did a quick check of all the rooms, but there was no sign of anyone, so I called the police.

***

Detective Susan Shay was not happy. That much she had made patently clear over the last two hours.

"We've been over this a dozen times," I said.

The two of us were in an interview room at Washbridge police station. I was tired, hungry and very cheesed off.

"And we'll go over it another dozen times if need be."

She thumped the table. "Why didn't you contact the police the moment you learned of the kidnapping?"

"Because, as I've already told you, the client asked me not to."

"That's irrelevant. You should have contacted us."

"Yes, well, it's too late now."

"You're dead right it's too late. It's now a murder case, thanks to you."

"Hold on. You can't blame me for his murder. I didn't kill him."

"We only have your word for that."

"Now you're just being ridiculous."

"Tell me again, how you found out where he was being kept."

"From the CCTV."

"And how exactly did you gain access to that?"

"I told you before. I can't reveal that. And anyway, how is that relevant? Shouldn't you be trying to find out who murdered him?"

And so the conversation continued: Around and around in circles. By the time I was allowed to leave the police station it was late afternoon, and my brain had turned to soft cheese. I rang Mrs V to check if there were any messages—there weren't—and to let her know I was going to call it a day.

Even though I was exhausted, I wanted to check with Aunt Lucy on how Grandma was doing.

"Aunt Lucy, it's me. Any news?"

"No change, I'm afraid."

"Are you still at the hospital?"

"No, I'm back home. I thought I should have dinner

with Lester. I plan to go back there tonight."

"Okay. What time were you thinking of —?"

"It can't be." She shouted down the phone. "How?"

"Aunt Lucy? Are you okay? What's happened?"

"I think you'd better get over here. Straight away!"

Something was clearly wrong, so I magicked myself over there. Aunt Lucy was in the lounge, staring out of the front window.

"Aunt Lucy, are you okay? What's the matter?"

"Your grandmother."

"What about her? Have you heard from the hospital? Is she alright?"

"She just walked down her driveway."

"I think you need a lie down." The stress had clearly got to her. "Why don't I take you upstairs?"

"I know what I saw, Jill. She just walked down the driveway and into her house."

"But she's in hospital."

"Come on." Aunt Lucy charged out of the house and around to next door. She didn't bother knocking. Instead, she just opened the door and stepped inside.

Grandma was in the kitchen, slicing a loaf of bread.

"Mother?" Aunt Lucy's eyes were as wide as saucers. "What are you doing?"

"Making myself some toast. What does it look like? Do you have any strawberry jam? I'm all out."

"But you were in hospital?" I said.

"Don't you think I know that? Whose bright idea was it to take me there?"

"You were in a coma."

"Don't be ridiculous."

"You were. You have been for days."

"I was *not* in a coma. I was witchbernating."

"You were *what*?"

"Considering the two of you are supposed to be witches, you seem to know very little about the subject. It's a well-known fact that witches have to witchbernate once every thousand years. Those doctors and nurses are pretty clueless too. They seemed quite surprised when I sat up in bed."

"What does that even mean? Witchber — err — ?"

"Witchbernate. The clue is in the name. It's similar to when an animal hibernates."

"Are you telling me you've just been asleep?"

"Yes, and some lovely dreams I had too."

"Did you know you were going to witchbernate?"

"Of course I knew."

"And you didn't think to tell us?"

"Why would I?"

Unbelievable! "What about the dark hazel? Why do you have that in the house?"

"How do you know I have it?"

"Because when we thought you were in a coma, we were trying to find out what might have caused it."

"Not that it's any of your business, but I use dark hazel to get rid of the rats. They're pretty much immune to the ordinary poison, but that soon sees them off. Now, is someone going to get me that strawberry jam or not?"

Chapter 14

The next morning, by the time I eventually managed to drag myself out of bed, Jack was already downstairs. He couldn't have had much sleep because he'd worked late the night before, and he hadn't been home by the time I'd gone to bed.

"Morning." I yawned. "What time did you get in last night?"

"Just before midnight."

"Poor you. I didn't hear you come up."

"You were dead to the world when I got into bed."

"What were you working on?"

"A missing child. Suspected abduction."

"Oh no."

"It's okay. He turned up fit and well at one of his friends' houses."

"That's good."

"I heard about the Warne murder, Jill. You were bang out of order."

"Don't you start on me. I had Sushi on my back all yesterday afternoon."

"She called me and gave me a mouthful, too."

"She had no right to do that. You had nothing to do with it."

"That's as maybe, but she has a point. You should have reported the kidnapping."

"Look, Detective Maxwell, I'll tell you the same thing I told your colleague. My client said she didn't want the police involved, so I had to respect her wishes."

"*Detective Maxwell?*"

"I assumed this was a formal interview. It certainly feels

like one."

"I'm sorry. It's just that I can see it from both sides. A man died."

"Don't you think I know that?" I exploded. "I feel bad enough without you piling it on too."

"I'm sorry. You're right." He came over and tried to take me into his arms, but I pulled away.

"You can't do this, Jack. I know you're a policeman, but you're my husband too. I don't expect you to agree with everything I do, but I shouldn't have to fight you too."

"Fair enough. Point taken. But this cuts both ways."

"How do you mean?"

"You can't keep asking me to help you with your cases. Like you did with the CCTV thing, which I assume was connected to this case."

"You refused anyway."

"That's not the point. If I had helped you, how would that have looked now this has happened? You shouldn't put me in the position of having to refuse."

"Okay, you're right. I won't do it again."

"Can I have a hug now?"

"Of course you can."

We'd always known that our respective jobs would bring us into conflict occasionally, but that didn't make it any easier when it happened.

***

We had planned to go into town, but Jack had been told he had to work in the afternoon, so we abandoned our shopping plans, and instead had a lazy Saturday morning at home.

"I still can't get over your grandmother." He chuckled. "All that time, she was just dozing?"

"It's typical of her. She never gave a moment's thought to how it might upset the family. She's so unbelievably selfish."

"But you're still glad she's okay?"

"Of course I am. I don't know what I would have done if I'd lost her, but that doesn't alter the fact that she drives me to distraction." Jack's mention of losing Grandma reminded me there was something I needed to speak to him about. Now seemed like as good a time as any. "You'll never guess who I bumped into at the launch party for Cakey C."

"Did Mad come up from London?"

"No, she couldn't make it. It was Yvonne."

"Mum?"

"Yeah."

"Why didn't you say something before now?"

"Because I wanted to wait until we had the time to talk about it properly."

"How is she? Apart from being dead, I mean?"

"She's fine. She looked really well."

"That's so good to hear." His eyes began to well with tears. "What did she say?"

"I asked why she hadn't made contact with me before. She said she wanted to get settled in GT first."

Jack grabbed a tissue. "You don't know how much it means to me to know she's okay."

"She wants to see you."

"Is that possible?"

"Yes, but only if it's something you're sure you want to do."

"Are you kidding? Of course I'm sure. What do I need to do?"

"I have to let her know that you're okay with the idea. After that, she'll get in touch with you."

"What does that entail, exactly?"

"It's hard to describe, but you'll know it when it happens. You'll feel the temperature drop, and you'll just kind of sense it."

"Is that all?"

"Not quite. You have your part to play too. The important thing is that you believe. If there are any doubts in your mind, it won't work. And don't be disappointed if it doesn't happen the first few times. It may take a while."

"When can we do it?"

"That's up to Yvonne. The chances are it'll happen when you're alone."

"I can't wait." As he gave me another hug, the tears began to flow. For both of us.

I left Jack in the lounge with his thoughts while I went through to the kitchen to make us both a cup of tea.

What the−? I was sure that I had eight packets of custard creams, but there were only six in the cupboard.

"Have you been at my biscuits?" I handed him his drink.

"I wouldn't dare."

"Are you sure? There were eight packets in the cupboard yesterday, but there are only six now."

"You must have eaten them."

"Two packets in one day?"

"You say that like it would be unusual."

"I've never eaten that many in one day."

"Well, someone must have, and it wasn't me."

The idea that I could have eaten so many custard creams in a single day was just too ridiculous for words. But then something occurred to me. The surveillance imps had been really taken with my custard creams. Had they sneaked into the house and stolen them? Although Daze seemed to have complete faith in the imps, I still had my doubts about them. I would have to keep my eyes peeled.

It was eleven o'clock, and Jack had just got changed for work.

"How long has that been there?" He pointed out of the window.

"What?"

"The post box across the road."

"It wasn't there yesterday."

"It must have been installed earlier this morning. I suppose it'll save us having to walk around to the corner shop." He gave me a kiss. "What are you going to do with yourself this afternoon?"

"I thought seeing as how you're going into the office I might as well do some work on the case of the green cars."

"Take care."

"And you. I'll see you tonight."

***

Wilde Cars were located not far from Kathy's house, so it occurred to me that I could kill two birds with one stone.

Who came up with that saying? First, why would you want to kill a bird? And second, how would you kill two of them with one stone? You'd have to somehow calculate the trajectory of the stone so that it hit the first bird at precisely the right angle to then go on to kill the second bird. Very unlikely if you ask me.

What? I know you didn't ask. I'm just saying is all.

"Jill?" Britt looked surprised to see me.

"I'm sorry to trouble you. I wanted to ask a small favour."

"Of course. What is it?"

"The other night at your housewarming party, I think I may have lost an earring."

"I haven't seen it."

"It's a pair my mother gave to me." I held out an earring for her to see.

"You're welcome to come inside if you like. We can both look for it."

"Thanks. I wouldn't ask but it has sentimental value."

"No problem. Come on in."

We spent a few minutes searching the lounge for the 'missing' earring. Unsurprisingly, we had no success.

"Britt, do you think it might be quicker if we split up?"

"I—err—guess we could."

"I'll just nip upstairs and take a look around your gym room. I might have dropped it in there."

"Okay."

I sprinted upstairs before she could change her mind. Once inside the room, I closed the door behind me.

"Gerald! Are you here? Gerald?"

"Hello again." The cute little gremlin poked his head out from behind the cross trainer. He was wearing another charming duffle coat; this one was yellow. "I didn't expect to see you again."

"I have a proposition for you."

"Oh?"

"You said you were bored because the couple who live here are so tidy."

"That's right."

"How about I take you somewhere there'll be lots of tidying for you to do?"

"You'd do that for me?"

"Yes, but you have to make your mind up right now."

"I want to do it."

"Are you sure?"

"Definitely."

"Okay. Climb into my jacket pocket."

He'd no sooner done that than Britt came through the door. "Any luck, Jill?"

"Yes, I found it." I showed her the two earrings. "Thanks very much. I'd lose my head if it was loose."

"Jill?" Kathy was still in her dressing gown. "I wasn't expecting you, was I?"

"Jack has to go into the office this afternoon, and I'm going to be working on a case close by, so I thought I'd pop in for a coffee. I hadn't realised you'd still be in bed."

"I wasn't in bed. I just haven't got around to getting dressed yet."

"Nice work if you can get it." I grinned.

"It's my day off from the shop, and Pete has taken the kids out, so I figured I'd have a lazy day."

"Do I get a coffee or not?"

"Yeah, come in."

"I just have to nip up to the loo."

"Okay. I'll put the kettle on."

Once I was upstairs, I went into Mikey's bedroom. Oh boy! Kathy hadn't been exaggerating. The room was a complete tip.

"Gerald. You can come out now." The gremlin poked his head out of my pocket. "How does this room look to you?"

His face lit up. "This is more like it."

I lifted him out of my pocket and put him on the unmade bed.

"There are more rooms like this one."

"Really? That's brilliant. Thank you so much."

"Don't mention it."

When I got back downstairs, the coffee was waiting for me.

"What are you working on?" Kathy said.

"It's a bit of a weird case involving green cars."

"Aren't most of the cases you work on a bit weird?"

"It sometimes feels that way."

"Did you see there had been another murder in Washbridge?"

"Yeah, I did hear something about it." Time to change the subject. "How are the kids?"

"As untidy as ever. Otherwise, they're as happy as Larry."

"Is he, though?"

"Is who what?"

"Larry? Is he happy? How can we be sure?"

"Don't start with that stuff again, Jill."

"Anyway, call it a premonition if you like, but I have a feeling the kids are going to be much tidier from now on."

"I won't hold my breath."

***

As soon as I stepped onto his car lot, Harry Wilde came over to introduce himself.

"Wilde by name, and wild by nature, that's me." If by wild he meant that he looked like he'd just been dragged through a hedge backwards, then he wasn't wrong. "Do you have anything in mind, young lady?"

"Nothing in particular. How much would you give me for my car?"

"Where is it?"

"Over there."

"*That* thing?" He frowned. "It would depend on what you decide to buy. What about this little beauty? Low mileage, one owner and a lovely little runner."

"I'm not keen on red."

"How about that one over there by the gates? I'm practically giving it away at that price."

"I really had my heart set on something green."

"It's not a very popular colour. I'm not sure I have anything in green just at the moment."

"Oh well, never mind. Thanks anyway."

"Hold on! Before you go, come and take a look around the back. I've got a few cars around there that I'm selling at thirty percent off."

"Is there something wrong with them?"

"No, of course not. They're all mechanically sound. It's just that—err—well, you'll see for yourself." He led the way around the back of his office building.

"They're all purple." I looked up and down the row of

cars. "Why do you have so many purple cars? Is it a popular colour?"

"Not particularly. That's why I'm offering them at such a big discount."

"I still don't understand. If purple isn't a popular colour, why did you buy in so many of them?"

"Are you interested or not?"

"No, thanks."

"Please yourself." He started back to the office. "You'll never get anything for that rust heap of yours."

Rust heap? The cheek of the man.

Burt Claymore had suggested that Harry Wilde might be behind the green car incident, but having spoken to Wilde, and having seen his stock of cars, I now considered that to be unlikely. In fact, even though Harry Wilde hadn't been very forthcoming, it seemed obvious to me that Wilde Cars were experiencing the same issues as Bestest Cars. The only difference was that someone was respraying Wilde's cars purple.

The mystery thickened.

When I got back to the house, I was surprised to see Jack pulling onto the driveway in front of me.

"I didn't think you'd be back yet," I said.

"Neither did I. I don't know why they asked us to go in. It could have waited until Monday. How was your afternoon?"

"Pretty uneventful. I did see a lot of purple cars, though."

"I thought the problem was with *green* cars?"

"So did I."

"Yoo hoo, Jill." Kimmy came hurrying across the road. "I'm glad I've seen you."

I wasn't. "Hi, Kimmy. We were just about to go inside to make dinner."

"I won't keep you. I just wanted to remind you to let us know when you have the dates for your play."

Jack glanced at me and mouthed the word, "Play?"

"Right, yes. I'll do that just as soon as they're finalised."

"We do enjoy the theatre, and the title sounds so very intriguing: The Invisible Fairy. We can't wait to see it."

"Neither can I." Jack grinned.

Chapter 15

It was Monday morning and Jack was still on cloud nine.

Yvonne had made contact with him for the first time yesterday. He'd been so keen to see her that she'd managed to make the connection on only her second attempt. I'd said a quick hello, but then I'd left them alone to catch up. Although she hadn't been able to stay for very long, it had been enough to leave Jack happier than I'd seen him since the day she died.

"When do you think she'll come again?" he asked over breakfast.

"I've no idea, but I do know that it'll be exhausting for her the first few times she does it. Over time, it definitely gets easier. My mother, father and the colonel experienced the same thing."

"I'm so lucky to have you."

"I've been telling you that for ages."

"If I hadn't met you, I would never have seen my mother again because I never used to believe in ghosts."

This probably wasn't the right time to point out that if we hadn't got together, his mother would probably still be alive.

"I thought you were going to say you were lucky to have me because I'm so smart, sexy and beautiful."

"That too, obviously."

"What else did the two of you talk about?"

"I don't even remember. Isn't that weird? I was just so thrilled to see her. Do you think she might contact me again while I'm at work?"

"I wouldn't think so. In my experience, ghosts prefer to

return to the same place. She's more likely to make contact while you're in the house."

"I'd better be making tracks." He grabbed his coat. "I have an early meeting."

"Take care. Love you."

"Love you, too." He gave me a quick kiss and then he was out of the door.

Not long after Jack had left, the postman popped a letter through the door — no doubt a bill, that's all we seemed to get these days.

I was wrong.

The world was now officially crazy because Rhymes had won first prize for his poetry book.

As I was on my way out of the door, I spotted an envelope on the hall table. It was a congratulations card for one of Jack's colleagues who'd just had a baby. I wasn't one for sending greetings cards, but Jack just couldn't get enough of them. He'd obviously been so engrossed with thoughts about his mother's visit that he'd forgotten to take it with him. Not a problem; I'd post it for him in our new post box across the road.

"Morning, Jill." The large bowling ball called from next door.

"Morning, Clare. It looks like you're ready for TenPinCon."

"We can't wait. Tony is in the house, calling some of the suppliers to make sure everything is in place. You and Jack must be excited too?"

"Absolutely. I'm counting the minutes." Until it's over.

"You will be wearing your tenpin costume, won't you?"

"Just try stopping me."

"That's good to hear. I didn't think you sounded too keen on them."

"What? Are you kidding? I love those costumes."

And no, I hadn't lost my mind. I had a cunning plan. Watch this space.

Snigger.

Once I'd managed to shake off the bowling ball, I hurried across the road and popped the card into the post box. Before I could walk away, the card flew back out.

What the —?

I popped it in again. And it flew back out *again*.

"It's me, Jill," a familiar voice said from inside the post box.

"Mr Hosey?"

"What do you think of it?"

"This is your new camouflage, I take it?"

"So much better than the tree, don't you think?"

"It looks very authentic, but I can see one slight problem."

"Oh?"

"If you throw the mail back out, don't you think that might make people suspicious?"

"I suppose so. I hadn't considered that."

"Might I make a suggestion?"

"Of course."

"Why don't you hang onto the mail, then when you go off duty, you can post it in the real post box?"

"That's pure genius. That's what I'll do."

"Excellent. Here's your first card." I popped it through the slot. "Make sure you catch the last post."

"Will do."

***

Mrs V's school reunion had been held on Saturday, so she would no doubt be full of it. Great! The only thing worse than going to a school reunion was having to listen to someone talk about theirs.

Still, I was nothing if not polite, so I felt I should enquire how it went.

"Morning, Mrs V."

"Good morning, Jill."

"How was the school reunion?"

"Okay."

"Was that old flame of yours there? What was his name? Roland?"

"Yes, I think so. Would you like a cup of tea?"

"Err, yeah. That would be nice."

"I'll bring it through."

Could she have been any less enthusiastic about the school reunion? That wasn't at all what I'd been expecting. Something must have occurred. But what? Now my curiosity was piqued, and I really wanted to know what had happened.

"What do you think of Pluto?" Winky was on the sofa, reading a book.

"Sorry?"

"Pluto? What do you think?"

"I always thought Goofy was funnier."

"Not *that* Pluto." He held up the book so I could see the cover: Astronomy for Felines.

"Oh? You mean the planet?"

"Strictly speaking, it's a *dwarf* planet."

"I didn't know that."

"So, what do you think of it?"

"I've never given it a moment's thought. Why are you so interested all of a sudden?"

"Unlike you, I like to broaden my mind. To learn new things."

"And today, it's astronomy, is it?"

"A fascinating subject, wouldn't you agree?"

"Fascinating."

Just then, Mrs V brought my cup of tea through. "I didn't realise you were interested in astronomy, Jill?" She'd spotted the book on the sofa next to Winky.

"Oh yeah. I've always been interested in it. Did you know that Pluto is actually a dwarf planet?"

"Of course I did. In the Kuiper belt if I'm not mistaken."

"Err, yeah. Obviously."

Winky went back to his book, leaving me to contemplate two questions: First, what had happened at Mrs V's school reunion for her not to want to talk about it? And second, how come she knew so much about Pluto?

My phone rang; caller ID showed an unknown number.

"Is that Jill?"

"Belladonna?"

"Hi. I've spent all weekend thinking about what you said, and I've decided I want to go through with it."

"To change your identity? Are you absolutely sure? It's a big step."

"It wasn't an easy decision, and to be honest, I wish I

didn't have to do it, but if I don't, I'll never get another job."

"I understand how difficult this must have been for you, but I think it's the right decision."

"I hope so. What happens now?"

"I want to let the twins know what's happening first, and then I'll pop over to see you later today, to talk through what you need to do."

"Okay, great. Thanks, Jill."

I magicked myself straight over to Cuppy C where the twins were both behind the counter.

"Can you believe Grandma?" Pearl rolled her eyes.

"She's unbelievable," Amber said. "She doesn't care that we were all frantic about her."

"At least she's okay." I was busy eyeing the cake display. "Are those muffins new?"

"They're chocolate pecan."

"They look delicious. I'll have one of those and a caramel latte."

"The two of us went over to Grandma's house to see how she was." Amber grabbed one of the chocolate pecan muffins.

"Shouldn't you pick that up with the tongs?"

"Normally I would, but it's only for you." She shrugged.

Charming. "Was Grandma pleased to see you both?"

"Not really," Pearl said. "She said we were disturbing her."

"She did show us something interesting while we were there, though." Amber grinned. "Her new candle."

The twins both pulled a face and shuddered.

"How could you, Jill?" Pearl said. "Ear wax? Yuk!"

"I didn't know that's what it was. She tricked me into doing it."

"Was it worse than treating her bunions?"

"It was a close call. Do you mind if we change the subject? This is putting me off my muffin."

"Did you talk to Belladonna?" Pearl said.

"Yes. In fact, that's why I came over. I've just heard back from her."

"What did she say?"

"She's decided to go through with the change."

"I wasn't sure she would," Amber said.

"Neither was I. It can't have been an easy decision for her."

"What happens now, then?"

"You'll need to let all the parents know that Belladonna has resigned, but that you already have a replacement sorted out."

"They won't be happy that Belladonna has left."

"I realise that, but they'll soon get over it when they see her replacement is every bit as good."

"What's her new name going to be?"

"I still have to sort all that out with Belladonna. I'm going to see her later today."

"How long will we have to wait for her to come back?"

"With a bit of luck, I'm hoping your 'new employee' will be with you within a couple of weeks."

"It's not ideal." Amber shrugged. "But I guess we can use an agency to get temporary cover in the meantime."

***

The chocolate pecan muffin was delicious.

I was just about to magic myself back to Washbridge when the sound of a trumpet almost made me jump out of my skin.

Moments later, Edna appeared on my shoulder. "Was that better?"

"Why were you blowing a trumpet?"

"You said you wanted me to warn you when I was coming."

"I've changed my mind. Dump the trumpet."

"As you wish. Anyway, I have news."

"On Tonya?"

"Indeed. Your client was right to have his suspicions. The little madam is up to no good."

"What's she doing?"

"Come and see for yourself. She's at it right now."

"I'm not sure I should—err—I mean, I don't want to walk in on anything—err—"

"Come on. Hurry up."

I held onto Edna as we magicked ourselves back to Washbridge.

"Where are we?" I glanced around.

"Washbridge park. Tonya is over there, behind those bushes."

"Are you sure?"

"Hurry up or you'll miss her."

I sneaked over to the line of bushes, and then crept slowly around them.

The huge dog barked, and pulled on the lead that Tonya was holding.

"It's okay," she reassured me. "Tiny is quite friendly really."

Tiny? I'd seen smaller horses.

I thought I might have blown my cover, but then I remembered that Tonya had the memory span of a gnat. I'd encountered her many times at WashBet, but she'd never remembered me from one visit to the next.

"He's a big lad," I said.

"He's an Irish wolfhound."

"Is he yours?"

"No. I wish he was. My husband hates dogs. He reckons he's allergic to them. I've just borrowed Tiny."

"Borrowed him?"

"Yeah, there's a website which matches you up with people who need help walking their dogs. I take a different one out every day."

"Doesn't Norman mind?"

"How do you know my husband's name is Norman?"

That was a very good question. "I—err—I didn't say *Nor-man*. I said *your man*."

"Oh? Right." She laughed. "I thought it was strange that you'd know his name. Norman doesn't know I'm doing this. If he did, he'd complain that dog hairs set his allergy off."

"But they haven't so far? You must have had some on your clothes."

"No, I'm beginning to think that he isn't allergic to dogs at all. It's just an excuse not to get one."

"I'd better be going. Bye, Tiny."

"What did I tell you?" Edna said.

"You told me she was up to no good."

"And so she is. Clandestine dog-walking? It doesn't get much worse than that."

Hmm? I wasn't so sure about that. "You did well to find out what she was up to."

"It was a piece of cake."

"And now, there's just the matter of your payment."

"There's no need. I've already taken it."

"When? How?"

"Cash is of no use to me at my age. I have more than I'll ever spend. That's why I've taken payment in kind."

"You have? Sorry, I'm confused."

"The custard creams of course. I assumed you would have realised."

"No, I thought it was the — err — never mind." Although I was a little annoyed that Edna hadn't told me she'd taken the biscuits, I was more than happy with the cost of her services. "So, is that the going rate, then? Two packets of custard creams?"

"Don't be ridiculous. I come cheap but not that cheap. The two packets were just a down-payment. I'll be collecting the other three packets later today."

"Oh? Right. Okay."

And with that, the custard cream thief disappeared.

Chapter 16

There was no sign of Mrs V in the outer office, but there *was* a very strange looking man. He was quite elderly, probably a similar age to Mrs V, but he was wearing clothes more suited to a much younger person. The open-necked shirt, gold medallion and ponytail were not a good look.

"Can I help you?"

"Oh, hello there. I'm looking for Annie. I believe she works here."

Annie? "You mean Annabel Versailles, I assume?"

"That's right. Do you know where I can find her?"

"Can I ask your name?"

"Of course." He offered his hand. "I'm Roland Brass. Annie and I went to the same school."

"Nice to meet you, Roland." Normally, I would have invited him to wait until Mrs V got back, but there was something about the way she'd been acting that morning that had put me on my guard, so I decided to play safe. "I'm afraid she isn't in today. Can I give her a message?"

"How very disappointing. Yes, would you tell Annie that I enjoyed seeing her again, and that I hope we might get together for lunch." He gave me a wink. "Or something."

The guy made my flesh crawl.

"I'll pass on the message."

"Goodbye then, young lady."

"Bye."

It was hard to believe that Mrs V had once had the hots for that creepy guy. Speaking of Mrs V, where was she?

Winky was on the sofa, and he appeared to be scowling at my desk for some reason. I was just about to enquire why when—

"Has he gone?" Mrs V's voice came from beneath the desk.

"Roland? Yes, he's gone. Why are you under there?"

"I'm hiding from that awful man." She crawled out. "I was just on my way back from lunch when I saw him headed towards the office."

"What exactly happened at the school reunion?"

"Nothing."

"Something clearly did."

She took a seat at my desk, and I joined Winky on the sofa.

"I told you that Roland used to be an old flame of mine, didn't I?"

"You most certainly did."

"I just thought it would be nice to catch up with him."

"To flirt with him, you mean."

"I intended to do no such thing."

"Of course you didn't. I'm sure there was another, perfectly innocent explanation why you didn't want Armi there with you. So, what actually happened?"

"You've seen the man. He still dresses as though he's twenty."

"The open shirt and medallion cut quite the look."

"He looks ridiculous. As soon as I saw him, I gave him a wide berth, but he homed in on me, and I couldn't shake him."

"It looks like he still has the hots for you."

"It appears that way. I thought if I told him about Armi that he might get the message."

"Didn't he?"

"Quite the opposite. He said the fact that I'd decided to go there by myself was proof that my marriage was on the rocks."

"You did rather ask for that."

"There's no need to rub it in. I already feel bad enough."

"Sorry. So what happened then?"

"He said he thought he and I had a future together, and that I should dump Armi. I told him I would do no such thing, and that I didn't want to see him again."

"Something tells me he didn't get the message."

"What shall I do, Jill?"

"There's nothing much you can do other than to stand firm. Oh, and it wouldn't do any harm to come clean with Armi."

"I can't do that."

"You don't have any choice. What happens if Medallion Man turns up again while Armi is with you? How is that going to look?"

"You're right. I'll talk to Armi tonight."

"Okay, I give up." Winky shook his head. "You're going to have to explain it to me."

"Explain what?"

"How someone can have the hots for the old bag lady."

"Mrs V is a fine figure of a woman."

"No, seriously." He laughed. "I assume the man is some kind of nutjob?"

"Probably. He was wearing a medallion."

"Hey, don't diss the medallion. I've been known to sport one from time to time."

"Please never wear one in my company."

I was still trying to purge the image of Winky with a gold medallion when Mrs V came back into the office.

"Have you seen this, Jill?" She was holding a newspaper. "Roland must have left it behind."

"What the—?" I stared in disbelief at the main headline in The Bugle.

Private investigator responsible for my husband's death.

The quote was from Cheryl Warne. As I read the article, I could feel my blood pressure rising, and by the time I'd finished, I was spitting feathers.

"I don't believe it! She says she wanted to go to the police, but that I persuaded her not to. That's an outright lie. And she reckons her husband was only killed because the kidnappers must have seen me and panicked."

"Have you spoken to her?"

"No. I've tried to phone her a couple of times, but she didn't respond. I assumed she'd be too busy grieving. Not too busy to talk to The Bugle, though, apparently."

"What are you going to do?"

"What can I do? Who's going to believe me now if I deny it?"

Thirty minutes later, I was still seething. Cheryl Warne had done me up like a kipper, but I couldn't for the life of me work out why. The only thing that made any sense was that she didn't want anyone to blame her for her husband's death. So, instead of admitting she'd been the one who insisted the police weren't involved, she'd told everyone it was my idea.

"Would this be a bad time to tell you we're short of

salmon?" Winky looked up from his astronomy book.

"What do you think?"

I glanced again at The Bugle's story. The first time I'd read it, I hadn't paid much attention to the accompanying photo. Cheryl Warne, looking suitably distraught, was centre stage; at her side was a sombre looking Jonathan Langer.

At this point, the sensible thing to do would have been to forget all about the Warne case. It would all blow over eventually — these things always did. The very worst thing I could have done under the circumstances would be anything that kept the story in the headlines.

So, the question was, did I walk away, or did I keep on poking the wasps' nest?

What's that buzzing sound?

***

Mrs V popped her head around the door. "I have Reginald here to see you, Jill."

"*Reginald*? Oh, you mean Reggie."

"I told him you might be busy."

"No, it's okay. Send him in, would you?"

If I wasn't mistaken, Reggie had treated himself to a new suit.

"You're looking very smart today, Reggie."

"Thanks, Jill." He did a little twirl to show off his new blue suit. "Do you like it?"

"Very sharp. Have a seat. Can I get you a drink?"

"No, thanks. I just thought I'd pop in and let you know my news. I've handed my notice in to Pete."

"Why would you do that? Has something happened?

Peter hasn't done anything to upset you has he?"

"No, he's been great, but the job just isn't right for me."

"You haven't really given it long enough to know that for sure, have you?"

"The work is okay, and I like the people I work with, but—" He hesitated.

"What?"

"I miss Candlefield. The human world simply isn't for me."

"What will you do for work?"

"I've had a bit of luck there. I bumped into an old school friend. He manages Candlefield Park Hotel. Do you know it?"

"I've seen it, but I've never been inside."

"It's quite upmarket. Anyway, we got talking, and he mentioned that the guy in charge of his maintenance had recently retired. He asked if I'd be interested in the job. It's a fantastic opportunity—I couldn't turn it down."

"Of course not. It sounds great."

"I feel bad about letting Pete down. And you, of course. You were the one who got me the job in the first place."

"Don't be daft. You mustn't give it a second thought. I'm just pleased that you've landed a job you really want. And don't worry about Peter. He'll be fine with it."

"Thanks, Jill. I really do appreciate everything you've done for me. While I'm here, do you have any news on the school governors?"

"Not really. I've had them under surveillance, and it seems that the three of them recently met up in a pub."

"What happened?"

"I don't know. The surveillance imps, who were following them, were unable to get inside the room where they were meeting. I've asked the imps to continue with their surveillance, and to let me know if the governors meet up again. If they do, I'll be straight over there, to see what they're up to."

"What do you think is going on?"

"Honestly, Reggie, I don't know, but I did discover that all three of them have been acting oddly recently. At least, according to people who know them."

"Will you keep me posted?"

"Of course I will. And the best of luck in your new job."

***

Having spoken to Harry Wilde at Wilde Cars, it was clear that the car respraying issue at Bestest Cars wasn't an isolated problem. The question now was how widespread was it? Was it affecting all the car dealers in Washbridge? It would have taken me forever to check on each of them in turn, but I'd come up with an ingenious plan.

What do you mean: *another one*? I'll have you know that my earlier reference was to a *cunning* plan which is an entirely different animal to an *ingenious* plan, as you'll find out in due course.

So, back to my plan of the ingenious variety.

A phone call to Burt Claymore revealed that he used a company called We-Spray to respray the green cars to a more marketable colour. Another phone call to the guy in the service department at Wilde Cars confirmed they used the same company. Learning that, made life a little easier for me, as I could talk to just the one resprayer, to try to get a feel for how widespread the problem was.

The young man on reception at We-Spray looked as though he was in need of a respray himself. The left side of his hair was green; the right side was red.

"Do you like it?" He'd caught me eyeing his mop.

"Err, it's very — err — colourful."

"It's a charity thing. I'm being sponsored to keep it like this for a month."

"Well done you. That's a very brave thing to do. You must have attracted a few strange looks."

"No kidding, but it'll be worth it."

That's when I spotted the large framed photograph on the wall behind him. It was a group shot of the staff at We-Spray. My new friend with the green and red hair was on the front row.

"It was unfortunate for you that they decided to take the company photo while you have your hair like that."

"Actually, that was taken last year."

"Oh?" I took a closer look. And then it registered. In the photograph, the left side of his hair was red, and the right side was green. "You've swapped the colours around?"

"That's right. You wouldn't believe how people stare at me now."

"Right. Anyway, I was hoping to see the owner or manager."

"That would be Lee Black. I'm afraid he isn't here today. He'll be back on Wednesday, though. Is there anything I can help you with? My name is Eric."

"Maybe. It was just a general enquiry, really. I've been speaking to the people at Bestest Cars and Wilde Cars, and I understand from them that they've both had a lot of work done by your company recently."

"That's correct. We've been incredibly busy."

"Mainly with work from those two businesses?"

"Not just them. We've been getting work from dozens of different companies."

"Right, thanks."

It was beginning to sound like this problem was widespread.

"It's weird, really," Eric said. "A few months ago, we had hardly any work, and it looked like the business might fold."

"What caused that to change so dramatically? Did your company run some kind of marketing campaign?"

"Not as far as I'm aware. The work just started to flood in. The contrast between now and then is unbelievable."

"It sounds like it. And you say Mr Black will be back the day after tomorrow?"

"That's right. Would you like me to make an appointment for you?"

"Thanks, but that won't be necessary. I'll pop in on spec."

After leaving reception, I made myself invisible, and walked over to the workshops where the respraying took place. Outside the buildings was a large area designated for the cars that were waiting to be resprayed. They appeared to be grouped by colour: green cars, purple cars, orange cars and beige cars.

It appeared that someone, at least, was benefitting from the work of the phantom car sprayer.

Chapter 17

It was time for my dental appointment.

Despite what Winky had said, I wasn't scared of dentists, but I did have doubts about whether the new guy was fully qualified because he looked very young. And why would anyone with the name of Max Payne choose a career in dentistry?

It was only one small filling after all. I probably wouldn't feel a thing once he'd given me the anaesthetic to numb my gum. But that would mean having a needle first, and those things were awfully big.

I was standing outside the door of the dental practice, psyching myself up for the ordeal ahead. Deep breath, Jill! There's absolutely nothing to be scared of. Twenty minutes from now and it would all be over.

Okay, here goes.

The young woman on reception flashed me a smile with her oh-so perfect teeth.

"I have an appointment at three with Mr Payne."

"I'm afraid Mr Payne has had to cancel all his afternoon appointments."

"Oh? No one called me."

"I'm really sorry about that, but he was forced to go home twenty minutes ago."

"Is he okay?"

"Yes, he's not ill. He just developed the most awful toothache."

Was this some kind of wind-up? I was half expecting someone to jump out and say I'd been punked.

"But he's a dentist."

"Dentists get toothache too."

"I'm sure they do, but isn't there more than one dentist at this practice?"

"Yes, there are two others, but I'm afraid you can't see either of those because they're fully booked today."

"I didn't mean for me. Couldn't Mr Payne have got one of the other dentists to see to his toothache?"

"Yes, err—well, that wasn't possible."

"Why not?"

She was clearly becoming exasperated at my line of questioning, and I half-expected her to ask me to leave, but then she beckoned me to come closer, and whispered, "Max is scared of dentists."

"How can he be scared of dentists? He is one!"

"Shush!" She was clearly not impressed with my outburst. "Would you like me to make you another appointment?"

"Don't bother. I'll make alternative arrangements."

***

While I considered what to do about my dental situation, I gave Norman a call.

"It's Jill Maxwell."

"Who?"

"The private investigator. You hired me, remember?"

"Sorry. I didn't realise that was your surname. I thought it was—err—"

"Gooder?"

"Gooder than what?"

"No, that used to be—never mind. Are you okay to talk at the moment?"

"Yes. I'm in the shop. Tonya has gone to get her eyebrows knitted."

"Threaded."

"What?"

"They thread your eyebrows; they don't knit them. Where is she having it done?"

"She didn't say."

"Will she be back soon, do you think?"

"I doubt it. She only left a few minutes ago."

"Okay. I'll come over to see you now."

When I arrived at Top Of The World, Mastermind was busy with a customer. While I waited for him to finish, I took a look around. I still found it hard to believe that people actually collected bottle tops, but even more astounding was the price of some of the offerings.

If the customer paying for his purchase was anything to go by, the bottle top fraternity were a strange breed. He was wearing a beret covered in bottle tops.

"Sorry to keep you waiting, Jill."

"That's okay, Norman. Was that your first sale of the day?"

"No. We've been really busy today. In fact, the last couple of weeks have been exceptionally good."

"Are there a lot of collectors in this area?"

"Quite a few, but people travel from far and wide to visit the shop."

"Don't you have a website?"

"Of course, but most toppers like to feel the goods. There's nothing quite so exciting as getting your hands on a new bottle top."

Had a sadder sentence ever been spoken? "Anyway, I

thought I should report back on Tonya."

"Is it bad news?" He was clearly bracing himself for the worst.

"No, not at all. Can I ask you a question?"

"Okay."

"How do you feel about dogs? Do you like them?"

"They're okay."

"Are you allergic to them?"

"I was as a kid, but I seem to have grown out of it. What does this have to do with Tonya?"

I told Norman what my 'assistant' had discovered while watching his wife. Needless to say, I didn't mention that my assistant was an elderly fairy named Edna because I didn't want to blow what was left of his tiny mind.

"Tonya has been walking dogs?"

"That's right. I think she'd really like one of her own."

"She should have told me."

"Are you sure she hasn't tried to?" His head was probably too full of bottle tops to pick up on any subtle hints.

"What do you think I should do, Jill?"

"Why don't you suggest she gets a dog?"

"Shall I tell her that you told me to suggest it?"

"That's probably not such a good idea because then you'd have to tell her that I've been following her."

"Oh yeah. I hadn't thought about that."

"Right, well I think that's me done. I'll let you have my bill, shall I?"

"Yes, please. Thank you. Would you prefer payment in cash or bottle tops?"

"Cash will be fine, thanks."

***

It was Barry's exhibition tonight, so I called Mrs V to let her know I'd be going straight home.

When I pulled onto the street, I spotted Norm Normal standing next to the new post box. He had a pile of letters at his feet, which he was feeding into the post box one at a time. Each time he posted a letter, he checked the address, and then wrote something in his little notepad.

If I'd had even a modicum of sense, I would have ignored this strange behaviour, and made my way into the house. Unfortunately, as so often happened, curiosity trumped common sense.

"You have a lot of letters there, Norm."

"Hello, Jill. I most certainly do. This new post box is a godsend. You're probably wondering what all these letters are?"

"It's none of my business." But tell me anyway.

"They're to my penfriends."

"I didn't realise people still had those. I thought it was all email and Facebook these days."

"Not at all. Some of us still prefer the tried and tested methods of communication. Those new-fangled things like Facesnap are just a fad. They'll go the same way as hula hoops, mark my words."

"You may be right. I never did like hula hoops. You have an awful lot of penfriends."

"This is only one half of them. I write to half at the beginning of the month, and the other half midway through the month."

"I see."

"That's why I keep this notebook, so that I can make

sure I don't miss anyone."

"Good idea. Well, I'd best leave you to it."

Poor old Mr Hosey. By the time Norm had posted that lot, there would barely be any room inside the post box for him.

Tee-hee.

***

Jack arrived home not long after I did.

"I see you've made the front page again," was his opening gambit. "You told me that your client didn't want you to go to the police."

"She didn't, but now she's decided to lie about it, and throw me under the bus."

"Why would she do that?"

"I wish I knew."

"They seem to be suggesting that the kidnapper only killed the hostage because you were getting close."

"I know what they're saying, thanks. It doesn't mean it's true."

"Have the Washbridge police been in touch?"

"Not yet, but I'm expecting a visit from Sushi anytime."

"The best thing you could do would be to keep a low profile for a while."

"Hide, you mean? Why should I? I've done nothing wrong."

"I'm just trying to look out for you."

"I know, but if I go into hiding, it would be as good as admitting that I'm in some way responsible, and I'm not."

"What do you intend to do, then?"

"I don't know, and even if I did, I wouldn't tell you.

You were the one who said I shouldn't put you in a difficult situation, so the less you know, the better."

"Fair enough. Just don't go doing anything stupid."

"When do I ever? And before you answer that, the question was rhetorical."

"You won't hear another word on the subject from me. By the way, what happened to the card I left on the hall table? I meant to post it this morning."

"Your darling wife posted it for you."

"Thank you." He gave me a peck on the lips. "What would I do without you?"

"Speaking of which, you'll never guess what arrived in this morning's post?"

"Was it my bowling magazine subscription reminder? It must be due about now."

"No, it was from the company that published Rhymes' book. It was the results of the poetry competition."

"Who won?"

"Guess."

"Don't tell me it was Britt?"

"Nope. None other than Mr Robert Hymes."

"You're joking, right?"

"I wish I was. How can Rhymes have won it? His stuff is terrible. The other entrants, including Britt, must have really sucked."

"Are you going to tell her?" Jack said.

"Of course I'm not. What would I say? Hey, Britt, how do you feel about losing out to a tortoise?"

"What do you think we should do about the trophy?"

"I'd forgotten about that. We'll just ignore the letter."

"We can't do that."

"Are you volunteering to pose as Robert Hymes to go

and collect it?"

"Well, err—no, but shouldn't you at least tell Rhymes that he won? The little guy would be thrilled."

"We can't. If we do, he'll want us to get the trophy. Trust me. This is the only way."

What do you mean I'm heartless? I don't see any of you volunteering to impersonate a tortoise.

***

"This is going to be so embarrassing." I sighed.

We were on our way to Washbridge Art Gallery for Barry's exhibition. Jack had insisted we both break out our glad rags for the occasion.

"It might be fun."

I never ceased to be amazed at Jack's unrelenting optimism.

"It's an art exhibition by a dog. How is it going to be fun?"

"Have you actually seen any of his work? He might be talented."

"I've seen tons of it papered all over Aunt Lucy's walls. Lizzie could do better. With one hand tied behind her back. And blindfolded."

"It can't be that bad. Didn't you say Barry had been mentored by someone?"

"Yes, by Dolly. The world's worst artist. Talk about the blind leading the blind."

"There'll probably be nibbles and drinks."

"There'd better be. I'm going to need something to numb my senses."

"It's just a pity that Barry can't be there. Couldn't you

have magicked him over?"

"You're missing the point. Getting him over here isn't the problem. Explaining that he's the artist would be."

"I hadn't thought of that."

The nearest car park was a five-minute walk from the gallery, and wouldn't you know it, the heavens had opened. Fortunately, Jack had had the foresight to bring his umbrella.

"Are you sure you don't want to share this?" I said.

"That's okay. It's only big enough for one."

"That's the gallery over there."

"It looks crowded."

"It can't be." But it was. The gallery was choc-a-bloc; we could barely get through the door. I whispered to Jack, "Do you think we've come on the wrong day?"

"No, this is it. Look over there."

On the wall was a notice that read:

Reflections on life. An exciting new collection from the artist, Barry.

"Amazing, aren't they?" A woman wearing a white dress appeared beside us.

"We've only just arrived," Jack said. "We haven't had chance to look around yet."

"You really must. They're quite exquisite." She had a half-empty champagne glass in her hand. I could only assume she'd been at the bottle for some considerable time. "And if you're thinking of buying anything, you'd better get in fast. They're being snapped up extremely quickly."

She had to be having a laugh. That or there was more

than one artist exhibiting.

"How many artists' works are on display today?" I said.

"Just the one: Barry. Do you know him?"

The question caught me off-guard. "Well, I — err — "

"You do know him, don't you? What's he like? I hear he's something of a recluse, and that's why he goes by just the one name. To protect his privacy."

"That's true. He's had a bit of a *woof* life."

"Really?"

"Oh yes. He's had to work his fingers to the *bone* to get to where he is today."

"That's amazing."

"It certainly gives you *paws* for thought, doesn't it?"

"Jill!" Jack grabbed me by the arm. "I think I see someone over there we should say hello to."

"So very nice to meet you," the woman said. "Do tell Barry I think his work is excellent."

"If I manage to *collar* him, I'll do that."

"What are you playing at?" Jack said.

"What do you mean?"

"Don't come the innocent. Woof? Bone? Paws?"

"Don't forget *collar*."

"It isn't funny."

"Are you kidding? This whole thing is hilarious. Just look at this crowd, fawning all over these ridiculous pictures."

"I beg your pardon." A man, who clearly had a toffee firmly wedged up his nose, admonished me. "These are the work of a genius."

"And what qualifies you to decide?" I challenged him.

"I'm the art critic for The Bugle."

"That explains it."

Once again, Jack dragged me away.

"I can't take you anywhere, Jill."

"Someone needs to tell the emperor that he's butt naked."

"It doesn't always have to be you." Just then, his eyes got wider and his jaw dropped.

"What's wrong?"

"I've just seen the prices. Look!"

"*Fifty pounds*? Who'd pay fifty pounds for that monstrosity?"

"You must be due a trip to the opticians. That's not fifty. It's five-hundred."

***

"You seem a lot brighter," Jack said on the drive home. "I told you that you'd enjoy the exhibition."

"Are you serious? It was beyond awful."

"Why are you so chipper, then? You didn't overdo it with the champagne, did you?"

"No, I was quite restrained under the circumstances."

"So why the stupid grin?"

"I'm just thinking about all the money those paintings must have fetched today."

"What does that have to do with you?"

"Have you forgotten that Barry is my dog?"

"So?"

"What can a dog possibly do with that kind of money? He'll probably want to give it to someone who can put it to good use."

"You, for example?"

"That would be his decision of course."

"And you wouldn't try to influence him?"

"Certainly not. That would be unethical."

"I'm very pleased to hear it."

"I did think I might nip over to see him in the morning, though. Just to offer my congratulations on the success of his exhibition. I always knew he had talent."

Jack was giving me the strangest look.

"What?"

Chapter 18

The next morning when I arrived at the office, Armi was seated in a chair next to Mrs V's desk. He was drinking a glass of water, and he looked as white as a sheet.

"Armi? Are you okay?"

"He's had a nasty shock, Jill," Mrs V said.

"I'm okay," he insisted. He certainly didn't look it; his hands were trembling so much that the water was splashing out of the glass onto the floor.

"What happened? Has he had a funny turn?"

"He was almost killed." Mrs V took the glass from him. "We came into town together, and we'd just said our goodbyes. Armi was headed for Cuckoos Unlimited, weren't you?"

He nodded.

"Tell Jill what happened."

"I was going to see if they had any stock of the Tweetling3619. It's the latest in the line and it's proving to be very popular."

"Jill doesn't want to know about the Tweetling3619," Mrs V said. "Tell her what happened just after we'd gone our separate ways."

"I was on the pedestrian crossing. The little man had turned green, so I set off. Halfway across the road, a car came hurtling towards me. I only just managed to get out of the way in time."

"Did you get his registration number?" I said.

"No. It all happened so quickly. By the time I'd picked myself up, he'd gone."

"He could have been killed, Jill." Mrs V gave Armi a cuddle. "I could have lost him."

"Are you injured?" I asked. "Do you think you should go to A&E?"

"No." Armi waved away the suggestion. "Just a few scrapes on my knees. It's nothing to worry about. I just need to sit here until I've caught my breath."

"Stay as long as you like."

"I'll make us all a cup of tea." Mrs V picked up the kettle. "Lots of sugar for you, my little gingerbread man."

"Thanks, dewdrop."

It was nice to see the affection Mrs V and Armi felt for one another, but I still found the whole *dewdrop/gingerbread man* thing a bit much. Would that happen to Jack and me one day? Would we suddenly come up with cutesy names for each other?

Not. On. My. Watch.

Winky was working up quite a sweat on the punch bag.

"What happened to Arnie?"

"It's Armi, and he almost got run over."

"The old bag lady probably did it. She's after his life insurance."

"That's a terrible thing to say. You shouldn't judge everyone else by your own low moral standards."

"We'll see." He shrugged. "My money is still on her."

"How's the astronomy going?"

"Really well. I've ordered a telescope. With a bit of luck it will be here next week."

"I hope you didn't use my money to pay for it."

"I kind of did."

"What have I told you about using my credit card?"

"Keep your wig on. I meant that I used the money I won from you in our little hula hoop challenge." He grinned. "I assume you'll be wanting a rematch, by the way."

"No chance. I'm done with hula hoops."

"I see you've been making the wrong kind of headlines again."

"I don't want to talk about that."

"You need to get your act together or we'll all be out on the street. First, you get rid of the sign, so no one knows we're here, and now this." He held up a copy of The Bugle.

"I've already told you. I don't want to talk about it. Shouldn't you be preparing for the boxing match? It's tomorrow, isn't it?"

"Yep. Tomorrow night I'll be crowned the undisputed feline boxing champion of Washbridge. If you want my autograph, you'd better ask for it now. After tomorrow, I'll be charging fifty pounds a time."

***

I'd arranged to pay Belladonna a visit to discuss her new identity, but first I thought I should pop into Aunt Lucy's to offer my congratulations to Barry on the success of his exhibition.

What? You lot are as bad as Jack. Of course I wasn't only interested in the money.

Aunt Lucy and Lester were in the kitchen.

"Morning, Jill. Would you like a cup of tea?" Aunt Lucy said.

"No, thanks. I've not long since had one. I'm surprised to find you here, Lester. I thought you'd be chasing that bonus."

"I've given up on that stupid game, Jill."

"How come?"

"He's only given up because he knows he can't get the top spot," Aunt Lucy said. "He didn't do it for the reason he should have, which is because the whole thing is distasteful."

The two of them exchanged a look. There had clearly been a few heated discussions on the subject.

"Jim Dunston pretty much has it all sewn up already," Lester said to me. "He's got three times as many points as his nearest rival."

"Points?" Aunt Lucy shot him a look. "Did you hear that, Jill? These are *people* we're talking about. People who have passed away!" She stood up. "I can't listen to any more of this. I'll go and water the plants while you two talk about it." And with that, she stormed out of the room.

"I'm sorry, Lester," I said. "Touchy subject, I guess?"

"For Lucy, yes. I try not to talk about it in front of her if I can avoid it. And, anyway, like I said, it's pretty much done with. No one is going to catch Dunston now."

"How did he manage to get so many more points than anyone else?"

"I have no idea. I wouldn't have thought it possible. He does live in the human world, though. That gives him a slight advantage, I guess. And he's been unbelievably lucky too."

"Lucky how?"

"Some of the points he's picked up were sheer flukes. One guy was crushed to death when a tree fell onto his car. Then there was the man who fell down an open manhole. And another guy who owned a signage company was killed when his own sign fell on top of him."

"I knew that guy: Sid Song. He supplied my signs—all of them."

"It just goes to show you, doesn't it? Wrong place, wrong time, I guess. Or in Dunston's case, right time, right place."

Alarm bells were starting to ring in my head. Why had there been so many freak accidents in such a short period of time? And how come this guy, Dunston, just happened to be on-hand to mop up the points? Had Armi's near miss been another 'freak accident' in the making?

"And you say this Dunston lives in the human world?"

"Yeah. In Middle Wash, I believe. Why?"

"No reason."

Lester checked the wall clock. "I suppose I'd better be making tracks. I'll go and find Lucy to see if she's in the mood to kiss and make up."

"Okay. Bye, Lester. Good luck."

Five minutes later, Aunt Lucy came back into the kitchen.

"I'm sorry if I caused an argument," I said.

"It's not your fault, Jill. It's my problem. I shouldn't be so sensitive."

"Did you two make up?"

"Of course. I would never let him go to work without making up first. Are you sure you don't want a drink?"

"Go on, then. Just a quick one won't hurt."

"Anything to eat?"

"Do you have any custard creams?"

"You know I do. I get them in especially for you."

"Just a couple, then."

"Is that a *conventional* couple or *your* version of a couple?"

"Three will be fine. I don't want to be greedy."

Once we had our drinks, we went through to the living room.

"I hear Barry's exhibition was a success." Aunt Lucy handed me the plate of biscuits. "It was almost midnight when Dolly called over to tell him the exciting news."

"It was unbelievable. The people there just couldn't get enough of his work."

"It appears you have one very talented pet."

"Two, actually."

"What do you mean?"

"You're never going to believe this, but Rhymes won the poetry competition."

"Really? Does he know?"

"No, and I'm not going—"

"I won it?" The little tortoise popped his head out from under the armchair I was sitting in.

Oh bum!

"Rhymes? I didn't realise you were under there."

"You just said I won the competition."

"I did say that, didn't I?"

"Do you have my trophy?"

"Err, no."

"When will I get it?"

"I believe it has to be collected from the publisher's offices in London."

"Will you collect it for me, Jill? Please."

"I—err. I'm not sure if—"

"Please, Jill! I've never won anything before. Please!"

"I'm sure Jill will collect it for you," Aunt Lucy chipped

in, helpfully.

"Yes, okay, but the presentation isn't for a couple of weeks."

"Thanks, Jill. You're the best."

Hmm.

"Ouch!" I winced. The custard cream had found my cavity.

"What's wrong, Jill?"

"It's nothing. Just a bit of toothache."

"You should get that seen to before it gets any worse."

"I've tried, but when I went to get it filled, my dentist had gone home with toothache."

"That's crazy."

"I know. I need to find someone else. It's just a matter of finding the time."

"Have you considered using the tooth fairies?"

"I didn't think they were real. I thought that was just something parents tell their kids when they lose a tooth."

"I can promise you they're very real. I wouldn't go anywhere else. I can give them a call and make an appointment for you if you like?"

"Err, okay then. Why not? Thanks."

After I'd finished my drink, I went to find the artist otherwise known as Barry.

As soon as he saw me, he came rushing over. "Were you at the exhibition, Jill?"

"Of course. Jack and I were both there."

"What did you think of it?"

"I thought it was incredible. And what a turnout."

"Dolly said it was the most successful exhibition she'd ever been involved with. We sold all of the pictures."

"That's fantastic! But then, I always knew you had talent."

"Did you? Did you really?"

"Of course. The first time I saw one of your pictures, I said to Aunt Lucy, this is the work of a genius."

"Thanks, Jill. That means a lot to me."

"I imagine you must have made a lot of money from the sales?"

"Tons and tons."

"You must be thrilled."

"I'm not bothered about the money. It's all about the art."

"*The art.* Of course. You'll probably need some help to manage the cash? If you wanted me to, I could —"

"It's gone."

"Sorry?"

"The money. It's already gone."

"Gone where?"

"Dolly suggested I donate it to Candlefield Dogs' Charity, so that's what I did."

"All of it?"

"I held back a few pounds to buy Barkies with."

"That's great! Absolutely great!" I felt like crying. "Right. I suppose I should be making tracks."

"Aren't we going for a walk? I love walks."

"I don't have the time right now, sorry." I started for the door.

"Wait, Jill! I have something for you."

"Oh?"

"I kept back a few pictures to give to family and friends." He handed me a framed picture. "This one is for you."

"Thanks, you shouldn't have."

"It's my way of thanking you for being so kind to me."

That dog sure knew how to make me feel bad.

I didn't really want to have to cart the picture around with me for the rest of the day, so I magicked myself back to the office, planning to leave it there.

"What have you got there?" Winky said.

"It's nothing."

"Let me see."

"Before you start to criticise it, it isn't one of mine."

"I'll buy it off you."

"Very funny."

"I'm serious. How much do you want?"

Only then did it occur to me that the previous night I'd seen Barry's paintings going for five-hundred pounds each. Maybe I could come out of this on the right side for once.

"Five-hundred pounds."

I expected him to laugh, but instead, he said, "Okay. Deal."

Maybe I'd misheard. "What did you just say?"

"I said you have a deal."

I hadn't been expecting that, but if he could come up with the money, it would save me having to hawk it around all the dealers in Washbridge.

"Let's see the cash first."

He disappeared under the sofa for a few seconds, and then re-emerged with a wad of ten-pound notes. "There you go."

"Where did that come from?"

"My mini-safe."

"How long have you had a safe in the office?"

"Do you want to sell the picture or not?"

"Yeah, okay." I snatched the cash, did a quick check to make sure the banknotes weren't fake, and then handed over Barry's masterpiece.

Result!

**

I was back in Candlefield, minus one picture, but five-hundred pounds the richer.

Belladonna and I couldn't meet at Cuppy C, just in case any of the parents spotted her, and asked her why she wasn't working in the creche. I had offered to meet her at her place, but she thought her housemates might be at home, so we'd arranged to meet at In a Jam, a tea room I'd been to only once before.

Belladonna was waiting for me outside.

The tea room had obviously had a revamp since my last visit, and it appeared to be doing a steady trade.

"I'll get these," I offered. I was feeling generous after my five-hundred pounds windfall.

"Thanks, Jill. Just a coffee for me, please."

"Those cakes look delicious. Are you sure you wouldn't like one?"

"No, thanks. I try not to snack in-between meals."

"Me too. Just the coffees, then."

We found a quiet table at the back of the shop, and got straight down to business.

"Have you come up with a new name?" I said.

"Yeah. I thought I could call myself Belle Madonna."

"That isn't going to work. It's too close to your real

name."

"What about Donna Bell?"

"Same problem, I'm afraid."

"I'm running out of ideas."

"How about — err — Rita?"

"I'm not sure I could live with Rita."

"Why not? Rita is a nice name."

"It just doesn't feel right."

"Shirley?"

"No."

"Amanda."

"Err, no."

"Paula?"

"My best friend at school was called Paula."

"There you go, then. Perfect."

"She stole my first boyfriend. I could never call myself Paula."

Fifty minutes, and two thousand names later, we finally had it.

"So, it's decided?" I had everything crossed.

"Yes. Definitely. Jemima it is. Jemima Tuck. I like it."

"Me too. It suits you."

"What happens now?"

"You'll need to find somewhere new to live."

"Couldn't I just stay where I am?"

"I'm afraid not. If this is going to work, you have to make a fresh start under your new identity."

"Okay. Then what?"

"You'll need to contact me again, so I can cast the spell which will change your appearance forever."

"I'm really nervous about that part."

"That's understandable, but it's the only way."

"What if I change my mind, will I be able to revert to how I look now?"

"I'm afraid not. Once I've cast the spell, you won't be able to go back to the way you look now."

"That's a really scary thought."

"It must be. There's still time to back out. You can change your mind at any time until I've actually cast the spell."

"I won't. I know I have to do this."

"Okay. I'll wait to hear from you, then."

After Belladonna had headed home, I made my way to Cuppy C where Amber was behind the counter.

"Hey, Jill. Your usual?"

"No, thanks. I've just had a drink at In A Jam."

"Traitor."

"I was there to meet Belladonna, or should I say Jemima Tuck."

"Who?"

"That's Belladonna's new name."

"She doesn't strike me as a Jemima."

"Well, she is now. I just wanted to keep you posted."

"Thanks. I hear you have two very talented pets."

"Some people seem to think so."

"I bet you expected to get your hands on some of Barry's money, didn't you? You must have been devastated when you found out he'd given it to charity."

"Has he? I didn't think to ask. My only interest is in nurturing his talent."

"Yeah, right." She laughed. "So, what happens next with Belladonna?"

"When she's moved out of her flat, I'll cast a spell which

will change her appearance permanently."

"I wouldn't fancy that. I suppose it wouldn't be so bad if you were plain looking to start with."

"Why did you look at me when you said that?"

"I didn't."

"Hmm. I'd better get back to the office."

Chapter 19

Coincidences do happen. Freak accidents certainly do occur. Still, the more I thought about what Lester had told me, the more convinced I became that there was something sinister about the recent spate of so-called 'freak accidents'.

Fortunately, there was only one Jim Dunston listed in the Washbridge phone book. I gave him a call.

"Jim Dunston speaking."

"Hi, my name is Reece Porter. I work for Grim Tidings Monthly."

"I've never heard of it."

"We're a brand-new publication. In fact, I'm currently working on our launch issue. If pre-orders are anything to go by, we expect to make a big splash, and I'm hoping that I can persuade you to grant me an interview."

"Why would you want to interview me?"

"If my sources are correct, I understand that you're set to top the performance table that was recently introduced by the grim reaper authorities."

"Oh, I see. I am leading the table at the moment, but there's still a way to go until they declare a winner."

"I think you're being overly modest. My understanding is that you're so far in front that no one has a chance of catching you. And besides, because of the lead times we have to work with, we'll need to get the interview in the bag quickly or we'll miss the deadline for the first issue."

"I'm not sure about this. My bosses might not like it."

"You would be on the front cover."

"Really? Okay, then. What do I need to do?"

"I'd like to meet up with you later today if that's

possible."

"I—err—yeah, why not? When and where?"

"Where will you be working today?"

"I'm covering Washbridge Retail Park and the surrounding area."

"Okay. Do you know The Wash Tavern? It's near the retail park."

"Yeah, I know it."

"How about we meet there at four?"

"Okay."

"And Jim, would you do me a favour?"

"Sure."

"Send me a selfie, please."

"Why do you need that?"

"We can use it as a placeholder for the front cover until we get our photographer out to take a proper shot of you."

"Okay. I'll text it to you now."

"Great, thanks."

No sooner had we finished on the call than my phone beeped with a text message. The guy was clearly eager.

And ugly.

***

I was definitely missing something on the Warne kidnapping case, but I couldn't work out what it was. When I'd studied the town centre CCTV, I'd seen Robert Warne leave the cinema by himself, and make his way to the house where he was later to meet his death. No one had forced him to go there, which was why I'd been convinced he'd staged his own kidnapping, in order to extort cash from his wife. But if that was true, who had murdered him? The police, the newspapers and even my client were under the impression that he'd been killed by his kidnappers who had panicked when they'd realised I was onto them. That theory was all well and good, but only if you believed that Robert Warne had actually been kidnapped in the first place.

I needed to take another look at that CCTV footage, so I paid another visit to the city centre monitoring centre. This time, though, I didn't need the 'sleep' spell because the bald man, who was supposedly 'on-duty', was already asleep. Not only was he asleep, but he was snoring like a pig, making it impossible for me to focus on the footage. After a few minutes, I could take no more of the awful racket. I daren't nudge him in case he woke up, so instead, I used the 'shrink' spell on him and the chair in which he was sitting. Then I picked up the chair with him still in it, and placed it inside the bottom drawer of the filing cabinet.

No matter how many times I watched the footage, I didn't spot anything new. All it did was confirm what I already knew: The man had left the cinema alone and made his way to the house where he would later meet his death.

Before I left the monitoring centre, I burned the relevant footage onto a disc, so that I could review it again later if necessary.

***

As Jim Dunston had kindly sent me a photo of himself, I had an advantage over him. I knew who I was looking for, but he had no idea what I, AKA Reece Porter, looked like. That meant I could search for him in and around the retail park without worrying that he might recognise me.

It had just turned two o'clock, so I had a couple of hours before our scheduled meeting at four. If my hunch was correct, Dunston was boosting his points tally by staging what appeared to be freak accidents. The question was, where would he have the best chance of doing that? The retail park itself seemed unlikely because there were way too many people around. If he tried anything dodgy there, it would probably be noticed.

I'd been walking around the streets that surrounded the retail park for the best part of an hour, and I was beginning to think I'd struck out when I caught a glimpse of the man himself on Havermore Street. If anything, he was even uglier in real life than in the photograph he'd sent to me. He was short too. Short and stubby.

At the end of the street, there were a number of empty office buildings. They'd been unoccupied for at least two years to my knowledge. When Dunston drew level with them, he ducked down the small alleyway that ran between two of the buildings. If I followed him down there, he'd realise I was tailing him, so I cast the 'invisible' spell.

Around the back of the building, several of the windows had been boarded up. Dunston had obviously been there before because he knew that the boards on one of the windows had been forced open on one side— maybe he'd done it himself earlier. Once inside, he made his way up a dusty staircase to the third floor. The huge open-plan room, which spanned the whole of the floor, was empty.

What was he up to?

I watched as he leaned out of one of the glassless windows, which overlooked the street. In order to get a better view of what he was doing, I went to the adjacent window.

Dunston was undoing one of the bolts that secured the large sign. Once he'd released it, the weight of the sign would pull it from the remaining fastenings and send it plunging to the ground below. This must be how he'd killed poor old Sid Song.

Dunston seemed to hesitate, and for a moment, I couldn't figure out why, but then I saw a young woman walking along the street below us. In a few seconds, she'd be underneath the sign, and he would release the bolt.

There wasn't enough time to get back down the stairs, so I used the 'levitate' spell to float down to the street. Still invisible, I threw myself at the young woman, knocking her backwards onto her bottom. The look of surprise on her face soon changed to one of horror as the sign crashed onto the pavement in front of her.

**

By the time Jim Dunston arrived at the Wash Tavern, I was already seated at a table. I waited until he had his drink before waving him over.

"Reece?"

"Pleased to meet you, Jim." We shook hands. "Have a seat."

"When will the first issue of your magazine come out?"

"It's two months away, but we have to have all our main features completed within the next couple of weeks."

"I can't believe I'll be on the front cover."

"Why wouldn't you? From what I hear, you're something of a superstar."

"It's nothing." He was grinning from ear to ear. "I was just doing my job."

"But if what I hear is correct, your numbers are nothing short of spectacular."

"I wouldn't go that far. I just got lucky I guess."

"Luck does seem to have played a part in it. I mean, what are the chances of someone being killed by a falling tree?"

"It doesn't happen often."

"Or falling down an open manhole?"

"I blame the careless workmen."

"And then there's the sign incident."

"That was rather tragic. Killed by his own sign."

"I wasn't referring to Mr Song's death."

"Oh?"

"No, I was talking about the young woman you almost killed less than an hour ago."

That revelation shocked him into silence for a moment, but then he said, "I don't know what you're talking about."

"Really? So you didn't loosen the bolts on the sign on the empty office building on Havermore Street?"

"What's this all about? Who are you?"

"Who I am doesn't matter, but I do have a couple of friends who are keen to meet you." I signalled to Daze and Blaze who had been watching from a table across the room.

"Who are they?" Dunston demanded.

"I think I'll let them introduce themselves." I turned to Daze and Blaze. "Can I leave this gentleman with you?"

"You most certainly can."

Daze had been delighted when she'd received my call. Rogue wizards, witches, vampires and werewolves were commonplace, but rogue grim reapers were considered something of a prize.

With Dunston behind bars in Candlefield, the people of Washbridge, including Armi who had had a lucky escape, would be able to walk the streets in relative safety.

Oh bum!

I suddenly realised that I'd forgotten to let the man out of the filing cabinet!

There was no time to lose, so I cast the 'invisible' spell, and magicked myself back to the control room.

There were two other men in there, and they were obviously trying to figure out where their colleague had gone.

"He must be skiving somewhere again," the taller of the two said.

"I don't know why they don't sack him."

"Did you check the loo?"

"Of course I did."

"I'm going to double-check."

As soon as they'd left the office, I opened the bottom drawer of the filing cabinet, only to find the man still fast asleep in his chair. I managed to take him out and restore him to full-size without waking him.

Just then, his two colleagues returned.

"Where have you been, Bill?"

"What?" He opened his eyes. "What do you mean? I've been here all the time."

"You're half-asleep. Have you been somewhere for a nap?"

"No, I just told you. I've never moved from this spot. I think I may have nodded off for a couple of minutes, though. You'll never guess what I dreamt."

***

"Not happening!" Jack said.

"You have to."

"No, I don't. He's your tortoise, so you should be the one to collect his trophy."

"But you were the one who got his book published."

"Watch my lips, Jill. I'm not doing it."

"But they're expecting a man. The author's name is *Robert*."

"In that case, you'll just have to use magic to turn yourself into a man."

"I don't know how to do that."

"Yes, you do. You just don't want to do it. I can't understand why you told Rhymes about it. You said you weren't going to."

"It seemed like the right thing to do."

He gave me a look. "I'm not buying that. What's the real reason you told him?"

"Okay. He was under the armchair when I told Aunt Lucy about his win, and he overheard."

"That reminds me. Did you manage to squeeze any cash out of Barry?"

"I can honestly say that it never occurred to me to try."

"I don't believe you. Come on, how much are you getting?"

"Nothing. He's given it all to charity."

"Poor you." He laughed. "That must have stung."

"All is not lost. He did give me a painting that I sold to Winky."

"How much for? Fifty pence?"

"Five-hundred pounds."

"You'll never see that money."

"I've already got it."

"Where does a cat get five-hundred pounds from?"

"His mini-safe under the sofa in the office."

"Of course. Silly me. I should have known." He held out his hand. "Where's my share?"

"You don't get a share. I'll need this to cover my costs for going down to London to collect Rhymes' trophy."

Before Jack could argue, Kathy rang.

"Hey, Sis." She sounded remarkably bright and breezy.

"Hi yourself."

"I rang to check on the arrangements for Saturday."

"*Saturday?*"

"Don't tell me you've forgotten?"

"Of course I haven't."

"Okay. What's happening on Saturday, then?"

"I—err."

"Who is it?" Jack mouthed.

"Kathy. She's asking me about Saturday."

"About TenPinCon?" He raised an eyebrow. "What about it?"

"Kathy, it's TenPinCon, obviously."

"I just heard Jack tell you that. What time should we be there?"

"Jack, what time are we meeting?"

"I've promised Tony and Clare that I'll be there at seven to help with the last-minute preparations."

"Kathy? Jack's going to be there at seven, but I'm not going that early."

"Shall we meet you there, then?"

"Yeah, I think that would be best. Ten o'clock?"

"Okay. I assume you heard that Reggie has resigned?"

"Yeah, he came to see me. It's probably for the best. The new job he's landed will suit him better."

"Do you know where that is? Pete did ask him, but he couldn't get a straight answer out of him. Something about a job in a hotel somewhere."

"No, he didn't tell me where he was going."

"Okay, not to worry. We'll see you on Saturday morning."

"Okay."

"Oh, and Jill."

"Yeah?"

"You'll never guess what's happened?"

"You've decided to adopt a llama?"

"What? No. The kids seem to have turned over a new leaf."

"What do you mean?"

"It's incredible. Ever since the weekend, their rooms have been tidier than I've seen them in years."

"Your nagging must have finally paid off."

"I guess so. Either that or they've been abducted, and these two are aliens who just look like Lizzie and Mikey."

"Or maybe a gremlin did it?"

"Don't you know anything about gremlins, Jill? They wreck places. They don't tidy them up."

"Sorry, my bad."

Chapter 20

"You do realise that this is weird, right?" Jack said over breakfast.

"It's just a boxing match."

"For cats!"

"It's not like I approve of it, but I did promise I'd take Winky there tonight."

"What am I supposed to tell the guys at work when they ask how you are and what you're up to? I can hardly say: She's fine. In fact, she's off to a feline boxing match tonight."

"Why not? It's no more embarrassing than me having to tell people about your ten-pin bowling fetish."

"That reminds me, I was supposed to go around and see Tony and Clare this morning about TenPinCon."

"What else can there possibly be left to talk about?"

Before he could answer, my phone rang.

"Is that Jill Maxwell?"

"Speaking."

"This is Dee from the Tooth Fairy Dental Practice. We were contacted by one of your relatives, I believe?"

"Right. That would have been my Aunt Lucy."

"I understand you're having a few problems."

"Not really. Well, just the odd twinge. It's probably nothing."

"She seemed to think you needed a filling?"

"Maybe. It comes and goes."

"It's probably best to get it seen to before it gets any worse."

"I guess."

"We have a cancellation this afternoon at two o'clock if

you could make that."

"Err—yeah, I can do that."

"It'll be with Maureen Lars."

"Okay, great. I'll be there. Bye."

"Who was that?" Jack said.

"The tooth fairies."

"How am I supposed to have a conversation with you if you won't be serious?"

"I am being serious. That really was the tooth fairies. They're going to see to my filling this afternoon."

"And I thought feline boxing was crazy."

Jack was still at Tony and Clare's house when I left for work. Before I could get into the car, I heard the dreaded tooting sound of Mr Hosey's train. Bessie was headed down the street, and before I could make my escape, Mr Hosey called to me.

"Did you give any more thought to Henry, Jill?"

"*Henry*?"

"My hurdy-gurdy. You were going to decide if you wanted me to give you lessons."

"Oh yeah. *That* Henry. Tempting as the offer is, I'm going to pass."

"What instrument will you play, then?"

"I'll decide on the night. Anyway, how come you aren't on post box duty today?"

"Unfortunately, I've had to abandon the post box camouflage."

"Really? I thought it was very effective."

"Too effective unfortunately. The sheer volume of mail I was having to repost was simply too great. Do you know how many penfriends Norm Normal has?"

"If the pile of letters I saw is anything to go by, it must be hundreds. What will you do about neighbourhood watch surveillance now?"

"Fear not, Jill. The streets are still safe in my hands. I have my eye on another camouflage already."

"What's that?"

"I'm afraid I'm not at liberty to say, but trust me, this will be the best yet."

***

"How's Armi, Mrs V?"

"He's fine now, thanks. He was just a little shaken up."

"That's understandable."

"What are your thoughts on magic, Jill?"

The question completely threw me. Had Mrs V somehow worked out I was a witch?

"Magic? I don't—err—"

"It's just that Armi has decided he needs a new hobby, and he's thinking of becoming a magician. An old friend of his used to be a children's entertainer of sorts, and he's selling all his old props. Armi wants me to be his assistant."

"I thought you two were invested in becoming clowns?"

"We were, but ever since the stolen clown shoe incident, Armi seems to have lost interest, and I don't really want to do it by myself. What do you think? Should I be his assistant?"

"Definitely. It'll be fun."

Winky was at my desk, on my computer.

"What have I told you about using my computer?"

"Shush! This is at a critical point."

"What are you doing?" I walked over to the desk, so I could see what he was up to.

"Wait! There's only a few seconds left on the auction."

"What are you buying?"

"I'm not buying anything."

And that's when I saw the photo on screen.

"You're selling Barry's painting."

"Ten, nine, eight, seven, six, five, four, three, two, one. Bingo!" He punched the air.

"Let me see that." I moved him to one side. "Two-thousand, one-hundred pounds?"

"Nice, eh?"

"But I sold it to you for five-hundred."

"Correct. A profit of sixteen-hundred pounds, less seller's fees. Result!"

"I should get half of that."

"Why?"

"Because—err—because it's only fair."

"Dream on. You named your selling price and I paid it fair and square."

"But, but—"

How? How could I have allowed that cat to get the better of me again?

***

It was time to pay another visit to We-Spray where the owner, Mr Lee Black, should be back at his desk. Although I'd never met Mr Black, I had a hunch that I knew something important about him, and if I was right, it might explain the issues that Bestest Cars had been experiencing.

First, though, I cast the 'block' spell to prevent any sups from realising I was a witch.

"Hello, again." It was Eric. He of the red and green hair.

"Hi. Is Mr Black in?"

"Yeah, he's in his office. Shall I go and get him for you?"

"There's no need. Just point me in the right direction."

Once I'd realised that We-Spray were doing both the original and the subsequent respray, it was just a question of working out how the cars were being moved back and forth from the car sales lots. The only explanation that made a lick of sense was that magic was being used. As soon as I reached Lee Black's office, and saw him through the glass panelled wall, my hunch was confirmed: He was a wizard.

I knocked on his door.

"Come in."

"Hi. My name is Ruth. Ruth Lesser. Do you have a minute?"

"Of course. Take a seat, Ruth. What can I do for you?"

"I have a car sales business in West Chipping. Ruth's Motors. You might have heard of it?"

"Err, yeah. I think I have."

"I'm looking for someone who can handle my respraying business, and I've heard good things about you. Would you be interested?"

"Absolutely. I'm always on the lookout for new clients."

"Excellent. The thing is, Lee — is it okay to call you Lee?"

"Of course. We're all friends here."

"The thing is, Lee, my requirements are a little out of

the ordinary."

"I'm sure we'll be able to accommodate you. What exactly is it that you need?"

"I'd like you to collect a number of cars from my lot each month. Maybe a dozen."

"Okay, that's no problem."

"And then, I'd like you to spray them all the same colour. Let's say green, for argument's sake."

"Green? All of them?"

"There's more."

"Okay?"

"A few days later, I'd like you to collect the same cars, and respray them back to their original colour."

"I — err — I don't understand."

"But, Lee, isn't that precisely what you do here already?" I reversed the 'block' spell.

"You're a witch. How did you do that?"

"That's not really important."

"Who are you?"

"My name is Jill Maxwell."

"I've heard of you. You're that superstar witch, aren't you?"

It wasn't often someone called me that, but I have to say that I kinda liked it.

"I'm not here to talk about me. I'm more interested in discussing your dubious business practices."

"Who are you working for?"

"Burt Claymore at Bestest Cars."

"Just my luck. Of all the people Burt could have hired, he had to choose a witch. I suppose you're going to call the rogue retrievers?"

"Give me one good reason why I shouldn't."

"Eric. He's the young guy who works for me. If I get taken away, the business will fold, and he'll be out of a job. He and his wife, Lorraine, have just had their first child."

"What possessed you to do this in the first place?"

"I was desperate. All the work had dried up."

"That's no excuse."

"I know, but I just couldn't bear the thought of telling Eric I was going to have to let him go. Please, Jill, don't call the rogue retrievers. There must be another way."

Call me a big softy, but I actually felt sorry for the guy. And, I certainly didn't want to see Eric out of a job.

"Okay, how about this? You respray all the cars you've sprayed green, purple or whatever other colour you've dreamed up. And you do it free of charge."

"It'll cost me a fortune."

"Tough. You should have thought of that before you started this."

"Okay. I agree, but I'm not sure how I'll keep this place going."

"Everyone I've talked to is impressed with the quality of the work you do here."

"That's good to hear, at least. I do take great pride in what we do."

"So get off your backside, and go out and sell your services."

"I've never been very good at selling."

"Well you'd better get good at it, and quick. Failing that, employ a salesman willing to work on commission. You have a great service to offer, so go out and sell it!"

"You're right. I know you are."

"And no matter what happens, don't be tempted to try

anything like this again because if you do, I'll find out, and the next time, it'll be the rogue retrievers who are knocking on your door."

"I promise. And thanks, Jill."

My problem is that I'm just too nice.

What? It's true. Take what just happened for example. Taking pity on Lee and letting him off with a slapped wrist was all well and good, but I couldn't tell my client, Burt Claymore, what I'd done. Instead, I was forced to tell him that, although I didn't find out who was behind the respraying, I felt sure it wouldn't happen again. Needless to say, he was less than impressed, and he told me not to bother billing him.

Brilliant, Jill! Just brilliant!

***

Back in Washbridge city centre, who should I bump into on the high street but the two masterminds, AKA Norman and Tonya.

And their dogs. All five of them.

"Hello, you two."

"Hi, Jill." Norman was trying to hold back the Great Dane, which looked as though it thought I was its lunch.

Tonya looked nonplussed, so I prompted her.

"We met in the park."

"Did we? Oh yeah, I remember."

She clearly didn't.

"Whose are all these dogs?"

"They're ours." Tonya was holding onto a dachshund, a poodle, a westie and a bichon frise.

"All five of them?"

"Tonya couldn't decide which one she wanted." Norman was still struggling to control the huge hound. "So we ended up with all of them."

"Right. I'd better let you get going. This big guy looks as though he's hungry."

***

Back at the office, it was a case of déjà vu.

Armi was sitting next to Mrs V's desk. He was as white as a sheet, and had a glass of water in his hand.

"What's happened, Mrs V? Has he had a flashback to the near miss with the car?"

"No. He was almost killed by a piano."

"When?"

"Just now, as he was walking from the car park. It fell out of the window of the Arial Building."

"Are you sure?" I said.

"Do you think he's making it up?" Mrs V fixed me with her gaze. "Just look at the state of him!"

"Sorry, I didn't mean—err—sorry." This didn't make any sense. Daze had taken Jim Dunston away to Candlefield where he'd be behind bars. So who could have done this? Were there other grim reapers chasing the bonus? I had to find out. "Is there anything you need, Armi?"

"No, thanks, Jill." He took a sip of the sweet tea Mrs V had made for him. "I'll be alright in a few minutes."

"I've just remembered something I meant to do." I made for the door. "I won't be long."

At this rate, I'd soon be spending more time at the city centre CCTV monitoring centre than I did in my own office.

Once again, the 'invisible' spell got me into the control room where I found my bald friend on duty. This time, though, he was actually awake on the job.

But not for long.

Once I'd sent him to sleep, I took over the controls, and began to view the footage taken around the Arial building earlier that day. It didn't take long to spot Armi, walking down the street on his way to my offices. Suddenly, a large object hit the ground just a few feet behind him; the piano disintegrated on impact. Armi, and several other passers-by, stared in disbelief at the carnage, and then one by one, they looked up to see where the piano had fallen from.

I was more interested in knowing which of the grim reapers had been behind the attempt on Armi's life. Whoever it was would rue the day they were born when I'd finished with them.

I rewound the footage so that I could watch the main entrance of the Arial building. Hopefully, I'd be able to narrow down the suspects based upon the time they entered and left. It wouldn't be easy because that particular building was home to several businesses.

In the event, though, it proved to be much easier than I'd expected.

"Got you!"

I made a quick call to Mrs V to check on Armi, and also to ask her for an address. She seemed surprised at my request, but I promised to explain all later.

***

He answered the door wearing his trademark open-necked shirt and gold medallion.

"Can I help you?"

"Don't you remember me, Roland?"

"I don't think so, and I never forget a pretty face."

"You came to my office the other day, looking for Mrs V—I mean Annabel Versailles."

"Of course. I remember you now. What brings you here today? Has Annabel sent you with a message for me?"

"No. Annabel doesn't want anything to do with you. Let me see, what was it that she called you? Oh yes, the oldest swinger in town."

His smile evaporated. "Why are you here, then?"

"I thought you'd like a lift to the police station."

"What are you talking about?"

"I can run you down there now if you like."

"I don't have time for your nonsense." He tried to close the door, but my foot was in the way. "Do you mind?"

"It might be an idea to get changed before you hand yourself in to the police. First impressions, and all that."

"If you don't leave right now," he yelled, "I'll call the police."

"Good idea. You can tell them how you tried to run Armi over, and when that didn't work, how you tried to kill him by pushing a piano out of the Arial building. You were captured on CCTV both times."

All the colour drained from Roland's face as he realised the game was up. "Annabel and I were made for one another."

"I very much doubt she'd agree."

By now, all the fight had gone out of Roland. He put up no resistance when I drove him to the police station, where he informed the officer on duty that he wanted to confess to attempted murder.

Chapter 21

For some reason, I'd assumed that the Tooth Fairy Dental Practice would be in a fairy-sized building, and that I'd have to shrink myself before I could pay it a visit.

It turned out that I was wrong.

The practice was just off the marketplace in Candlefield, in-between an estate agent and a solicitor. The young woman behind reception was a witch; her name badge read: Dee Kay.

"Hi, I'm Jill Maxwell. I think we spoke this morning. I have an appointment with Maureen Lars at two."

"That's right." She checked her computer. "Mo is just with another patient at the moment. Would you like to take a seat?"

"Thanks."

At least the waiting room didn't have any light aircraft magazines, but to be honest, Potions Quarterly wasn't much of an improvement.

"Mrs Maxwell, we're ready for you now." The dental nurse led me through to the surgery.

I'm not sure what I'd been expecting, but the room looked just like every other dentist I'd ever visited. After I was seated in the reclining chair, the dental nurse put a bib around my neck and handed me a pair of shades.

"I'm very pleased to meet you, Jill."

The tiny voice made me jump. I hadn't noticed the fairy until she flew across the room and perched on my shoulder.

"Hi. Sorry, I didn't see you there."

"I'm Mo. It's an honour to have such a celebrity as a

client."

"It's very good of you to see me at such short notice."

"I understand you need a filling?"

"Maybe. Probably not. It's most likely nothing."

"Why don't I take a look? Open wide."

I've encountered a few weird things over the last few years, but having a fairy flying around inside your mouth is right up there. I was terrified in case I breathed in through my mouth and swallowed her.

"Yes." She was back on my shoulder. "There's definitely a small cavity back there, but I'll soon have it sorted."

I knew what was coming next: the dreaded needle.

Obviously, I'm not scared of needles. It's just that my gums are particularly sensitive, which is why I find them more painful than everyone else does.

"Open wide again, please," the dental nurse said. "Stick your tongue out."

I did as she said, and she put a drop of strawberry flavoured liquid on my tongue.

"What's that?"

"It will make sure you feel no pain," Mo said.

"No needle?"

"Goodness no." She laughed. "Do they still use those things in the human world?"

"Usually. Should my mouth be going numb yet?"

"It won't. There's no need for any of that. The fairy juice will make sure you don't feel any pain."

"Are you sure?" Much as I hated needles, I was even less keen on the idea of having a filling without any anaesthetic.

"Trust me. There's nothing to worry about. Open wide again."

As soon as I did, Mo flew inside.

I'm not sure if it was the fairy juice or not, but I didn't feel a thing. After a few minutes, I was beginning to wonder if she was still in there, but then she reappeared. "All done."

"That's it?"

"Yes. Good as new."

"Thanks."

"My pleasure. If you have any more problems, just give us a call. Otherwise we'll see you in six months for a check-up."

When I got back to reception, it occurred to me that I couldn't use my debit or credit cards in Candlefield.

"I'm sorry about this, but I'm going to have to pop out to get some cash."

"There's no need," Dee Kay said. "We have special arrangements in place for our patients who live in the human world."

***

"I can't believe Roland would do something like this." Mrs V was still in shock from learning that her old flame had been behind Armi's 'near misses'.

"He obviously thought if he could get rid of Armi, you'd go running to him."

"He was wrong. Even if I was all alone, I wouldn't want anything to do with Mr Roland Brass. How did you work out he was the one behind it?"

"Just a hunch. How is Armi?"

"Physically, he's okay, but this experience has unnerved him a little."

"Understandably."

"How's the tooth?"

"All sorted now."

"Is it really or are you just saying that because you're scared to go to the dentist?"

"Honestly, I've just come back from there."

"Maybe you'll cut back on the muffins and custard creams now."

"Yeah. Maybe."

Winky was skipping around the office, shadow-boxing.

"There's still time to change your mind about this stupid boxing match," I said.

"No chance. That belt is as good as mine. What time are we leaving?"

"What time do you need to be there?"

"Five."

"We'll set off in half an hour, then."

"Four-thirty? Will that be early enough?"

"Yeah, that'll give us plenty of time."

"Who's this crowd?" He glanced over at the window through which the three surveillance imps had just made their entrance.

"They're imps."

"They look like over-sized wasps."

"Why don't you go and punch your bag? We have business to discuss."

Ray, May and Jay landed on my desk.

"That cat of yours is very rude," Ray said.

"Don't take it personally. He's rude to everyone. Do you have some news for me?"

"We do." Jay glanced around the office as though he

was looking for something.

"Well?" I was eager to hear their news.

"Do you happen to have any of those custard creams here?" May said. "Surveillance can be hungry work, can't it, guys?"

The other two nodded.

It was obvious that I wasn't going to get any information out of this crew until I fed them, so I broke open my secret stash of custard creams and put them on a plate.

"Hmm, yummy," Ray said through a mouthful of crumbs.

"So? What do you have to tell me?"

"You said we should let you know when the school governors visited the Whisperer's Horse again."

"Right."

"They're there now."

"Okay. In that case, I'd better get over there."

"Do you remember where it is?"

"I—err—?"

"It's between Bryan's Irons and Bart's Tarts, and across the road from June's Spoons."

"How could I forget? I'd better magic myself straight over there. Are you guys okay to see yourselves out?"

"Sure, we'll be fine."

They looked fine and judging by the way they were devouring my custard creams, I doubted there'd be any left for me by the time I got back.

I'd assumed that Bryan's Irons sold smoothing irons, but I was wrong. It was in fact a golf shop, which was doing a brisk trade. June's Spoons, on the other hand, was deserted except for the woman behind the counter, who may or may not have been June — I didn't have the time to go inside to enquire. Bart's window display was full of delicious-looking tarts, and I was tempted to nip inside to avail myself of one, but there simply wasn't time. Instead, I made my way into the Whisperer's Horse.

On their previous visit to the pub, the school governors had met in a private room. It appeared they'd done the same thing again because there was no sign of them in the bar, but there were two werewolves standing guard over a door at the rear of the room.

How best to get in there?

After careful consideration, I nipped outside and found a quiet spot where I used the 'doppelganger' spell to take on the appearance of Cornelius Maligarth, headmaster of CASS.

"You can't go in there." One of the werewolves blocked my way.

"I'm Cornelius Maligarth."

"I don't care if you're the king of the elves. You're not going in there."

"But my three colleagues are already inside: Randolph Straightstaff, Francesca Greylock and Adrian Bowler. Tell them I'm here. They'll vouch for me."

"Wait there." The same werewolf went into the room and closed the door behind him.

"Nice weather," I said to his buddy.

He scowled. Like me, he obviously wasn't big on small talk.

After a couple of minutes, the door opened again. Standing behind the werewolf were three people, one woman and two men, none of whom I recognised.

"Cornelius? What are you doing here?" the woman said.

"Let me in, and I'll tell you."

"It's okay." The woman nodded to the werewolf. "Let him in."

"What's wrong?" one of the men said, after the werewolves had left us alone.

I had no idea what was going on. I'd expected to find the school governors inside the room, but instead I was confronted by three strangers. And yet, they all seemed to recognise Cornelius Maligarth. It was time to call on my poker bluffing skills.

"Don't pretend you don't know what's wrong," I said.

"Is it about that reporter, Maggie Mantle?"

For a moment the name threw me, but then I remembered it was the cover I'd used when I'd approached the school governors. These three strangers in front of me must have somehow posed as the school governors. I decided to play along and see where it led.

"Of course it's about her."

"She came sniffing around, asking questions."

"What did you tell her?"

"Nothing, of course. She has no idea what's going on."

That was my cue to reverse the 'doppelganger' spell, leaving the three of them to stare at me in disbelief.

"Maggie Mantle?" the woman said. "How did you do that? Are you a shifter?"

"No, but I assume you three are. Oh, and by the way, my name isn't Maggie Mantle. It's Jill Maxwell."

"Are you a reporter?"

"No, I'm not."

"What do you want, then?" the woman said.

"I'm here to do you a massive favour."

"What do you mean?"

"By rights, I should give my friends, Daze and Blaze, a call. Do you know them?"

They didn't need to answer. The looks on their faces confirmed they did.

"What do you want?" said the taller of the two men.

"Several things. First, I want to know what you've done with the real school governors, and then I need you to tell me what Maligarth is up to."

"He'll kill us."

"Maybe you'd prefer that I called Daze."

"No, don't do that."

The three of them were caught between a rock and a rogue retriever, but in the end, they decided their best hope was to co-operate with me.

"Why don't we start with you three telling me your real names?"

"Cory Withers. I pretended to be Adrian Bowling."

"Nigel Green. I was Randolph Straightstaff."

"Beth Spokes."

"AKA Francesca Greylock, I assume?"

"Correct."

"Okay, now that I know your names, how about we talk about the real school governors? Are they still alive?"

"We believe so." The woman seemed to have nominated herself as the spokesperson.

"Where are they, then?"

"As far as we know, Maligarth is holding them at the school."

"At CASS?"

"That's what he said."

"And what does he plan to do with them?"

"He said he'd release them once he had his hands on the Core."

"So, what you're saying is he had the three of you replace the real school governors, to ensure he'd be appointed headmaster, just so he could get his hands on the Core?"

"Yes."

"If you knew he was going to do that, why would you agree to help him?"

The three of them exchanged the same puzzled look.

"For the money of course."

"What good would money be to you if Maligarth uses the Core to destroy the sup world?"

"What are you talking about?"

"I've seen the Core. According to the previous headmistress, in the wrong hands, it could wreak untold havoc in Candlefield. And yet, you've aided and abetted Maligarth in his attempt to get hold of it."

"Wait a minute! I knew nothing about that." She glanced at the other two who both shook their heads. "I don't think Maligarth knows it has that kind of power."

"Just how naive are you? Of course he knows. Why else would he go to such lengths to get his hands on it?"

"For the money. The stone is worth a king's ransom."

"Says who?"

"Maligarth."

"And you believed him?"

"Yes, why would he lie?"

"Maybe because if he'd told you the truth, you would have wanted nothing to do with it."

I would have liked nothing better than to have handed those three idiots over to the rogue retrievers. The only reason I didn't was because they could still prove useful, and in doing so, compensate, in some small way at least, for their crimes.

"Are you still in contact with Maligarth?"

"Yes. He hasn't paid us yet."

"So you could get hold of him right now?"

"Well, no, but he phones us every Thursday without fail."

"Okay, this is what's going to happen. Tomorrow, when he calls, you're going to insist on a face-to-face meeting at CASS."

"On what pretence?"

"Say that you want proof that the real school governors are still alive and well."

"What if he won't agree to it?"

"If he refuses, tell him you'll go to the authorities and you'll spill the beans."

"He's not the kind of man who reacts well to threats."

"I don't care. It's either that or I call the rogue retrievers right now."

"Okay. Then what?"

"Once you've set up the meeting, you give me a call."

Back in the human world, I stopped off for a drink at Coffee Games. It wasn't like I needed to rush back to the office for anything.

Chapter 22

When I got back to the office, Winky was not a happy — bunn — err — pussycat.

"Do you know what time it is?" he yelled. "I'm going to be late."

Oh bum! I'd forgotten about his stupid boxing match. There was no way I could tell him I'd just spent the last thirty minutes in the coffee shop.

"Sorry, there was something important that required my attention."

"More important than my boxing match? I don't think so."

"It's probably too late to bother now."

"Not if you magic us both there."

"I don't use magic to travel in the human world unless it's a matter of life and death."

"This *is* a matter of life and death. If you don't get me there on time, I'll kill you."

Charming.

"Okay, but only this once."

"It won't hurt, will it?"

"Stop being a wimp. I thought you were a big tough boxer."

"Come on. Let's get it over with."

"I don't even know where I'm supposed to be going. Where is the Feline Quarter?"

"How long have you lived in Washbridge?"

"All my life, but I've never had occasion to go to the Feline Quarter."

"Look, it's right there." He held up his phone, which was displaying a map of Washbridge. "Got it?"

"Yeah. Okay, hold tight."

More by luck than judgement, we landed in a quiet alleyway next to the gym where the boxing match was to take place.

"That was really trippy." Winky shook his head. "I feel like I've just been inside a spin dryer."

"You probably shouldn't go ahead with the fight, then."

"I'll be fine."

"How do we get inside?"

"*We* don't. It's strictly felines only."

"I thought I could sit ringside and cheer you on."

"I don't need anyone cheering me on, and besides, they won't allow two-leggeds in there."

"I'm not hanging around out here until you come back."

"That's okay, there's no need. I'll make my own way home."

"It's a long walk to the office from here."

"Who said anything about walking? I'll call a CatBer."

"Is that like —"

"Uber? Yeah. Yet another case of humans stealing feline ideas."

"Okay, then. Good luck, and try not to get hurt."

"Winky doesn't need luck." And with that, he shot off down the alleyway.

Despite his infuriating habit of referring to himself in the third person, I couldn't help but worry about him. If he got injured, I'd be partly to blame. The only reason he'd got it into his head that he could make it as a boxer was because of the way I'd got rid of Bruiser.

It was no good. I couldn't just leave him there. What would happen if he was badly hurt? I'd never forgive myself. I had to get inside that building so that I could keep an eye on him. But how? Maybe invisibility?

I abandoned that plan as soon as I realised that the cat gym, which was actually in the basement of the building, was cat-sized. I suppose I could have shrunk myself, and then made myself invisible, but why overcomplicate things? There was a much simpler solution.

"Hello, sexy."

I ignored the feline bouncer who was standing by the door.

Being a cat felt kind of weird, but I figured it would allow me to blend in without drawing attention to myself. That was before I realised that ninety percent of those inside were male.

Temporary seating had been installed on all four sides of the boxing ring, and as far as I could tell, there wasn't a seat to be had.

Perfect! Just perfect!

"Over here, beautiful!" A ginger tom pointed to the vacant seat next to him.

"I'm okay, thanks."

"You won't find another seat. The only reason this one's free is because my brother cried off at the last minute."

He was right, the place was packed, and the vacant seat was on the front row, so I'd have a great view.

"I'm Tommy." My new friend introduced himself.

"I'm—err—Lovely."

"You most certainly are. Where's your boyfriend?"

"He—err—had to work."

"You're here to see Driller, I assume?"

"Sorry?"

"Driller Dale, the reigning champion. He's fighting

some no-hoper, so it shouldn't last long. Maybe I could take you for a drink afterwards?"

"Is he good then? This Driller guy?"

"The best. Thirty fights and still undefeated. Twenty of those were won by a knockout."

Gulp! "Who's he fighting today?"

"I don't remember his—err, wait a minute. Wonky, that's it." He laughed. "He'll certainly be wonky after Driller has finished with him."

The more I heard, the worse it got.

My friend continued to try to chat me up, but I wasn't really listening to him. I was too busy worrying about what was going to happen to Winky.

"Gentlemen and ladies, welcome to Feline Boxing HQ. Tonight's match promises to be a belter."

The crowd roared their approval.

"How many bouts are there tonight?" I asked Tommy.

"Just the one."

"Gentlemen and ladies, please show your appreciation for the brave challenger. In the blue corner, we have Wonky!"

Winky appeared through a door to my left, and made his way into the ring, where he whispered something to the MC.

"Gentlemen and ladies, my apologies. In the blue corner, we actually have *Winky*."

Winky took a bow, but no one was paying any attention to him. They were all waiting for his opponent to appear.

Suddenly, the place erupted. Driller Dale was a monster. I'd thought Bruiser was huge, but he had nothing on Driller, who would have made three of Winky.

"Gentlemen and ladies, in the red corner, your reigning champion, and still undefeated, give it up for Driller Dale."

The already enthusiastic crowd cheered even louder.

Winky, who had been full of confidence all week, now looked terrified. It seemed the reality of what he'd signed up for had finally sunk in. I was hoping that he'd jump out of the ring and make a run for it, but the bell rang, and the fight was underway. Winky's only hope was to keep moving and to try to avoid his opponent's punches.

Halfway through the round, he'd managed to do just that, much to the frustration of his opponent and the crowd who were baying for blood.

"Stop running and fight!" Tommy yelled.

I was hoping that Winky would make it through the first round. Maybe then I could get him out of there.

But it wasn't to be. Winky seemed to be running out of steam, and he failed to dodge an uppercut. Fortunately, it only landed a glancing blow, but it was enough to send him to the canvas.

I'd seen enough. I couldn't just stand by and watch this massacre.

Much to the surprise of the audience, the referee, and above all to Driller Dale, I jumped out of my seat, and leapt into the ring.

"What are you doing, girl?" The boxer flashed me a gumshield smile.

"Leave him alone." I gestured to Winky who was clearly still dazed.

"Are you his girlfriend?" Driller laughed. "You've got yourself a real loser there."

"Think you're a tough guy, don't you?"

"Driller Dale isn't scared of anyone."

What was it with cats and the third person?

"You should be scared." I put up my paws.

"Don't be a silly little girl." The patronising fleabag laughed.

I cast the 'power' spell, and then landed a punch under his jaw, which sent him flying across the ring, and into the ropes.

A silence fell across the room, as everyone stared in disbelief at the champion who was now spark out.

"Winky, come on!" I grabbed his paw, and pulled him to his feet.

"Is it Easter? I can see pink rabbits."

Oh boy!

I dragged him from the ring, and then out of the building.

"What's going on?" He was starting to come around.

"It's me, Winky." By now, I'd reverted back to my natural form.

"Jill? What happened?"

"I'll explain later." I grabbed him by the paw, and magicked us both back to the office.

Phew! That was a close call. Another few minutes in the ring, and Winky would have been a goner.

"Are you okay?" I said.

"No, I'm not okay. What do you think you were playing at?"

"I just saved you."

"I didn't need saving."

"You were on the deck. He would have killed you."

"That was all part of my game plan. I went down so

he'd think he had the better of me."

"You didn't know what day it was. You were talking about Easter bunnies!"

"Rubbish."

"Well, that's just great. I save your skin, and this is all the thanks I get."

"You've made me a laughing stock. How will I ever be able to hold my head up again? Everyone will point, laugh and say, there goes Winky who needed a girl to come to his rescue."

Sheesh! Why did I even bother?

***

"This is just too hilarious." Jack was in near hysterics. "My wife, the feline boxer."

"It's not funny."

"Do you have a ring name? You should definitely give yourself one. How about Deadly Delia? Or Killer Kim?"

"I'm so very pleased you're enjoying this. I risked my skin to save that cat, and the ungrateful little furball just gave me a hard time for helping him."

"I'm sure he was grateful really. He just didn't like to admit it."

"I'm done with him. The next time he gets himself into a tight corner, he can get himself out of it."

"I wish you'd taken a selfie when you were a cat. I bet you were hot."

"You're a very sick man."

Jack was chuckling to himself on and off all evening. When I challenged him about it, he swore that he was laughing at something on TV, but I knew different.

"Do you think we should try our costumes on again?" he said.

"Is this another joke about cats? If it is, I *will* kill you."

"I meant our tenpin costumes."

"I'm not putting that thing on."

"You have to wear it on the day."

"Yes, but not until then."

"You promise you won't try to get out of wearing it on Saturday?"

"I said I'd wear it, didn't I? I'm a woman of my word."

Little did Jack know that I had a cunning plan.

Snigger.

It was bedtime, and I was pleased to be putting the day behind me.

"Do you have any cash?" I said.

"What for?"

"I need to put fifty pounds under the pillow."

"Why?"

"For the tooth fairy."

"You've got it all wrong, Jill." He grinned. "The tooth fairy leaves *you* money not the other way around. But only when you lose a tooth."

"Actually, you're the one who has it wrong. Sups who live in the human world pay tooth fairy bills by leaving cash under their pillows."

"So how come I always thought the tooth fairy gave us money?"

I climbed into bed. "I was thinking about that. I reckon what must have happened is that a human found cash under their sup partner's pillow, and asked what was going on. The quick-thinking sup must have come up with the story that it was the tooth fairy who had left the cash. And the myth grew from there."

"Wow, you learn something new every day. By the way, are you still getting aggro about the kidnapping case?"

"Not really, but I still feel like I'm not done with it yet."

"Wouldn't it be better just to let it lie?"

"I can't. I'm missing something. I just can't put my finger on it." I shot up. "Wait a minute! That's it!"

"What's it?"

"I know what I've been missing." I started for the door.

"Where are you going?"

"There's something I have to check."

"I thought we might play kitty cats."

"So sick."

Chapter 23

The next morning, Jack and I were at the kitchen table, both enjoying a bowl of muesli.

What? Of course I'm joking. I was in a hurry to get out of the door, so it was just toast and jam for me.

"What time did you come to bed last night?" he said.

"Just after midnight. You were dreaming about ten-pin bowling."

"How can you possibly know that? Is that some kind of witchy thing?"

"No. You were shouting spare, split and strike."

"No, I wasn't. You've just made that up. What were you doing until that hour, anyway?"

"I think I've worked out what happened with the Warne case."

"The kidnapping? Do you know who murdered him?"

"I think so."

"Who?"

"I can't tell you that."

"Why not?"

"Because we agreed not to mix our personal and professional lives, remember? In fact, as I recall, you were the one who made such a big deal about it."

"Yes, but this is different. If you know who the murderer is, you have to tell the police."

"And I will, but not until I'm one-hundred percent certain, and I have the evidence to back it up."

"How are you going to get that?"

"Oh no you don't. I've already told you I'm not going there. Let's talk about something else."

"Okay. I could talk you through the schedule of events

for TenPinCon."

"Is that the time? I'd better get going."

***

Mrs V appeared to be deep in thought.

"Morning, Mrs V."

"Morning, Jill. Sorry, I was miles away."

"Is everything okay?"

"Yes, it's just Armi and this magician thing of his."

"He's going through with it, then?"

"Yes, he's already bought all the props. We can barely move in the house for them."

"Is that what's bothering you? Couldn't he put some of the equipment in storage?"

"It's not that. He's going to clear out the garage this weekend, so he'll be able to keep most of it in there."

"What's the problem, then?"

"He wants to practise his act on me."

"It would be nice for you to do it together, wouldn't it?"

"I suppose so. It's just that some of the stuff is scary. This morning, just as I was leaving for work, he said he wanted to saw me in half."

"There's really nothing to it." I smiled. "I didn't feel a thing when I did it."

"When did you get sawn in half?"

Oh bum! There I went again, shooting my mouth off before my brain was engaged. I could hardly tell her that Winky, AKA The Great Winkini, had once sawn me in half, only a few feet from where we stood.

"I — err — I went to a magic show with Jack."

"And you volunteered to go on stage?"

"Yeah, why not? It's just an illusion after all."

"Weren't you scared? Not even a little bit?"

The vision of Winky wielding a chainsaw popped into my head.

"Of course not. It's a piece of cake."

"You're right. I'm probably worrying about nothing. I'll tell Armi that I'll do it."

"Good for you."

"You don't happen to remember the name of the magician who sawed you in half, do you, Jill?"

"The Great Winkini."

"That's a strange name."

"He's a strange character altogether."

"What do you mean I'm a *strange character*?" Winky demanded.

"That's quite a shiner you have there."

He touched his swollen eye. "It's nothing. Like I said yesterday, everything was going to plan until you stuck your oar in."

"You're welcome."

"And you should be very careful about giving advice on a subject you know nothing about."

"What are you talking about?"

"I heard you telling the old bag lady she should let Arnie cut her in half."

"How many more times do I have to tell you his name is *Armi*? And, if you can do that trick, I'm sure someone as intelligent as he is will be able to."

"It isn't a *trick*. It's a very complicated illusion, which requires years of practice to master."

"Whatever. I'm sure he'll be fine."

"On your head be it."

***

Now, to put stage one of my brilliant plan into action.

What do you mean you're confused by all these different plans? Okay, here's a quick refresher: For TenPinCon, I had come up with a *cunning* plan—more of which later. To solve the car spraying case, an *ingenious* plan was required. And now, in an attempt to resolve the Warne kidnapping case, I would be employing a *brilliant* plan. I know I make this stuff look easy, but it takes a genius to match the right plan to the right circumstances.

Got it? Good! On with the story, then.

First stop, Washbridge General Hospital. After donning a white coat, which I'd *borrowed* from the laundry, I was able to wander the corridors unchallenged. As always, the place was very busy, and most of the private rooms were occupied. On the third floor, though, I found a vacant room. After a quick check that no one was watching, I hurried inside.

Ten minutes later, I'd completed stage one of the brilliant plan. Now, to call Cheryl Warne.

"Jill? I didn't expect to hear from you again."

"I don't imagine you did."

"What do you want?"

"Just to thank you for the hatchet job you did on me in the press."

"I don't know what you're talking about. I'm sorry, but I don't have time to—"

"I know who murdered Robert." Her silence spoke

volumes. "Cheryl? Did you hear what I said?"

"Err, yes. Who?"

"I'm sorry to have to tell you this, but Robert was murdered by Jonathan Langer."

"Jonathan?" She laughed, but it sounded false. "That's ridiculous."

"The evidence says otherwise."

"What evidence?"

"I'd rather not discuss that over the phone."

"Have you told anyone else about this? The police?"

"Not yet. Despite what's happened, you're still my client. I wanted to tell you first. Maybe you could come to my office, and we—"

"Not your office. You'll have to come to my house."

"Okay. When?"

"This has come as a bit of a shock. I need a little time to get my head around it. How about we do it tomorrow?"

"What time?"

"One o' clock?"

"Okay, I'll see you then."

Result!

***

I'd no sooner left the hospital than my phone rang.

"Jill, it's Cory Withers. I was the one who pretended to be the school governor, Adrian Bowler."

"I know who you are. What's happened?"

"We've just spoken to Maligarth."

"How did it go?"

"Not great. He went ballistic when we told him we wanted to see the school governors."

"I hope you stuck to your guns."

"We did, but it wasn't easy. He made all kinds of horrible threats."

"But did he agree that you could go over there?"

"Yes, that's why I'm calling. He says we have to go right now."

"What did you say?"

"That we would. What else could I say?"

"What about the airship? Is it even running today?"

"Maligarth said he'd give instructions for one to be waiting for us in an hour."

"Okay. I'll meet you at the airship station."

"We'll be there."

"The other two don't need to come. It'll be just you and me."

"I don't understand."

"I'll explain everything once we're on the airship."

"I'm really scared, Jill."

"There's no need to be. I have it all under control."

I hoped that I sounded more confident than I actually felt.

***

I had an hour to kill before the airship would be ready for us, so I called in at Cuppy C.

"One of your most excellent blueberry muffins, please, Amber. And a cup of your finest coffee."

"Aren't we all la-di-da today?" Amber rolled her eyes. "Since when were you so formal?"

"It's the new me."

"Yeah, right. What are you working on?"

"When I leave here, I'm going over to CASS."

"You have the life of Riley. Swanning around when and where you want."

"Are you joking? I put my life on the line every week."

"If you say so. Just wait until you have a kid, then you'll know what real work is."

"Yeah, well, that's a way off yet."

"Have you and Jack talked about what you'll do when the time comes?"

"We're both familiar with the birds and bees, thanks."

"I didn't mean that. I meant your jobs. Will you give up the P.I. business?"

"What? I—err, no, of course not."

"What will you do, then?"

"I've no idea. We've never really discussed it. Now, are you going to give me that muffin and coffee, or do I have to climb over there and get it myself?"

"That's more like the Jill I know."

Sheesh! What was with the twenty questions on my childcare plans? Now, instead of being able to relax before my visit to CASS, Amber had got me thinking about the future. Jack and I both wanted kids, but we hadn't really thought beyond that. What would happen to my business? I couldn't imagine giving it up.

***

Cory Withers was waiting for me at the airship station, as arranged.

"I don't think this is a good idea, Jill."

"It's too late to turn back now."

"How come Nigel and Beth get to stay behind?"

"We're going to tell Maligarth that Nigel has stayed in Candlefield as insurance."

"Insurance against what?"

"If we don't return, Nigel will go to the authorities and tell them what he knows."

"He won't do that. He'd be too scared."

"Maligarth doesn't know that."

"What about Beth? How come she isn't coming to CASS?"

"She is." I cast the 'doppelganger' spell. "She's right here."

"Wow! You even sound like her."

"When we get to CASS, let me do all the talking."

"Don't worry. I intend to."

The airship journey was about as good as it gets: There was little or no turbulence, and not a dragon to be seen. The company, though, left a lot to be desired. All Cory did was pace up and down the deck and bite his nails.

"It's time to pull yourself together," I said, as we came in to land.

"I'll do my best."

"You'll have to do a lot better than that. Come on. Maligarth is waiting for us."

The headmaster was standing at the edge of the playing field, and he wasted no time in making his displeasure known.

"This is a waste of my time." He growled.

"It needn't take long," I said. "Once we've seen the school governors, we'll be on our way."

"Where's the other one?"

"Nigel is back in Candlefield. If we don't return safely,

he has instructions to take what he knows to the authorities."

The look of frustration on Maligarth's face left me in no doubt that he'd been hoping that all three of the phoney governors would make the trip. He'd no doubt intended to dispose of them, as they were now surplus to requirements.

"Follow me." He led the way into the school.

Cory hadn't spoken since we'd got off the airship, which was just as well because he was trembling with nerves and would probably have given the whole game away.

Even though I was now a semi-regular visitor to CASS, I'd still only seen a fraction of the building. Maligarth led the way through the north wing into an annexe. After walking along numerous corridors, and going up and down several flights of stairs, I was beginning to think that he was leading us on a wild goose chase. I was just about to challenge him when he stopped outside a steel door.

"They're in here." He took a key from his pocket.

Conscious that this could be a trap, I was still very much on my guard.

"After you," I said to Maligarth.

"Very well." He led the way into a room that was more sleazy motel than prison cell. Cowering on their respective beds, were the three school governors.

"Satisfied?" Maligarth turned to me.

"Not quite." I walked over to the terrified captives. "Are you three okay?"

"Of course they're okay!" Maligarth's temper erupted. "You can see they're okay."

"I'd like to hear it from them."

"We just want to go home," Francesca Greylock said. "Have you come to take us back?"

"No, she hasn't, you stupid woman!" Maligarth yelled at her.

"Actually, you're the stupid one." I turned to face him. "Because taking them home is precisely what I intend to do."

"Over my dead body." He laughed.

"If necessary, yes." I reversed the 'doppelganger' spell.

"You?" He stared at me in disbelief.

"The game's up, Maligarth. You might as well give it up now and come quietly."

"Never." As he spoke, his eyes began to glow orange.

This time, though, I was ready for him. Before his power could eat its way into my mind, I used the 'power' spell to fling him backwards across the room. He hit the wall with a sickening thud, leaving him unconscious on the stone floor.

"Cory, take these three to the airship, and make sure they get back to Candlefield safely. If anything happens to them, I'll hold you personally responsible."

He didn't need telling twice. He couldn't wait to get away from CASS, and Maligarth.

"Just a minute," the 'real' Francesca Greylock said. "What's going to happen to him?" She gestured to the prone figure of Maligarth.

"He's going to spend a very long time behind bars."

"What about the school? Who will be head now?"

"That will be for you three to decide."

"Come on!" Cory urged her. "Let's get out of here."

Once I was alone with Maligarth, I made a phone call.

"Daze, it's Jill. How do you fancy a trip to your old school?"

"I'd love that. It's ages since I was there. What's the occasion?"

"Strictly business, I'm afraid. I have a gentleman here who I think you should meet."

"Who's that?"

I talked her through Maligarth's exploits: how he'd kidnapped the real school governors, had their replacements elect him to the post of headmaster, and tried to get his hands on the Core.

"Sounds like that gentleman will be spending some time behind bars. It may take me a while to get over there, though. I'm not sure when the airship runs."

"Don't worry. He won't be going anywhere. You'll find him in the head's office."

After I'd finished briefing Daze, I made another phone call. The person on the other end of the line was clearly surprised to hear from me, and even more surprised by what I asked of her.

Once Maligarth had been arrested and taken back to Candlefield, I made my way to the staffroom. Fortunately, it was break time, so most of the teachers were in there.

"Everyone! Could I have your attention, please?"

"I didn't think it was your day to teach, Jill?" Natasha Fastjersey was eating a cupcake.

"It isn't. I'm here on rather more serious business today."

Once I had everyone's attention, I told them how Maligarth had taken the school governors captive, and used shifters to impersonate them in order to secure his appointment. As I was speaking, I noticed three men at the back of the room stand up and leave. They had been recruited by Maligarth, and they now no doubt saw the writing on the wall.

"Who will take over as head now?"

"That will be up to the real school governors, but until then, I'm pleased to tell you that I've just spoken to Ms Nightowl who has agreed to stand in for the time being."

Chapter 24

The next morning, Jack was in panic mode about TenPinCon.

"What if the caterers don't turn up? What if the roof leaks? That roof definitely looked dodgy to me. What if the lights fail?"

"Relax, Jack. I'm sure everything will go swimmingly."

"I can't believe it's happening tomorrow. There are still so many things I have to sort out."

"I have a suggestion that might help."

"What's that?"

"You just said you still have lots of things to sort out, right?"

"Yeah, dozens."

"In that case, let's not bother going to the community band thing tonight. I'd hate to miss it, obviously, but it's a sacrifice I'm willing to make if it helps you."

"That's exceedingly generous of you."

"I know. That's just the kind of person I am."

"But I wouldn't hear of it. I know how much you've been looking forward to tonight."

"I don't mind, honestly."

"Thank you for that magnanimous offer." He grinned. "But I simply couldn't live with myself if you were to miss out just because of me."

Drat! That man knew me too well.

"Alright, but if the Normals turn up with their alphorns, I'm leaving."

"They won't. I bumped into Norm yesterday, and he said they were going to choose new instruments for the band. Something a little more portable than the horns."

"That shouldn't be difficult."

"What's going on out there?" Jack was staring out of the front window.

"What are you looking at?" I couldn't see anything out of the ordinary.

"The woman walking a dog."

"What about her?"

"She's the third person to walk by with a dog in the last ten minutes."

"Why are you counting them?"

"I'm not. It's just that you rarely see dog-walkers on this road. As far as I'm aware, no one on the street has a dog."

"Much as I'd like to stay here and hold a census on the dog-walking contingent of Smallwash, I have work to do." I gave him a kiss. "I'll see you tonight."

"Love you."

"Love you back."

"Look, there's another dog-walker."

"Bye, Jack."

I was just about to get into the car when someone bid me good morning.

I turned around to see who had spoken to me. The woman, who I didn't recognise, was walking a toy poodle.

"Morning."

"Lovely day."

"It is."

"Benjy loves his morning walk."

"That's nice."

Maybe Jack had a point. I'd never seen that woman before. Why had all the dog-walkers suddenly decided to include our street in their itineraries? Whatever the reason, I had more important things to attend to.

***

I arrived at the office to find Mrs V typing one-handed. Her other arm was bandaged at the elbow.

"What happened, Mrs V? Did you have a fall?"

"That's the last time I listen to your advice."

"Me? What did I do?"

"You told me that the *saw a woman in half* trick was perfectly safe."

"Did something go wrong?"

"I would say so, yes." She held up her injured arm as Exhibit A. "Armi clearly hadn't read the instruction manual thoroughly enough."

"Is it badly injured?"

"Luckily not. I screamed out as soon as the saw made contact. Another few seconds, and I could have lost my arm."

"Surely, that's a bit of an exaggeration?"

"You weren't there, Jill. There was blood everywhere."

"Sorry. I'm sure it was horrible. How's Armi? Is he going to give up the magic now?"

"Quite the contrary. He suggested we give it another go tonight."

"What did you say to that?"

"Nothing I'd care to repeat. I didn't even realise I knew some of those words."

"Oh dear. Will you be okay to work?"

"I'll manage, but I might be a little slower with my knitting than usual."

"Couldn't you call that friend of yours? The one who

helped out the last time you injured your arm? What was her name?"

"Doreen Daggers? I'm afraid she's incapacitated herself at the moment. A mishap with a blender, I believe."

"I'm sorry to hear that. Just take it easy."

"I will."

"And don't drip any blood on the paperwork."

What? It was clearly a joke. Granted, Mrs V didn't see the funny side, but you can't please everyone.

"What did I tell you?" Winky was sitting on the window sill. "Didn't I say that illusion required years of practice?"

"Yes, you were right. As always. What are you doing on there?"

"Talking to Harold."

"Who's Harold?"

"My buddy." Winky stuck his head out of the window. "Hey, Harold, come and say hello."

"I don't want any more cats in here," I shouted.

"Harold isn't a cat."

"What is — ?"

"Pleased to meet you. I'm Harold. Winky has told me a lot about you."

"You're a pigeon."

"What did I tell you?" Winky rolled his eye. "Nothing gets past this woman."

"Hey, Winky, give the lady a break," Harold said. "She's a successful private investigator. That's no mean feat."

This bird was starting to grow on me. "Thank you, Harold. I'm glad someone appreciates me. Do you live around here?"

"Just along the window ledge, actually. Me and the Missus, Ida."

"Oh? Did you move in recently?"

"No, we've lived there for two years. If I'd realised you could talk to animals, I would have said hello before now."

"And you're friends with Winky? Isn't that a little unusual?"

"Why would it be unusual?" Winky chipped in.

"You know why."

"No, I don't. You're going to have to elaborate."

"Because cats hunt birds, don't they?"

He shook his head. "That's yet another myth created by two-leggeds."

"I've seen them. Cats are always trying to catch birds."

"They're just playing a game of tag."

"What about when a cat brings an injured bird into the house?"

"He's trying to rescue it. He takes it home in the hope that the two-legged will help."

"Are you sure about that?"

"Winky's right," Harold said. "Cats and birds are bosom buddies."

"Hold on a minute. When I had that cuckoo clock in here, you were doing your best to get hold of that bird."

"First, I knew that wasn't a real bird. I was just putting on an act for your benefit. And second, cuckoos are different. They're untrustworthy birds with whom cats will have no truck."

I wasn't sure I bought any of that, but I didn't have the time or inclination to debate the issue further. "It's nice to have finally met you, Harold."

"Likewise, Jill."

***

Cheryl Warne had opened the door before I'd had a chance to press the bell. There were no greetings and no small talk. Instead, she told me to follow her through to her study.

"What's all this nonsense you mentioned on the phone?" she demanded. "I would have thought you'd done enough damage by getting Robert killed without trying to blame an innocent man for his murder."

"You seem very sure that Jonathan didn't do it."

"Of course I'm sure. He would never do anything like that."

"But then I guess you would say that, seeing as how you were in on it too."

"What are you talking about?"

"You and Jonathan cooked up this plan. You knew that sooner or later I'd get around to viewing the CCTV footage. You wanted me to see him leave the cinema alone, and make his way to the house, didn't you? You knew I'd track him down, and that allowed you to claim that the kidnappers panicked and killed him. Except of course, that the man who accompanied you to the cinema wasn't Robert, was it? It was Jonathan. My guess is Robert was already being held captive in the house where he would eventually meet his death."

"This is crazy."

"I don't think so. You and I both know it was Jonathan, don't we?"

Before she could respond, the door flew open, and in walked Jonathan Langer.

"It's no good, Cheryl. She knows too much."

"Hello, Jonathan. I wondered how long it would be before you showed up."

"What are we going to do?" Cheryl turned to Jonathan.

"Shut up! I'll deal with this."

"Is that what you did with Robert, Jonathan? *Deal* with him?"

He picked up the paperweight from the desk.

"You can't do it in here!" Cheryl screamed at him.

"We don't have any choice."

"Before you do anything you might both regret, there's something you should know about Robert."

It was clear that Jonathan wasn't interested in anything I might have to say because he began to walk towards me, paperweight poised to strike.

"Wait!" Cheryl grabbed his arm. "Listen to what she has to say."

"Thank you, Cheryl." I took out my phone.

"If you try to call anyone, I'll kill you." He raised the paperweight.

"I have a video I'd like you both to see."

"This is nonsense," Jonathan said.

"Actually, I think you'll both find this very interesting indeed."

"Get on with it, then," he barked.

I played the video and watched as their expressions changed from shock to fear.

"You thought you'd killed Robert, but actually, he was still alive when the paramedics got to him. It was touch and go for a while, but he pulled through, as you can see from the video. The police and I have been working together since then." I glanced at my watch. "In fact, they should be here any minute now."

"You said you'd killed him!" Cheryl screamed at Jonathan.

"I did kill him. He was dead when I left him."

"He can't have been. You just saw him on the video."

Just then, there was a pounding on the front door.

"I'll get that. You two clearly have a lot to discuss."

"Hello, Detective Shay. Prompt as always."

"This had better be good, Maxwell."

"Listen to this." I clicked the play button on the digital recorder I'd had hidden in my pocket.

"You said you'd killed him!"

"I did kill him. He was dead when I left him."

"Where are they?" Sushi demanded.

"Follow me."

Cheryl and Jonathan looked like a pair of rabbits caught in the headlights.

"Cheryl Warne and Jonathan Langer, I'm arresting you for the kidnap and murder of Mr Robert Warne. You are not—"

"You can't do that!" Langer interrupted. "Robert's not even dead."

That comment clearly caught Sushi off-guard. She'd no doubt expected to hear claims of innocence, but not a denial that the murder had ever taken place.

"Of course he's dead. He's lying in the mortuary as we speak."

"No, he isn't!" Cheryl insisted. "He's in hospital. She

just showed us a video of him."

Sushi turned to me.

"I have no idea what she's talking about." I shrugged.

Sushi beckoned to the police officer who was standing at the door. "Take these two to the station."

As they were led away, Cheryl and Jonathan were still protesting their innocence.

"Why do I get the feeling that there's something you aren't telling me, Maxwell?" Sushi said.

"I have no idea. Your suspicious nature, maybe?"

"I need you to come down to the station to answer a few questions."

"It will be my pleasure, as always."

Normally, when Sushi dragged me down to the police station, she made sure I spent as long as possible kicking my heels there. Today, I was hoping she would do just that. Jack could hardly complain if I had to cry off the community band meeting because I was being held at the police station. But the one time I was hoping for a long stay, Sushi allowed me to leave after only a couple of hours. Apparently, once Cheryl and Jonathan had realised that Robert was indeed dead, and they'd heard the digital recording, they both confessed to his kidnap and murder.

Sushi clearly wasn't happy, and she made that clear in no uncertain terms.

"I still think there's something you're not telling me, Maxwell."

"I'm hurt that you'd even think such a thing."

"Why do they both insist they saw a video of her husband alive?"

"Who knows how their sick minds work? You checked

my phone yourself, didn't you?"

"Yes, but —, never mind. You can leave."

"Are you sure? I don't mind hanging around a little longer if it will help."

"Just go."

***

"I'm really tired, Jack." I faked a yawn. "Can't we just stay at home and relax?"

"No. We've both been saying for ages that we should find a common interest, and this is our chance."

"The community band? Seriously?"

"It'll be good."

"I doubt that. Where is it being held, anyway?"

"The old Scout hut."

"Where's that?"

"Near The Corner Shop."

"I don't remember seeing it."

"Yes, you do. It's directly across the road from the shop."

"Hold on. Are you talking about that old wooden building?"

"Yes, that's it."

"I thought that was derelict. It's falling to bits."

"It just needs a lick of paint."

"I definitely don't think we should go. That place could fall down at any moment."

"Don't be ridiculous. It's perfectly safe. Come on, we'd better get going. We don't want to be late."

"Don't we?"

"No, and you can tell me all about the murder case on

the way over there."

"I don't understand why Cheryl Warne came to you in the first place," Jack said, as we made our way to the Scout hut.

"They wanted me to stumble across Robert's body, so they could blame me for spooking the 'kidnappers'. They thought by doing that they'd redirect attention from themselves. And it worked. The press and police were so busy blaming me for his death that no one thought to question the kidnapping story."

"How did you work out that Warne hadn't been kidnapped?"

"It was Langer who had accompanied Cheryl Warne to the cinema. They'd obviously studied the location of the CCTV in advance. By wearing a hat, and not facing any of the cameras, Langer was able to pass himself off as Robert Warne. They knew I would work out that he'd left the cinema of his own accord, and that I'd draw the conclusion that he'd staged his own kidnapping. They must have been watching me, and as soon as I made a move towards the house where he was being held, Langer killed Robert."

"But how did you know it wasn't Robert Warne on the CCTV footage?"

"His fingernails gave him away. Langer is the same build as Robert Warne, but he has a bad habit of biting his fingernails to the quick. Robert Warne had long, well-manicured nails. I'd noticed them on the photograph that Cheryl had given me."

"Why on earth would you notice his fingernails?"

"Normally, I wouldn't have, but this particular

photograph was a close-up of him holding a trophy. His fingers were wrapped around the cup."

"The one thing I don't understand is how you got them to confess."

"That took a little magic. I made a video of Robert Warne in hospital, reading a copy of the newspaper dated yesterday."

"Did you bring him back from the dead?"

"Nothing so gruesome. I just made myself look like him."

"That's a pretty neat trick. Can you make yourself look like anyone you want?"

"More or less."

"Hmm, interesting." He grinned.

"And before you get any ideas, I'll tell you now, it's never going to happen."

"Spoilsport. What did they do when they saw the video you'd faked?"

"Cheryl tore into Jonathan because he didn't make sure Robert was dead. He insisted that he had."

"And you just happened to record their conversation?"

"Correct."

"What about the video? Didn't Sue Shay ask to see it?"

"What video would that be?"

"You do realise that it's a crime to destroy evidence, don't you?"

"I have no idea what you're talking about, officer."

"Okay, I can see that I'm wasting my time with that line of questioning, but I still don't understand why they did it."

"Me neither; all I can do is speculate. Cheryl was obviously having an affair with Robert's business partner,

Jonathan Langer. She wanted Robert gone."

"Why didn't she just divorce him?"

"I've asked myself the same question a hundred times, and I keep coming up with the same answer. It has to come down to money. My guess is that Robert knew about Cheryl's affair, but wouldn't agree to a divorce unless she gave him half of her fortune."

"Didn't they have a pre-nup?"

"They did, but they're notoriously difficult to enforce. Faking the kidnap and murdering Robert made sure he didn't get a penny."

Chapter 25

The exterior of the Scout hut was even worse when we got up close.

"Are you sure we're going to be safe in here?" I pulled away a piece of rotten wood. "This place should be bulldozed."

"It'll probably be better inside." Jack, always the optimist.

It wasn't.

"It's colder in here than it was outside." I had to rub my hands together to get the feeling back into them.

"You're exaggerating. It's a good turnout, isn't it?"

He was right. Practically all of our neighbours were there, and many more from the surrounding streets.

"Where are the refreshments?" I was starving.

"I doubt there'll be any."

"Of course there will. Maybe they're behind that screen?"

Before I had a chance to take a look, Kit called for order.

"Welcome neighbours, one and all. I'm so excited to see so many of you here today. When Britt and I came up with the idea for the community band, we never realised it would prove to be so popular."

"But where are the cakes?" I said, under my breath, earning myself a gentle dig in the side from Jack.

Kit hadn't finished yet. "You're probably wondering what's behind this screen."

Actually, I was trying to work out who I'd need to trample over to make sure I reached the cakes first.

Britt, the other half of Team Lively, took over. "It's my great pleasure to introduce you to Melody Rock, the owner of Washbridge's premier music shop, High Note."

A young woman, wearing trumpet-shaped earrings, stepped forward.

"Hi, everyone. When Britt and Kit approached me and explained what they had planned, I was only too eager to get involved."

"I bet she was. She could probably see the pound signs." That whispered comment earned me another silent rebuke from Jack.

At long last, Melody took hold of the screen and slid it to one side.

What the —?

There was a collective gasp, as a table laden with all manner of instruments was revealed.

"Wow!" Jack was clearly impressed. "Look at all those!"

Melody continued, "I know how difficult it can be to decide which instrument to take up, so I brought these here today for you to try out. Feel free to experiment until you find the one that suits you best. Are there any questions?"

Jack gave me a look and said in a hushed voice, "Don't you dare ask where the cakes are."

There was no point in asking; it was obvious that no thought had been given to the question of refreshment provision. Downright selfish if you ask me.

Everyone scrambled to choose their instrument. Everyone except me that is. I simply couldn't summon up enough enthusiasm. I'd take whatever was left when the others were finished.

"Am I late?" Mr Hosey had just arrived.

"Not much. You haven't missed anything important.

And, in case you were wondering, there aren't any refreshments."

"What's going on over there?"

"Everyone is choosing an instrument. You'd better get in there quick before they're all gone."

"There's no need. I have Henry with me." He pointed to the strange-shaped case at his feet. I should go and apologise to Britt and Kit for my tardiness, though. I hate being late, but I've had a rather traumatic day."

"Has Bessie been playing up?"

"No, she's on tip-top form, but I'm afraid I may have made an error of judgement vis-à-vis my new camouflage acquisition."

"Why? What happened?"

"I don't suppose it would hurt to tell you because I won't be using it again." He looked around. "As long as you promise not to tell anyone else. It's all rather embarrassing."

"I won't say a word."

"I was sure this particular disguise would be a success. It's not like I hadn't done my homework. All my studies showed there were no dogs in the immediate vicinity."

"*Dogs*? Sorry, I don't follow."

"My post box disguise failed because too many people used it to post their mail, particularly Norm Normal. After that experience, I figured I needed something that no one would try to interact with."

"Right? I'm still not sure how dogs come into any of this." But then, the penny dropped, and I laughed. "Oh no! You don't mean? You can't possibly mean?"

"I'm afraid so, yes."

"Oh dear." By now I was in tears. "That explains why

we've suddenly seen so many dog-walkers on our street. They were all headed for your dog poo bin."

"Shush, Jill!" He glanced around to see if anyone had overheard.

No one had; they were too busy checking out the instruments.

"Let me get this straight." I wiped the tears from my eyes. "The dog-walkers were posting little bags of—"

"Not always so *little*. It was horrible."

"It must have been. What are you going to do now? Will you take the camouflage back for a refund?"

"If only I could. It was on special offer, so I can't return it."

"That's a really tough break. You must be considering giving up the undercover surveillance after that horrible experience?"

"Certainly not. It will take more than a few setbacks to defeat Hosey. I'll be back."

"What camouflage will you use next time?"

"I don't know, but you can be sure it won't be canine related."

Jack appeared carrying an instrument.

"What's that?" I said. "A banjo?"

"Close. It's actually a ukulele." He gave it a little strum. "Hi, Mr Hosey. Have you chosen your instrument yet?"

"I'll be playing Henry." He pointed to the case at his feet.

"Your hurdy-gurdy?"

"That's right. If you two will excuse me, I must go and find Britt and Kit to explain why I was late."

"Is he okay?" Jack asked once Hosey was out of earshot.

"He does look a little *woof*, doesn't he? But then, he's

had a *dog* of a day."

"Why? What happened?"

"I can't tell you that. He swore me to secrecy."

"Fair enough. I wouldn't ask you to break a confidence."

"Okay, seeing as you've twisted my arm, I'll tell you. You'll never guess why there have been so many dog-walkers on our street."

Twenty minutes later, Jack was deep in conversation with Tony and Clare. They were discussing TenPinCon, so they didn't notice when I sneaked away to a quiet corner. With a bit of luck I would go unnoticed there for the rest of the evening.

But it was not to be.

Norm and Naomi Normal had made a beeline for me.

"Haven't you chosen your instrument yet, Jill?" Norm said.

I couldn't respond because I was too busy staring at the instruments in their hands.

"Jill? Are you okay?" Naomi shook my arm.

"Err, yeah. Sorry, I was miles away."

"We decided to go for the triangles." Norm held his proudly aloft.

"So I see. After the alphorns, aren't they rather — ?"

"Small?"

Evil more like.

"Yeah. Wouldn't you prefer a wind instrument?"

"We wanted a complete change, didn't we, Norm?"

"Yes, and these have a lovely sound. Listen." He hit the triangle with the wand.

That was my cue to escape.

"Great. I'd better go and choose my instrument."

There were very few left on the trolley by this time.

"Do you see anything that takes your fancy?" Melody Rock popped up beside me.

"I was hoping for a cupcake."

"Sorry?"

"I said I'm not sure what to choose."

"Can I recommend the tuba?"

"That big thing? Isn't it difficult to play?"

"Not at all. Why don't you give it a try?"

"Okay, why not?"

"Do you mind if I leave you to it? I promised I'd give that gentleman over there some tips on the ukulele."

"No problem. I'll be fine."

I dragged the monstrous instrument back to my corner. I figured I'd be able to sit there, unnoticed, until it was time to go home.

Foiled again.

"What have you got there?" Jack laughed.

"It's a tuba."

"You'll never be able to play that enormous thing."

"Of course I will. All you have to do is blow into it. How difficult can it be?"

"Go on, then. Let's hear you."

I could barely hold the giant thing, but when I did eventually manage to get a grip on it, I pursed my lips and blew.

Nothing.

"Still waiting." Jack was enjoying this way too much.

I tried again. Still nothing.

"You should have picked something smaller."

"It'll be fine. I just need time to practise. Why don't you go and play your ukulele while I work this thing out?"

"Okay. I won't hold my breath, though." He laughed. *"Won't hold my breath.* Get it?"

"You're hilarious."

I was determined not to be defeated by the stupid instrument, but no matter how hard I tried, I couldn't get a note out of it.

"Hey, do you mind?" I glanced all around, trying to work out where the voice had come from. "Over here!" Peeping out of the tuba's bell was a tiny creature. "Are you the one who's causing all the wind?"

"I — err — probably, but I was only trying to play this thing."

"That's all well and good, but it doesn't show much consideration for those of us who live inside."

"Sorry, I had no idea. What's your name?"

"Violet."

"Are you a fairy?"

"Do I look like a fairy?"

"I — err, I'm not sure. Are you?"

"I'm an elf."

"Sorry. It's very nice to meet you, Violet. I'm Jill. Is this your permanent home, then?"

"It was, but it looks like I'll have to move again now."

"How long have you lived in there?"

"A couple of years. Before that, I lived in a French horn for a while, but that was sold to a school orchestra. I assume you'll be buying this, will you?"

"Not if it's going to deprive you of your home. I'll go and swap it for one of the other instruments."

"You'd do that for me?"

"Of course. It's not a problem."

"That's very kind of you, Jill."

"Don't mention it."

"I see that you gave up on the tuba?" Jack was back.

"I swapped it for this penny whistle." I treated him to a few notes.

"I told you that you'd never be able to play that enormous thing."

"The only reason I couldn't play it is because there's an elf living inside it."

"Why don't you just admit it was too difficult?"

"It's true. Her name is Violet. I couldn't see her homeless, so I put the tuba back."

"Even by your standards, that's a whopper of a lie."

"Hey, you two." Kit had a saxophone in his hand. "We wondered where you were hiding."

"I see you chose the ukulele, Jack?" Britt said.

"Yes." He gave it a quick strum. "And, I've already had my first lesson with Melody."

"What about you, Jill?"

"The penny whistle." I held it up, but didn't offer to give them a demo.

"I thought I saw you with the tuba earlier," Kit said.

"I had to swap it because there was an elf living inside it."

"You're so funny, Jill." Britt laughed. "I don't know how you come up with this stuff."

"What time does today's meeting end?" I was desperate to get back home to my custard creams.

"We'll be wrapping things up any time now," Kit said. "We'll meet again in two weeks' time, to see how everyone has progressed with their instruments."

"Great. I can't wait."

I was just about to drag Jack back home when Britt remembered something.

"I see that friend of yours won the poetry competition, Jack."

"Err, yes. So I heard."

"He must be very proud."

"I imagine so, but I haven't actually seen him since the winner was announced."

"Maybe you could arrange for me to meet him?"

"I — err —"

"Jack would love to do that," I said. "Wouldn't you?"

"I — err —"

"Great." Britt was clearly delighted at the prospect of meeting Robert Hymes. "Let me know where and when."

As they walked away, Jack glared at me.

"What? What did I do now?"

Chapter 26

As you're no doubt already aware, I'm not one to complain, but no reasonable person should be expected to spend an evening at a community band meeting followed by a day at TenPinCon. Luckily for me, I had my cunning plan to fall back on.

What's that you say? You want to know what it is? Patience. Not long to wait now.

"Have you seen my TenPinCon folder?" Jack was rushing around the kitchen like a man possessed. He'd been up since the crack of dawn because he wanted to be at Washbridge Arena by seven o'clock. I'd tried to go back to sleep, but my brain wasn't having any of it.

"What does it look like?"

"It's a folder with 'TenPinCon' written across the front."

"What size is it?"

"A4."

"What colour is it?"

"Are you trying to wind me up?"

"It's up there, on top of the fridge."

"What's it doing on top of the fridge?"

"Someone must have put it up there."

"Right, that's everything, I think." He gave me a quick peck on the lips. "I'll see you at the arena at ten. And you won't forget to bring your costume, will you?"

"Of course I won't."

"Promise?"

"Cross my heart."

As I watched Jack drive away, I noticed there were two

dog-walkers on the pavement opposite. The man was pointing up the road, and the woman was shaking her head. They'd no doubt discovered that the new 'dog poo bin' had disappeared as quickly as it had appeared. What had Mr Hosey been thinking? Little wonder that particular disguise had been on special offer.

***

I'd arranged to meet Kathy, Peter and the kids outside Washbridge Arena at ten o'clock, but first I needed a caffeine boost.

"Hi, Jill." Sarah was behind the counter. "We don't often see you in here at the weekend."

"I'm going to Washbridge Arena for a convention."

"To TenPinCon?"

"Yeah, how did you know?"

"I love ten-pin bowling. I tried to get the day off so that I could attend, but no such luck."

I was tempted to tell her she could go in my place, but I wasn't sure the owners of Coffee Games would appreciate me taking over as their barista.

"Your usual, Jill?"

"Yes, please."

While I was waiting for Sarah to make my coffee, a young man approached me.

"Excuse me, could I ask your name?"

"Err, it's Jill."

"And do you live in Washbridge?"

"In Smallwash, actually."

"What car do you drive?"

"Hold on. What is this? Twenty questions?"

"Actually, that's precisely what it is." Sarah handed me my coffee. "But I don't think Frank has quite got the hang of it." She turned to the young man. "What have I told you about pestering the other customers?"

"Sorry." He skulked away.

"Will you be taking part in the cosplay?" Sarah glanced at my bag.

"Yes, but it wasn't my idea."

"I'm so jealous. What will you dress as?"

"A tenpin."

"You must take a selfie to show me."

"I will if I remember." Not. A. Chance.

As I approached the arena, Lizzie was the first to spot me.

"Auntie Jill! I've lost a tooth." She opened her mouth wide. "Look!"

"So you have."

"The tooth fairy is going to put some money under my pillow tonight."

"Actually, the tooth fairy doesn't do that."

"But Mummy said she would, didn't you, Mummy?"

"What, pumpkin?"

"Auntie Jill says the tooth fairy doesn't put money under the pillow."

"I'm sure that's not what Auntie Jill meant, is it, Auntie Jill?" Kathy shot me such a look.

"Err, no. What I actually meant is that the tooth fairy no longer puts *coins* under the pillow. What with inflation and everything, she now leaves a five-pound note."

"Five pounds?" Lizzie's face lit up.

"Sometimes even ten pounds."

"Wow! Mummy said it would only be one pound."

"Your mummy doesn't know Maureen as well as I do."

"Who's Maureen?" Kathy said.

"That's the tooth fairy's name, of course. Everyone knows that."

"Shall we go inside?" Peter was clearly keen to get going.

As we made our way into the arena, Kathy pulled me to one side. "Five pounds a tooth? You're going to bankrupt me."

"You can't put a price on a child's happiness."

"And how did you come up with Maureen? What kind of name is that for a fairy?"

As arranged, we met up with Jack at the main information desk.

"Hey, you lot. What do you think of it all?"

Even I had to admit, the end result of Jack, Tony and Clare's endeavours was very impressive. Several of the major players in the industry were present, and most of the smaller stands had been taken too.

"I've lost a tooth, Uncle Jack." Lizzie showed him her toothless gap. "The tooth fairy is going to give me ten pounds."

"Wow, I didn't realise that was the going rate."

"Neither did we." Kathy glared at me. "Not until Jill was kind enough to enlighten us."

"Hey, Peter, you'll never guess what." Jack was clearly bursting to tell him something. "Washbridge Bowl have installed a full-size bowling lane for us, and there's a trophy for the person with the highest score at the end of the day."

"Game on, buddy."

"I hope you two aren't going to desert us, to play that all day," Kathy chipped in.

"It's okay." Jack reassured her. "Everyone is allowed only one frame."

"What a motley crew!" said a familiar voice.

I spun around. "Grandma?"

"Oh yes," Jack said. "I meant to tell you that your grandmother was here."

"I've lost a tooth." Lizzie showed her.

"So you have." Grandma put her hand in the pocket of her cardigan. "It just so happens I have a spare one in here."

My blood ran cold, as all kinds of chilling images ran through my mind, but before I could intervene, Grandma had passed something to Lizzie.

"Look, Mummy. It's a tooth made out of chocolate."

"So it is. Say thank you."

"Thank you, Granny Millbright."

"I'm not really your granny. You can call me Mirabel."

"Do you have a moment, Grandma?" I took her by the arm and led her to one side. "What are you doing here?"

"Not that it's any of your business, but I'm scouting out the arena because I'm thinking of running my own convention here."

"What kind of convention?"

"EverCon."

"Are you serious?"

"Deadly."

"Just don't go doing anything to upset today's events."

"Like what?"

"I don't know, but Jack has put a lot of work into

making today a success. I don't want anything to spoil that."

"Have you forgotten that it was my marketing expertise that ensured this sad excuse for a show is a sell-out?"

"Of course not. I just don't want you to—err—you know."

"I have no idea what you're talking about."

"No magic! Do you understand? Under no circumstances must you cast any spells today."

"Okay, okay. No magic. Are we done now? I want to look around."

"Yes. Thanks."

"What was that all about?" Jack said.

"Nothing. Everything's okay. Where are Kathy, Peter and the kids?"

"They're taking a walk around, so this is our chance."

"To do what?"

"Get changed into our costumes."

"Already?"

"Yes, take a look around. There are lots of people in costume. We can change in the cloakroom."

"Okay, I suppose."

And so, we come to the point you've all been waiting for: The big reveal of my cunning plan.

I simply could not bear the thought of wandering around Washbridge Arena all day, dressed as a tenpin. That's why I'd spent most of Friday morning coming up with a brand-new spell. I like to call it the 'animation' spell.

What does it do, I hear you ask. I'll tell you. It allows me to make the tenpin costume come to life, just as if I was inside it. And before you point out all the potential pitfalls, I'm pleased to confirm that I'd already anticipated them and planned accordingly.

First, because so many people were wearing the same tenpin costume, no one would know which one of them was me. Second, if someone were to try to interact with the costume, the spell was designed to hold a simple yes/no conversation, and then to get away from that person as quickly as possible. And finally, I only intended to stay away from the arena for a few hours. When I got back, I would use a second spell to recall the costume to the cloakroom where I would pack it away.

Cunning or what?

All I had to do now was to wait until the cloakroom was empty, then I'd cast the 'animation' spell, and leave the costume to spend the rest of the day wandering around the arena. Meanwhile, I planned to sneak out, and spend a leisurely day in Washbridge.

Moments later, I saw my opportunity. I quickly took the costume out of the bag, and cast the spell. Finally, I used my lipstick to make a small cross on the front of the costume, so I'd know I had the right one when I returned. After the animated tenpin costume had exited the cloakroom, I sneaked outside via the fire escape.

Yes! Freedom!

***

All good things have to come to an end. Sigh.

Still, I had just spent a lovely few hours doing exactly what I pleased. I'd enjoyed a light lunch at a new restaurant close to the arena, followed by a little shopping. Finally, I'd called in at Tina's Tea Room for afternoon tea.

After using magic to sneak back inside the arena, I made my way to the cloakroom where I cast the spell that would see the animated costume return. I was a little nervous. What if my original spell had failed, and someone had realised that I wasn't inside the costume? Or if it didn't return, and I had to go in search of it?

Those fears were allayed when the tenpin costume came walking into the cloakroom. I quickly checked for the small lipstick cross on the front to make sure it was the right one—it was. All I had to do now was to reverse the 'animation' spell, pack the costume away, then go and find Jack and the others.

What the—?

Instead of collapsing to the floor, the costume didn't move; it just stood there.

Maybe I'd got the reversal wrong? I tried again, but still the costume remained standing. I was about to try it a third time when the zip suddenly started to undo itself.

This couldn't be happening.

But it was. The costume, which should have been empty, was occupied.

"Grandma?"

"These things are incredibly hot," she said. "I have sweat pooling in my armpits."

Doing my best to ignore that mental image, I said, "What are you doing in there?"

"Being a tenpin."

"Yes, but why?"

"When you were busy lecturing me earlier, what did you specifically tell me not to do?"

"I don't remember."

"Yes, you do. You spent five minutes lecturing me on the subject."

"I said you shouldn't use magic."

"And yet, you did exactly that."

"But this is different."

"Is it? Really? Or is it one rule for you and another for the rest of us?"

"Okay, I'm sorry. I shouldn't have lectured you, but I still don't understand why you decided to wear the tenpin costume."

"You'll find out soon enough," she cackled. And with that, she made her exit.

I found Jack near to the bowling lane; he had taken off his costume too.

"Hey, you." I waved to him. "Did you win the trophy?"

"No." His frown said it all.

"Peter didn't win, did he?"

"No, he finished halfway down the pack. I was in the lead until about ten minutes ago, but then someone beat my score."

"Unlucky. Who was it?"

"Him." He pointed.

"That young kid?"

"He's not so young."

"He looks about ten."

"Anyway, never mind the bowling competition. What on earth got into you today?"

"What do you mean?"

"I was sure you'd sneak away into a corner somewhere to hide, but you really got into the spirit of it, didn't you?"

"Did I? I mean — err — yeah, of course I did."

"I would never have thought that you'd enter the talent contest."

"The *talent* contest?"

"It's a pity you didn't win. Still, runner-up isn't too shabby."

"I suppose not."

"I didn't even know you could tap dance."

"I'm full of surprises today, aren't I?"

"And the exposure might be good for your business."

"What exposure?"

"The local TV were covering it. Didn't you see the cameras?"

"No, I didn't notice them. Anyway, no one is going to know it was me inside the costume."

"Of course they will. The MC asked your name. Don't you remember?"

"It's all slowly coming back to me now."

"Auntie Jill!" Lizzie came running up to me. Kathy, Peter and Mikey were following behind.

"Have you had a nice time, Lizzie?"

"Fantastic! Daddy didn't win the bowling, though."

"Never mind. It's the taking part that counts, isn't it?"

"That's what I told her," Kathy said.

I checked the time. "I suppose we should be leaving soon."

"We can't go yet," Jack said. "Not until the big charity finale is over."

"Aren't you scared, Auntie Jill?" Mikey said.

"Of what?"

"I still can't believe you volunteered," Kathy said.

"Volunteered? For what?"

"I for one am really proud of you." Jack put his arm around my shoulder. "I wouldn't fancy doing it."

"Doing what?"

Just then, a voice came over the loudspeakers.

"Ladies and gentlemen, it's time for the grand finale of TenPinCon. Could I ask our brave volunteers, Jill Maxwell and Stuart Crane, to come on stage?"

"Go on!" Kathy encouraged me. "Hurry up!"

Still in a daze, I followed the crowd, and that's when I saw it.

On stage, two ducking stools had been set up over a giant water tank. In front of the tanks, stood ten pins.

Before I knew it, Stuart Crane and I were being helped into the chairs. In front of us, the children in the audience were all armed with sponge bowling balls.

"Okay, children, on my word, throw your balls. When all the pins have been knocked down, our plucky volunteers will go for a dip. Are you ready? Three, two, one, go!"

A matter of only seconds later, the last of my tenpins had been knocked over, and I was dropped unceremoniously into the cold water. As I looked out through the glass, I saw a familiar face standing next to the tank.

Grandma was grinning from ear to ear.

ALSO BY ADELE ABBOTT

Murder On Account (A Kay Royle Novel)

The Witch P.I. Mysteries
(A Candlefield/Washbridge Series)

Witch Is When... (Books #1 to #12)
Witch Is When It All Began
Witch Is When Life Got Complicated
Witch Is When Everything Went Crazy
Witch Is When Things Fell Apart
Witch Is When The Bubble Burst
Witch Is When The Penny Dropped
Witch Is When The Floodgates Opened
Witch Is When The Hammer Fell
Witch Is When My Heart Broke
Witch Is When I Said Goodbye
Witch Is When Stuff Got Serious
Witch Is When All Was Revealed

Witch Is Why... (Books #13 to #24)
Witch Is Why Time Stood Still
Witch is Why The Laughter Stopped
Witch is Why Another Door Opened
Witch is Why Two Became One
Witch is Why The Moon Disappeared
Witch is Why The Wolf Howled
Witch is Why The Music Stopped
Witch is Why A Pin Dropped

Witch is Why The Owl Returned
Witch is Why The Search Began
Witch is Why Promises Were Broken
Witch is Why It Was Over

Witch Is How... (Books #25 to #36)
Witch is How Things Had Changed
Witch is How Berries Tasted Good
Witch is How The Mirror Lied
Witch is How The Tables Turned
Witch is How The Drought Ended
Witch is How The Dice Fell
Witch is How The Biscuits Disappeared
Witch is How Dreams Became Reality
Witch is How Bells Were Saved
Witch is How To Fool Cats
Witch is How To Lose Big
Witch is How Life Changed Forever

Susan Hall Investigates
(A Candlefield/Washbridge Series)
Whoops! Our New Flatmate Is A Human.
Whoops! All The Money Went Missing.
Whoops! Someone Is On Our Case.
Whoops! We're In Big Trouble Now.

Web site: AdeleAbbott.com
Facebook: facebook.com/AdeleAbbottAuthor